"You're familiar with the mandate of the Consortium, right?"

Grant nodded brusquely. "Yeah. To dig out old predark tech, and try to figure out a way to enslave your fellow human beings."

Gray frowned at him. "If you want to believe that about us, go ahead."

"Thanks," retorted Grant. "I will."

"Get back to the subject," Kane said impatiently. "Why were you patrolling out here with a silenced weapon?"

Fear flickered in Gray's eyes. "We didn't want to draw attention if we had to shoot at something."

"Whose attention?" Kane asked, a steel edge in his voice.

Gray inhaled deeply through his nostrils, fixed an unblinking gaze on Kane's face and whispered, "The ghost walkers."

Other titles in this series:

James Axler
Outlanders®

GHOSTWALK

A GOLD EAGLE BOOK FROM
W🌐RLDWIDE®

TORONTO • NEW YORK • LONDON
AMSTERDAM • PARIS • SYDNEY • HAMBURG
STOCKHOLM • ATHENS • TOKYO • MILAN
MADRID • WARSAW • BUDAPEST • AUCKLAND

First edition May 2008

ISBN-13: 978-0-373-63858-1
ISBN-10: 0-373-63858-2

GHOSTWALK

Special thanks to Mark Ellis for his contribution to
the Outlanders concept, developed for Gold Eagle.

GHOSTWALK

The Road to Outlands—
From Secret Government Files to the Future

Almost two hundred years after the global holocaust, Kane, a former Magistrate of Cobaltville, often thought the world had been lucky to survive at all after a nuclear device detonated in the Russian embassy in Washington, D.C. The aftermath—forever known as skydark—reshaped continents and turned civilization into ashes.

Nearly depopulated, America became the Deathlands—poisoned by radiation, home to chaos and mutated life forms. Feudal rule reappeared in the form of baronies, while remote outposts clung to a brutish existence.

What eventually helped shape this wasteland were the redoubts, the secret preholocaust military installations with stores of weapons, and the home of gateways, the locational matter-transfer facilities. Some of the redoubts hid clues that had once fed wild theories of government cover-ups and alien visitations.

Rearmed from redoubt stockpiles, the barons consolidated their power and reclaimed technology for the villes. Their power, supported by some invisible authority, extended beyond their fortified walls to what was now called the Outlands. It was here that the rootstock of humanity survived, living with hellzones and chemical storms, hounded by Magistrates.

In the villes, rigid laws were enforced—to atone for the sins of the past and prepare the way for a better future. That was the barons' public credo and their right-to-rule.

Kane, along with friend and fellow Magistrate Grant, had upheld that claim until a fateful Outlands expedition. A displaced piece of technology…a question to a keeper of the archives…a vague clue about alien masters—and their world shifted radically. Suddenly, Brigid Baptiste, the archivist, faced summary execution, and Grant a quick termination. For

Kane there was forgiveness if he pledged his unquestioning allegiance to Baron Cobalt and his unknown masters and abandoned his friends.

But that allegiance would make him support a mysterious and alien power and deny loyalty and friends. Then what else was there?

Kane had been brought up solely to serve the ville. Brigid's only link with her family was her mother's red-gold hair, green eyes and supple form. Grant's clues to his lineage were his ebony skin and powerful physique. But Domi, she of the white hair, was an Outlander pressed into sexual servitude in Cobaltville. She at least knew her roots and was a reminder to the exiles that the outcasts belonged in the human family.

Parents, friends, community—the very rootedness of humanity was denied. With no continuity, there was no forward momentum to the future. And that was the crux— when Kane began to wonder if there *was* a future.

For Kane, it wouldn't do. So the only way was out— way, way out.

After their escape, they found shelter at the forgotten Cerberus redoubt headed by Lakesh, a scientist, Cobaltville's head archivist, and secret opponent of the barons.

With their past turned into a lie, their future threatened, only one thing was left to give meaning to the outcasts. The hunger for freedom, the will to resist the hostile influences. And perhaps, by opposing, end them.

Chapter 1

Kane did not hear the shot or see anyone with a gun.

The shock of the bullet's impact high on his right shoulder jerked him around, his feet tangling, his back slamming hard against the adobe wall.

Kane let his body sag to the ground. He could hear only his own strained breath as he swallowed air into his emptied lungs. As quickly as he could, he crawled behind a heap of chipped masonry. Pain streaked up and down his arm like flares of heat lightning, but he didn't think any bones were broken. Still, he had to clamp his jaws tightly shut against a groan of pain. He fingered the small hole punched through his tricolor desert-camouflage blouse and winced.

His mind swam with anger. Your own fault, dumbass, he snapped at himself. He knew he should have checked out every structure in the ruins of the old village before leaving the shelter of the walls, but concern over a missing team member had made him reckless.

A single dirt lane led to the settlement, which was a cluster of small huts, most of them roofless, surrounding a well. The north wall had collapsed into rubble and dried mud bricks long ago. The place looked like a typical abandoned Outland village so Kane hadn't strolled through it with any particular caution.

He hitched around, careful not to dislodge any loose stones and give away his position. The lowering sun was a blinding red ball, and if nothing else, Kane appreciated his sunglasses. His eyes swept over the featureless sandy plain. Less than a hundred yards to his right rose a range of low hills with a rolling tongue of sand dunes between them.

High, rust-red mesas towered between the low hills. He resisted taking a drink from his canteen, straining his hearing for any sound of movement. He heard only the singing silence of the desert stirred by the constant hot breeze. Sand and the dry wind sapped all the juices from his body, parching the throat and dehydrating the flesh.

The sun dropped down behind one of the flat-topped outcroppings, and long shadows stretched toward him. Heat waves blurred the far horizon. The peaks of the Jemez Mountain Range were only a wavering mirage many miles to the south.

Kane had been walking point, a habit he had acquired during his years as a Magistrate because of his uncanny ability to detect imminent danger. He called it a sixth sense, but his pointman's sense was really a combined manifestation of the five he had trained to the epitome of keenness. When he walked

point, Kane felt electrically alive, sharply tuned to
every nuance of his surroundings and what he was
doing. Most of the time, he could sense danger
from far off.

Now he wondered if his senses, his instincts,
were failing him. In potential killzones, he normally walked with such care it was almost a form
of paranoia. He had grown accustomed to always
being watchful and alert, to expecting the unexpected. This time his pointman's sense had let him
down.

Or, he thought sourly, I'm just getting old.

Reaching up behind his right ear, he tapped the
Commtact, a flat curve of metal fastened to the mastoid bone by implanted steel pintels. Sensor circuitry
incorporated an analog-to-digital voice encoder embedded within the bone. Once the device made full
cranial contact, the auditory canal conveyed the
radio transmissions directly through the skull casing.

Kane touched the volume control and a hash of
static filled his head. Quickly he dialed it back
down, grimacing both in frustration and pain. A
frequency-dampening field spread out like a vast
umbrella over the village, blocking all radio communications. He could think of only a couple of
groups with access to that kind of tech.

Brewster Philboyd had volunteered to scout out
the zone to prove his suspicions. When Kane de-
clined to grant him permission, Philboyd had gone
anyway. He had not returned.

Clenching his teeth, Kane inched toward one of the lengthening shadows. Although his shoulder burned fiercely from the impact of the bullet, he carefully flexed the tendons of his right wrist. With the faint drone of a tiny electric motor, cables slid the Sin Eater from its forearm holster and into the palm of his hand. His fingers tingled with a painful pins-and-needles sensation and they barely stirred.

The Sin Eater, the official side arm of the Magistrate Division, was an automatic handgun, less than fourteen inches in length, with an extended magazine carrying 20 9 mm rounds. When not in use, the butt folded over the top of the weapon, lying perpendicular to the frame, reducing its holstered length to ten inches.

If the autopistol was needed, a flexing of wrist tendons activated sensitive actuator cables within the holsters and snapped the weapon smoothly into his waiting hands, the butt unfolding in the same motion. Since the Sin Eater did not have a trigger guard or a safety switch, the autopistol fired immediately when his index finger touched the firing stud.

The wrist actuators ignored all movements except the one that indicated the gun should be unholstered. It was a completely automatic, almost unconscious movement practiced by Kane.

Kane heard a faint crunch, as of a foot coming down on loose stone. Carefully he leaned over, peering around the base of the rock heap. The figure of a man stepped through a wide crack in the adobe wall. Because he was backlit by the shimmering corona of the setting sun, Kane couldn't pick out specific details beyond the very long-barreled pistol in the man's right fist. The man moved quickly and purposefully, walking heel-to-toe with expert ease, keeping the wall to his right.

Inhaling a deep breath through his nostrils, Kane pushed the Sin Eater back into the holster, hearing the lock solenoid catch with a pair of soft clicks. He noted the foot-long sound suppressor that was screwed into the bore of the man's autopistol. The silencer had successfully reduced the noise of the gunshot, but had also reduced the bullet's velocity sufficiently so it had only knocked Kane down rather than penetrating the Spectra fabric of his shadow suit.

A sound suppressor seemed a very strange attachment for a man on foot out in the wastelands of New Mexico, but Kane had no time to wonder about it.

With his left hand, he drew the fourteen-inch-long combat knife from the sheath at his waist. He gripped the Nylex handle tightly while he grimly tried to coax more feeling into his right arm. He waited, barely breathing, listening for sounds of the gunman's progress.

Built with a lean, long-limbed economy, most of Kane's muscle mass was contained in his upper body, much like that of a wolf. A wolf's cold stare glittered in his blue-gray eyes. A faint hairline scar showed like a white thread against the sun-bronzed skin of his left cheek. His thick dark hair glistened with sweat at the roots.

He listened to the stealthy tramp of feet, realizing that the way the man soft-footed through the loose gravel and sand indicated he wasn't sure of his shot. Kane felt pressure moving along his nerves and he rose to a crouch, favoring his injured shoulder.

A shadow crept slowly across the ground toward him, then it halted. Kane figured the gunman was eyeing the pile of rock, studying the tracks in the sand, guessing that his quarry more than likely hid behind it.

The man advanced silently in a smooth, fast rush. In his eagerness to get past the heap of stone, he grazed the wall with a knee and was thrown slightly off balance. He stumbled, reaching out to steady himself.

Kane slashed out with the knife, the razored edge penetrating the leather of a jump boot and slicing the tendon at the man's left heel. He uttered a strangulated screech and staggered forward, leg buckling.

The man's shoulder slammed against the wall, and a webwork of cracks spread out across the sun-baked clay. Kane caught an impression of a smooth, round face contorted in agony and surprise. The hollow bore of the sound suppressor swung toward him. Although he gave the handgun only the most fleeting of glances, he identified it as a Calico M-950 rimfire.

Kane dodged to one side, hearing a faint thump, then the sharp whine of a ricochet somewhere behind him. With his right hand, he knocked the pistol aside, then whipped the blade of the combat knife forward, stopping the razor edge a hairbreadth from the man's throat.

For a long second, the two men stared into each other's eyes. A round button on the man's dun-colored coverall glinted with dim sun sparks. The inscribed image showed a stylized representation of a featureless man holding a cornucopia, a horn of plenty, in his left hand and a sword in his right, both crossed over his chest. No words were imprinted on it, but none were necessary.

"The Millennial Consortium," Kane said softly. "I should've known."

The man's lips writhed back over his teeth in a sneer. In the same low tone he said, "The Cerberus crew. We *did* know."

Chapter 2

The millennialist struggled, trying to align the bore of the noise suppressor with Kane's head.

Kane tensed his wrist tendons and the Sin Eater slapped into his palm, the barrel smacking the side of the man's head as it popped from the holster. He cried out in pain and fear, squeezing his eyes shut in anticipation of a bullet plowing a path through hair, flesh, bone and brain.

Kane didn't depress the trigger stud or even increase the pressure of the knife blade. Calmly he said, "You're leaking a lot of blood, pal. If you want to keep enough of it in you to stay alive, I'm your only option."

The millennialist's lips twisted in pain and frustration. His skin was pinked by the sun, and his wispy blond hair was cut very short. He resembled most of the other consortium grunts Kane had met over the past few years. He looked to be in his early thirties.

"All right," he said hoarsely. "All right."

He opened his hand and the Calico dropped to the ground.

Picking up the man's pistol, Kane took the knife away from the man's throat. "What's your name?"

"What difference does it make?"

Kane shrugged. "None. I just thought it was the polite thing to ask of a man I've probably crippled."

Wincing, the man reached for the scarlet-seeping slash at the back of his boot. "Call me Mr. Gray."

Kane smiled slightly, recalling the pair of color-coded millennialists he had met in Europe. "You can call me—"

"Kane," Mr. Gray broke in harshly. "I've seen pix of you. Your file is black tagged."

"What's that mean?"

"It means you're a high-priority target. Big bonus pay for any of us who nails you."

He glanced sourly at the Calico in Kane's hand. "Guess I got too eager. But I could swear I got you."

"You did, just not as good as I got you." Kane eyed the man's injured foot. He popped the magazine out of the Calico and tossed the weapon over his shoulder. It clattered loudly against rock. "Let me see what I can do about getting that boot off."

Gray looked longingly toward the Calico. "They've been making us pay for every gun we lose."

"Yeah, the consortium has a reputation for squeezing every penny until it screams." Kane applied the edge of the knife to Gray's bootlaces, and after a quick sawing motion they parted easily.

"We're thrifty," Mr. Gray said defensively. "There's a difference."

Kane didn't reply as he carefully tugged off the man's boot. Blood acted as lubricant. Although the pain must have been excruciating, Gray didn't cry out, although he sank his teeth into his lower lip.

The Millennial Consortium was, on the surface, a group of organized traders who dedicated their lives to recovering predark artifacts from the ruins of cities. In the Outlands, such scavenging was actually the oldest profession.

After the world burned in atomic flame, enough debris settled into the lower atmosphere to very nearly create another ice age. The remnants of humankind had waited in underground shelters until the Earth became a little warmer before they ventured forth again. Most of them became scavengers mainly because they had no choice.

Looting the abandoned ruins of predark cities was less a vocation than it was an Outland tradition. Entire generations of families had made careers of ferreting out and plundering the secret stockpiles the predark government had hidden in anticipation of a nation-wide catastrophe. The locations of those hidden, man-made caverns filled with hardware, fuel and weapons had become legend to the descendants of the nukecaust survivors.

Most of the redoubts had been found and raided decades ago, but occasionally a hitherto untouched one would be located. As the Stockpiles became fewer, so did the independent salvaging and trading organizations. Various trader groups had combined resources for the past several years, forming consortiums and absorbing the independent operators.

The consortiums employed and fed people in the Outlands and gave them a sense of security that had once been the sole province of the barons. There were some critics who compared the trader consortiums to the barons and talked of them with just as much ill will.

Since first hearing of the Millennial Consortium a few years earlier, the Cerberus warriors had learned firsthand that the organization was deeply involved in activities beyond seeking out stockpiles, salvaging and trading. The Millennial Consortium's ultimate goal was to rebuild America along the tenets of a technocracy, with a board of scientists and scholars governing the country and directing the resources to where they saw the greatest need.

Although the consortium's goals seemed utopian, the organization's overall policy was pragmatic beyond the limit of cold-bloodedness. Their influence was widespread, but they were completely ruthless when it came to the furtherance of their agenda, which was essentially the totalitarianism of a techno-tyranny.

Nor were their movements restricted to the continental United States. Not too long before, Cerberus had thwarted a consortium operation in Slo-vakia.

Kane examined the knife wound. His blade hadn't completely severed Gray's Achilles tendon. Even so, Kane doubted the man would ever be able to walk without a limp again.

From a pouch pocket of his pants, Kane took out a long bandanna and folded it, then expertly knotted it around the man's wound to staunch the flow of blood.

Conversationally he said, "Once I hook back up with my team, I'll have access to a medical kit and get you some proper bandages and even a painkiller."

Gray responded only with a muffled groan.

In the same studiedly casual tone of voice, Kane continued, "You don't seem surprised to hear about my team….or even what I'm doing out here."

Gray's sweat-pebbled face tightened. "We expected you."

"And why is that?"

The millennialist sighed and said almost regretfully, "We found your spy."

Kane laid a hand on Gray's injured ankle. In a level voice he asked, "What spy?"

"He said his name was Philboyd, that he was a scientist and that we should back off."

Kane tightened his fingers around Gray's ankle. "Where is he?"

"He's not dead," Gray replied quickly. "I swear to you. We didn't kill him."

"I asked where he was."

Gray winced. "I can show you."

"I'm sure you can." Kane released the man's ankle and stood up. "And you'll show us a lot more besides."

He gazed beyond Gray. "You hear any of that?"

Mr. Gray's face registered momentary confusion, then he turned to see Cerberus Away Team Alpha stepping through a break in the wall.

THE SIX PEOPLE WERE ATTIRED in tricolor desert-camouflage BDUs and thick-soled, tan jump boots. All of them carried abbreviated Copperhead subguns attached to combat webbing over their field jackets. Under two feet long, with a 35 4.85 mm steel-jacketed rounds. The grip and trigger units were placed in front of the breech in the bullpup design, allowing one-handed use.

Optical image intensifier scopes and laser autotargeters were mounted on the top of the frames. Low recoil allowed the Copperheads to be fired in long, devastating, full-auto bursts. Four members of Team Alpha also carried XM-29 assault rifles.

Grant strode up to Gray and stared down at him, his eyes shadowed by heavy, overhanging brows. He towered six feet five inches tall in his thick-soled jump boots, and his shoulders spread out on either side of a thickly tendoned neck like massive planks, straining at the seams of his field jacket.

Although he looked too huge and thick-hewn to

have many abilities beyond brute strength, Grant was an exceptionally intelligent and talented man. Behind the fierce, deep-set eyes, the down-sweeping mustache, black against the dark brown of his skin, granite jaw and broken nose lay a mind rich with tactics, strategies and painful experience. Like Kane, he had lived a great deal of his life surrounded by violence. He had been shot, stabbed, battered, beaten, burned, buried and once very nearly suffocated on the surface of the Moon.

Kane nodded to Gray. "Gray, this is Grant. Grant, this is Gray."

"I know who he is," Gray snapped. "The consortium is very thorough when it comes to identifying its enemies."

Grant regarded him with no particular emotion on his face. In his lionlike growl he intoned, "All of you millennialists look like you were mass-produced. Same build, same haircuts."

"And you usually say the same things when we meet any millennialists," said a well-modulated female voice, purring with an undercurrent of humor.

"I almost forgot." Grant nodded to Gray and said almost apologetically, "I hate you guys."

Brigid Baptiste stepped between Grant and Kane, gazing down at Gray with bright emerald eyes. She was a tall woman with a fair complexion. Her mane of red-gold hair fell down her back in a long sunset-colored braid to the base of her spine. Like the other members of CAT Alpha, she wore desert camouflage. A TP-9 autopistol was snugged in a cross-draw rig strapped around her waist.

Kneeling down beside Gray, she lifted the lid of a square medical kit. "I think we can dress your injury a bit more properly."

Gray gave her a beseeching look of gratitude. "Something for the pain, too, please. I'm really hurting."

"I don't doubt it," Brigid replied sympathetically. She busied herself with the contents of the kit, then paused. "Of course, you'll have to give me something in return."

The expression of gratitude on Gray's face turned to resentment. "Like what?"

"What do you think, dipshit?" Edward barked. The ex-Mag from Samariumville marched forward and prodded Gray roughly in the ribs with a boot. "Information."

Edwards, whose head was shaved, wasn't as tall as Grant, but he was almost as broad, with overdeveloped triceps, biceps and deltoids. He usually served as the commander of CAT Alpha in the absence of Kane and Grant.

"I don't know anything," Gray retorted. "I'm just a grunt."

"That's the pat response we expected," Grant rumbled. "I'm sure you can guess *our* response."

He positioned his right boot over Gray's bandaged ankle and, balancing on his heel, slowly began exerting downward pressure.

Gray swallowed hard. "Okay, okay."

Grant lifted his foot, but kept the thickly treaded sole hovering over the millennialist's ankle. "Okay what?"

"If you're here at all, you probably know as much as I do about the operation."

Kane repressed the urge to exchange meaningful glances with Brigid and Grant. In truth, Cerberus knew very little. The information about sudden and suspicious activity on the outskirts of the little settlement near Los Alamos had reached them by the most inefficient of means—by word of mouth.

The information had been conveyed along a chain of Roamer bands until it finally reached the ears of Sky Dog in Montana. He in turn had brought it to the Cerberus redoubt, cloistered atop a mountain peak in the Bitterroot Range.

"Tell us what you know, anyway," Brigid said smoothly.

Gray gestured vaguely in the direction of the sand dunes and mesas. "You're familiar with the mandate of the consortium, right?"

Grant nodded brusquely. "Yeah. To dig out old predark tech, polish it up and try to figure out a way to use it to enslave your fellow human beings."

Gray frowned at him. "If you want to believe that about us, go ahead. It's not true, but keep on believing it if it'll make you feel better."

"Thanks," Grant retorted. "I will."

"Get back to the subject," Kane said impatiently. "Like for instance, why were you patrolling out here with a silenced weapon?"

Fear flickered in Gray's eyes. "We didn't want to draw attention if we had to shoot at something."

"Whose attention?"

Gray shifted uncomfortably, fingering the bandage around his ankle.

"Whose attention?" Kane asked again, a steel edge in his voice.

Gray inhaled deeply through his nostrils, fixed an unblinking gaze on Kane's face and whispered, "The ghost-walkers."

Chapter 3

"What the hell does *that* mean?" Kane demanded.

Mr. Gray swallowed the pentazocine tablet handed to him by Brigid before answering, "I don't really know much. Just what I was told."

"Which was?" Grant challenged.

"We've had reports from the locals that when anybody starts digging around Phantom Mesa, ghosts show up."

"Ghosts?" echoed Brigid, casting glance over her shoulder at the rock formations. "Which one is Phantom Mesa?"

"Third from the left…your left. The reports say the ghosts walk around like they're guarding the place. Supposedly they even kill people who defy their orders to leave."

"Folklore," Brigid stated matter-of-factly. "The whole history of the Southwest is a patchwork of legends and superstitions."

Mr. Gray flashed her a fleeting, appreciative smile. "That's what our section chief thought, too. But I figure it's called Phantom Mesa for a reason, right?"

The man's smile faded. "We've seen some strange-ass shit, though…enough so we take precautions. The locals claim the ghosts don't show up unless you make a lot of noise, so we use silencers on our guns."

"Speaking of them, where *are* the locals?" Grant asked.

Gray gestured out toward the sand dunes. "We gave them jobs, put them to work with our excavation crew."

"Right," Kane drawled. "I remember the employment opportunities offered by the Millennial Consortium. Another name for it is forced servitude. Just what are they excavating out here?"

Gray shifted uncomfortably. "I'm not sure about anything specifically. But this whole part of New Mexico was a testing site for all sorts of predark research—weapons, aircraft, even genetics."

"We know," Brigid said grimly, her face not betraying the involuntary surge of revulsion as she recalled the bioengineering facility known as Nightmare Alley hidden deep beneath the Archuleta Mesa. Several years ago, she had participated in its complete destruction.

"The consortium found a facility in almost pristine condition," Mr. Gray declared.

"A COG redoubt?" Grant asked skeptically. "Like the one you millennialists occupied in Wyoming?"

The predark Continuity of Government program was a long-range construction project undertaken by the U.S. government as the ultimate insurance policy should Armageddon ever arrive. Hundreds of subterranean command posts were built in various regions of the country, quite a number of them inside national parks. Their size and complexity ranged from little more than storage units to immense, self-sustaining complexes.

The hidden underground Totality Concept redoubts were linked by the Cerberus mat-trans network to the COG installations.

The Totality Concept was the umbrella designation for American military supersecret research into many different arcane and eldritch sciences, from hyperdimensional matter transfer to temporal dilation to a new form of genetics. The official designations of both the COG facilities and the Totality Concept redoubts had been based on the old phonetic alphabet code used in military radio communications.

In the twentieth century, the purposes of the redoubts were classified at the highest secret level. The mania for secrecy was justified since the framers of the Totality Concept feared mass uprisings among the populace if the true nature of the experiments was ever released to the public.

Before the nukecaust, only a handful of people knew the redoubts even existed. That knowledge had been lost after the global mega cull. When it was rediscovered a century later, it was jealously and ruthlessly guarded. A couple of years earlier in

Wyoming, the Millennial Consortium had discovered a COG-related storage depot.

Mr. Gray considered Grant's questions for a few seconds, then shook his head. "Don't think so. It's aboveground, not like most of the redoubts. It's more like a station of some sort, set in a little valley between Phantom Mesa and another one. Very well hidden, unless you know where to look."

"If that's the case," Kane said, "how'd *you* know where to look?"

Gray shrugged. "Our section chief knew where to look, not us grunts."

"Who's that again?"

"We just call her Boss Bitch…not to her face, though."

Kane's eyes narrowed, recalling the last time they had questioned a couple of millennialists. They had referred to a female section chief, too.

"How did *she* know?" Brigid asked.

"She took over from another chief…Mr. Breech. He laid the groundwork."

"And where is he now?" Grant inquired.

Gray hesitated before saying in a low tone, "A lot of us would like to know that."

Edwards edged closer. "What about Philboyd?"

Mr. Gray blinked up at him curiously. "What about him?"

Edwards bared his teeth in a silent snarl. "Where the fuck is he?"

"I don't know. He was taken away to be questioned. But he was alive." Gray coughed and asked, "Could I have a drink? That pill is stuck in my throat."

Kane nodded to Edwards. "Give him your canteen."

The big ex-Mag scowled, but he didn't object. Kane glanced meaningfully toward Brigid and Grant and jerked his head. The three people walked away, out of earshot of the consortium man.

Kane asked softly. "Do we believe him?"

Brigid sighed, running a hand through her hair. "I don't see why not. If the consortium is out here, something big has attracted their attention."

"I don't mean that," Kane retorted impatiently. "He could be giving us wrong directions."

Grant narrowed his eyes against the glare of the setting sun. "Even so, we've got to check out his story, no matter what."

Brigid smiled wryly. "Unfortunately."

Kane worked his shoulder up and down, wincing in pain. "Dammit."

Brigid eyed him questioningly. "What?"

"That son of a bitch shot me. Didn't get penetration, but it hurts like hell."

"Let's make sure," Brigid suggested.

Kane shucked out of his field jacket and opened a magnetic seal in the upper half of his bodysuit, peeling it down over his right shoulder. His upper torso still burned where the bullet had punched him.

A livid red-and-purple bruise spread in a star-shaped pattern around the impact point.

Brigid probed with gentle fingers at the injury. "I think you'll be all right, but your arm will be probably be very stiff in a couple of hours. When we get back to Cerberus, have DeFore look at it."

Kane resealed the seam, setting his teeth against a groan of pain. Brigid and Grant wore identical midnight-colored garments under their BDUs. Although the material of the formfitting coveralls resembled black doeskin and didn't seem as if it would offer protection from flea bites, the suits were impervious to most wavelengths of radiation.

Upon finding the one-piece garments in the Operation Chronos facility on Thunder Isle several years earlier, Kane had christened them shadow suits. Later they learned that a manufacturing technique known in predark days as electrospin lacing had electrically charged polymer particles to form a single-crystal metallic microfiber with a dense molecular structure.

Kane maintained the shadow suits were superior to the polycarbonate Magistrate armor chiefly for their internal subsystems. Also, they were almost impossible to tear or pierce with a knife, but a heavy-caliber bullet could penetrate them. And unlike the Mag body armor, the shadow suit wouldn't redistribute the kinetic shock.

Turning, Kane called to Edwards. The man strode toward him swiftly. "Sir?"

"Me, Baptiste and Grant will scout out ahead."

An uneasy expression settled over Edwards's face. "With our comm signals being jammed, you could walk into a trap and we'd be none the wiser."

"The jamming umbrella works both ways," Grant pointed out. "Gray couldn't have transmitted a warning, so the consortium is just as much in the dark about us as we are about them."

"Unless Brewster talked," Edwards said.

Brigid's eyes narrowed to slits. "Brewster is accident prone and he's pretty bad mannered even by ex-Mag standards, but he wouldn't betray us."

Edwards nodded contritely. "No, ma'am, I guess he wouldn't."

Kane said, "We'll only go a little way…just to get the lay of the land. Worst-case scenario is that we run into trouble and fire off a couple of shots to let you know."

Edwards didn't seem comforted. "Yes, sir."

Kane, Grant and Brigid moved away from the perimeter of the settlement and followed a scattering of footprints up along the face of a dune. The wind made the sand hiss around their feet.

"I don't know if firing off some signal shots is a good idea," Brigid commented. "Remember what Gray said about noise attracting ghosts."

Grant snorted in derision but said nothing.

The sand bogged around their ankles as they climbed. When they reached the crest of the dune, Kane studied the massive thrust of dark rock Gray called Phantom Mesa. It stood like a giant sentinel of the desert.

Brigid tested her Commtact and grimaced in frustration when she heard only static. Quietly but with a hint of reproach underscoring her tone, she said to Kane, "You never should have let Brewster go out alone."

"I didn't 'let' him," Kane answered. "And you know it. He waited until my back was turned and took off with the power analyzer. He thought he could trace down the origin of the jamming."

Brigid nodded, her emerald eyes clouded by worry. "Brewster is far too headstrong for a scientist."

"I don't know about that…but he's sure as hell clumsy."

Grant suddenly halted, indicating with a hand wave for his partners to do the same. He leaned forward, head cocked to the right, his expression intent. "Hear something," he whispered.

Kane strained his hearing, but only the sigh of the breeze touched his ears. Then he heard a faint groan, seasoned with garbled words. Through narrowed eyes, he scanned the ridge of the dune thirty feet ahead but saw nothing. At the very edge of audibility he heard panting, hard and labored.

Then a figure suddenly lurched over the top of the dune and fell awkwardly, his body digging a trench through the sand. Long legs thrashed. The shape rolled to the bottom and lay there, struggling feebly.

The Cerberus warriors scrambled down the dune and surrounded the figure, whose wrists were bound behind his back. Terrified and pain-filled gasps burst from split and bloody lips.

Kane clutched the man by the shoulders and said, "Take it easy. You're safe now."

Kneeling, Kane carefully eased the limp body over. He saw the man's face in the fading light and winced. It was Brewster Philboyd.

Chapter 4

Philboyd's face was contorted with feral terror, but when he recognized Kane, Brigid Baptiste and Grant, his tense muscles relaxed in relief. In a slurred voice, he said, "About time."

In his midforties, Brewster Philboyd was a little over six feet tall, long limbed and lanky. Blond-white hair was swept back from a receding hairline. Normally he wore black-rimmed eyeglasses. Like CAT Alpha, he wore desert-camouflage BDUs.

Brigid pulled him up and held him in a sitting position while Grant cut through the ropes binding his wrists. Philboyd's face was bruised, his left eye all but swollen shut. Dry blood caked the area around his nose and mouth. Though unsightly, his injuries were superficial.

"Are you all right?" Brigid asked.

"They just slapped me around some," Philboyd answered, striving for a tone of indifference.

"Who is 'they'?" Kane inquired, offering Philboyd his canteen.

"Four men jumped me about three-quarters of a mile from here. They tied me up."

Philboyd paused to take a sip of water, rinse out his mouth and then spit. "They asked me some questions and all I told them was my name. I thought I heard a woman's voice, but I couldn't be sure. After that, they started asking me about Cerberus, how many of us were out here and if you three specifically were in the vicinity."

"How'd they know about us?" Brigid asked, dismayed.

Philboyd took another drink of water before replying, "Beats the hell out of me."

Grant uttered a weary sigh but said nothing. Both Kane and Brigid could guess his thoughts. Brewster Philboyd was one of many expatriates from the Manitius Moonbase who had chosen to forge new lives for themselves with the Cerberus warriors.

Although the majority of the former lunar colonists were academics, they had proved their inherent courage and resourcefulness and wanted to get out into the world and make a difference in the struggle to reclaim the planet of their birth.

Nearly twenty of them were permanently stationed on Thunder Isle in the Cific, working to refurbish the sprawling complex that had housed Operation Chronos two centuries before and make it a viable alternative to the Cerberus redoubt.

The other Manitius expatriates remained in the redoubt concealed within a Montana mountain peak as part of the Cerberus resistance movement. For three years, Kane, Brigid and Grant had struggled to dismantle the machine of baronial tyranny in America. Victory over the nine barons, if not precisely within their grasp, did not seem a completely unreachable goal—but then unexpectedly, nearly two years before, the entire dynamic of the struggle against the nine barons changed.

The Cerberus warriors learned that the fragile hybrid barons, despite being close to a century old, were only in a larval stage of their development. Overnight the barons changed. When that happened, the war against the baronies themselves ended, but a new one, far greater in scope, began.

The baronies had not fallen in the conventional sense through attrition, war or organized internal revolts. The barons had simply walked away from their villes, their territories and their subjects. When they reached the final stage in their development, they saw no need for the trappings of semidivinity, nor were they content to rule such minor kingdoms. When they evolved into their true forms, incarnations of the ancient Annunaki overlords, their avaricious scope expanded to encompass the entire world and every thinking creature on it.

Even two-plus years after the disappearance of the barons, the villes were still in states of anarchy, with various factions warring for control on a daily basis.

A number of former Magistrates, weary of fighting for one transitory ruling faction or another that tried to fill the power vacuum in the villes, responded to the outreach efforts of Cerberus.

Once the Magistrates joined Cerberus, Kane and Grant had seen to the formation of Cerberus Away Teams Alpha, Beta and Delta.

"Do you have any idea of what the Millennial Consortium is looking for out here?" Brigid asked.

Brewster Philboyd waved to the desert at large. "I think we'll have to find our own answers."

"Nothing new about that," Kane said sarcastically. "How did you escape?"

"To be honest, I don't really know. About half an hour ago, I realized I was alone. Everybody had just left me."

He paused, high forehead furrowed in thought. "I sort of got the impression that the consortium had a bigger problem to deal with than just me."

"Something to do with ghosts?" Brigid ventured.

Philboyd swung his head toward her, his one good eye widening in surprise. "You know, I thought I heard one of the millennialists say something about ghosts, but I thought I misheard him. Figured he was talking about something else."

"Do you at least know if the consortium has found a base out here?" Grant demanded impatiently.

"Logically, I'd have to say yes," Philboyd retorted. "But I haven't seen it. But the energy emissions were strongest in the direction of that big mesa over there."

"How are they getting to and from the place?" Brigid inquired.

Philboyd opened his mouth to answer, then his shoulders stiffened. Grant looked at him quizzically, then tilted his head back to scan the darkening sky. "Everybody down."

They huddled into the shadow cast by the dune. In the distance, they heard the thumping beat of helicopter rotors. Craning his neck, Kane glimpsed a big transport chopper angling in from the south. Red-and-yellow navigation lights glowed along its undercarriage.

"An MH-6 transport…not a common piece of ordnance nowadays," Grant murmured.

He spoke very truly. After the atmospheric havoc wreaked by the nukecaust, air travel of any sort had been very slow to make a comeback.

The machine did not fly over them, but instead inscribed a half circle around Phantom Mesa and sank from view. The sound of its vanes faded away.

Kane straightened up, brushing sand from his clothes. "Brewster, do you think you can make it back to the settlement on your own?"

Philboyd frowned and slowly climbed to his feet, massaging his wrists. "I think so."

"Good," Grant said. "Tell Edwards to bring the team and follow our tracks. We'll head out toward the mesa."

"What about me?" Philboyd inquired.

"You'll stay behind and guard our prisoner."

"Prisoner?"

"Yeah, a guy named Gray," Kane replied. "He's hurt pretty badly, so he won't give you any trouble. Doesn't look like you can handle much more."

Wincing, Philboyd touched his bruised face. "If it's all the same to you, I'd prefer to go with you."

"It's *not* the same to me," Kane declared harshly. "You took off against my express orders to stay put. You got jumped and beat to hell and now you're no good to us."

Resentfully, Philboyd snapped, "Yeah, but the energy readings I picked up are localized in the area of that mesa. That's where the jamming umbrella is transmitting the white noise."

"We figured that out without being captured and having the crap kicked out of us," Grant retorted unsympathetically.

Kane pointed in the direction of the village. "Do as I say for once. Go back and stay put."

Philboyd looked to be on the verge of arguing, but then his shoulders slumped in resignation. Without another word or a backward glance, he began trudging up the face of the sand dune.

After he topped the rise, Brigid turned to Kane, her eyes glittering with anger. "There was no need to be so hard on him. He only wanted to pull his own weight."

"Brewster is an academic," Kane shot back coldly. "And every time he goes out into the field, something like this happens to him. If we weren't around to pull his ass out of the various fires he falls into, he would have been dead years ago."

"But this time," Grant interjected, "he gave us away to the millennialists."

Brigid pursed her lips thoughtfully. "Not intentionally. Somebody recognized him. Whoever it was would have recognized us, too. It was just Brewster's bad luck to be spotted first."

"Yeah," Grant grunted, "and either they didn't think Brewster was worth wasting a bullet on or they wanted to save all they had to settle a larger problem."

"Like what?" Brigid challenged.

Kane started forward. "Let's go see, why don't we?"

The three people marched swiftly toward the immense pinnacle of rock, noting the rubble piled high around its base. Brigid estimated it as nearly three hundred feet in height. As sunset progressed, the deep fissures scoring the surface of the gigantic monolith became fathomless black shadows. Alert for sentries or motion detectors, the Cerberus warriors didn't speak. The only sound other than the scrape of their feet against sand was the thin piping of the wind around the rocks.

Brigid Baptiste's steady gait suddenly faltered, then she trotted ahead. An unusual shape humped up from the ground. A small wave of sand had all but buried it, but in the dim light metal glinted. She picked up the rectangular power analyzer, a device designed to measure, record and analyze energy emissions, quality and harmonics.

"At least we don't have to charge this back to Brewster," she commented wryly.

She swept the extended sensor stem back and forth in short left-to-right arcs, then pointed it toward the mesa. The device's LCD glowed steadily and the readout indicated the energy signature was very strong.

"Whatever it is," Grant murmured, "we're almost on top of it."

The Cerberus warriors started walking again, scaling a shale-littered slope that led to a flat summit. They dropped to their hands and knees, then belly-crawled to the top. They stared for a long time in the fading light.

They saw a cuplike crater nestled at the base of Phantom Mesa, bracketed by broken edges of butte rock on the far side. The depression covered several acres and was surrounded by the remains of a chain-link fence. The floor of the crater was board flat. A road led toward a dark defile at the foot of the mesa. It was blocked by a metal gate.

Part of the open field was sheltered by a rooflike overhang of rock, jutting out from the side of the mesa. Metal gleamed under the roof, and a half dome of translucent Plexiglas reflected the dimming sunlight. The transport helicopter was parked near it, the rotors spinning.

Kane focused his attention on a large steel plate

at the bottom of the shallow crater. Several people clad in dun-colored coveralls stood around it, as if they were waiting for something to happen. On the far side of the crater, men bustled about with a military precision.

Suddenly, Brigid Baptiste put her mouth close to Kane's ear and breathed, "Hear something—"

Brigid Baptiste's warning whisper came a split second before Kane heard the grate of boot soles against rock. Kane turned his head slightly as a tall shadow stretched up to the lip of rock. He carried a sleek black Calico M-750 subgun, outfitted with a long noise suppressor.

Chapter 5

Kane remained flat on the ledge of rock as the man in the dun-colored coverall reached the summit. He paused and sneezed.

Swearing beneath his breath, the man juggled the Calico as he wiped his nose on the sleeve of his garment. Kane rose silently and slammed his Sin Eater-weighted forearm against the back of the man's head.

The sentry's breath exploded from his lips and he staggered, half-turning to topple off the rim. Kane caught him by one arm and yanked him forward. The Calico clattered on the rock and Brigid snatched it up. The man fell heavily on his face, only a few inches away from Grant.

The Cerberus warriors waited quietly for a handful of seconds, watching and listening for a general alarm to be raised. Men down in the crater shouted to one another, and the sound of the chopper's vanes increased in volume. The helicopter rose, the rotor blades whipping eddies of dust all over the crater. Swiveling, the aircraft's nose pointed eastward, banked to port, then arrowed away.

"I wonder who—or what—is aboard the chopper," Grant muttered. "They seemed to be in a hurry."

Brigid didn't answer. Moving swiftly, she removed a set of nylon cuffs from a pants pocket and slipped them over the unconscious man's hands, snugging his wrists tightly together. Grant fashioned a serviceable gag from a bandanna and knotted the ends at the back of the man's neck.

Kane gazed down at the activity in the depression, noting the swarthy complexions among the people standing around the gleaming metal plate. "It looks like they've got the locals busy."

Grant rose to a knee, his eyes narrowed. "Busy doing what?"

"I get the feeling they're packing up and moving out."

Brigid checked the Calico. "Should we stroll down and ask what they're up to or wait for the rest of the team? I'd like to avoid a firefight, if at all possible."

"Yeah, so would I," Kane replied.

Grant looked up at the sky. "No wonder our satellites couldn't locate this place…shielded by the rock this way, we could fly over it at a couple of hundred feet and never know the place was here."

Although most satellites had been little more than free-floating scrap metal for well over a century, Cerberus had always possessed the proper electronic ears and eyes to receive the transmissions from at least two of them.

The Vela-class reconnaissance satellite carried

narrow-band multispectral scanners. It could detect the electromagnetic radiation reflected by every object on Earth, including subsurface geomagnetic waves. The scanner was tied into an extremely high resolution photographic relay system.

The other satellite to which the Cerberus redoubt was uplinked was a Comsat, which for many months was used primarily to track Cerberus personnel when they were out in the field. Everyone in the installation had been injected with a subcutaneous transponder that transmitted heart rate, respiration, blood count and brain-wave patterns. Based on organic nanotechnology, the transponder was a nonharmful radioactive chemical that bound itself to an individual's glucose and the middle layers of the epidermis.

The telemetric signal was relayed to the redoubt by the Comsat, and the Cerberus computer systems recorded every byte of data.

Suddenly the air filled a painfully loud high-pitched whine, like a gigantic band saw. "Down!" Kane exclaimed, falling flat to the lip of rock.

The whining grew louder just as what was left of the sun's glow vanished below the horizon. But the crater was splashed by a multicolored shimmer. Down below, the laborers pulled aside the metal plate in the ground and then ran toward the gate at the base of the mesa. From a round aperture in the crater floor, a slender metal column rose straight up, pointing like a steel finger toward the sky.

"What the hell—?" Grant began.

The whining noise climbed to an eardrum-piercing crescendo. The top of the metal finger sprouted gleaming armatures, webworks of steel mesh unfolding and stretching outward. They formed shallow, disk-shaped dishes. The column continued to rise until it towered fifty feet above the crater floor.

Kane lifted his head, seeing activity by the gate at the base of the looming mesa. Movement shifted at the corner of his eye and he saw a man wearing the standard dun-drab coverall climb up to the ledge. A Calico was slung over his left shoulder and he stared downward at the crater.

As soon as Kane saw him, the millennialist turned his head and spotted Kane. Their eyes locked for what seemed like a long time. The sentry's mouth worked as he yelled something, but his voice was completely smothered by the electronic whine from below. He struggled to bring his Calico to bear, but the long sound suppressor made swift movement impossible.

Kane launched himself from the ground as the guard unslung his weapon. He slashed the noise suppressor at Kane's head, missed and hit his right shoulder. A fireball of pain exploded in Kane's shoulder socket and then he knocked the man down. They rolled and bumped down the slope, hitting big rocks with bone-jarring impacts.

They thrashed together down to the base of the slope, the man's breath hissing in his ear. Kane tried to hit him, but his right arm was numb, barely responsive. He grabbed the silencer of the Calico with his left hand, and the sentry twisted over with a steel-spring convulsion of his body. He threw his weight against the subgun, pressing the barrel across Kane's neck, pinning him against the ground.

Kane tried to break free by arching his back and bucking upward, but the sentry was heavy and surprisingly powerful. His teeth bared in a grin of triumph as he put more pressure on the metal across Kane's throat.

Kane glimpsed a shifting movement and even over the screeching whine from the crater, he heard a solid thump of metal colliding with bone. The millennialist cried out, went limp and fell half on top of him. Brigid stood over the man, feet spread, her appropriated subgun reversed in her hands. She had used to the blunt stock to club the man into unconsciousness.

Breathing hard, Kane elbowed aside the unconscious man. He staggered to his feet, rubbing his throat. "Thanks, Baptiste."

From a pocket he produced his own set of nylon cuffs and bound the man's wrists. While he worked, Brigid asked, "Why didn't you just shoot him?"

"Because you said you didn't want to start a firefight." He picked up the millennialist's Calico. "Now we have a matched set."

As they began climbing up the crater wall again, the mechanical whine ended. When they reached the top of the slope and rejoined Grant, they saw that the slender metal tower was slowly rotating, the disks made of mesh angling downward.

Grant glanced over his shoulder at them. "You okay?"

"Fine," Kane said hoarsely. "Thanks for all your help."

Grant shrugged. "I knew you could take him— with Brigid's help."

They eyed the metal tower. Although the electronic whine had faded, miniature skeins of lightning played along the rims of the dishes.

"What the hell is that supposed to be?" Kane asked.

Brigid shook her head. "I have no idea."

"My market for speculation is open."

"I'd sell it if I had it. At first glance, I'd say it looks like a microwave pulse transmitter. But my gut tells me it's something else entirely."

Grant hoisted himself to a knee. "Let's go take a closer look, since nobody is around."

"There could be a good reason nobody is around," Kane commented.

Brigid tried the Commtact frequencies again but heard only static. "There's no calling for help if he get ourselves trapped."

Grant snorted. "Since when do we call for help?"

Kane assumed the question was rhetorical. He rose and walked along the ridge until he found the path that the sentries had climbed. The Cerberus warriors descended into the crater, alert for other guards but they saw no one.

They strode across the crater, giving the steel column a wide berth. They heard a deep bass hum emanating from within the tower, a low throbbing that set up shivery vibrations within their eardrums.

The Cerberus warriors walked toward the metal gate and saw it hanging ajar, dim light spilling out from between the flat slats. The square-cut passageway beyond the door stretched away into gloom. Keeping close to the right-hand wall, they followed the curve of the tunnel until it ended at a circular well pit, with metal steps spiraling down.

"Why does it always have to be underground?" Brigid murmured with mock weariness.

Kane responded with a crooked half smile and took the first step, careful that the risers did not creak or squeak beneath his weight. The staircase corkscrewed down only a couple of yards before ending at a low-ceilinged foyer. Stenciled on the wall in red were the letters: Property OF DARPA, IEEE Approved. Must Have A-10 Clearance ID To Proceed.

Brigid's eyes darted back and forth as she read the words. "Definitely a predark scientific testing facility."

"What kind?" Grant asked, familiar with but annoyed by the fixation on acronyms.

She pointed to each letter, enunciating the words clearly, "Defense Advanced Research Projects

Agency and the Institute of Electrical and Electronics Engineers gave this place its seal of approval, if that means anything."

"It doesn't," Kane muttered, but he didn't question her.

Although Brigid Baptiste was a trained historian, having spent over half of her thirty years as an archivist in the Cobaltville Historical Division, there was far more to her storehouse of knowledge than simple training.

Almost everyone who worked in the ville divisions kept secrets, whether they were infractions of the law, unrealized ambitions or deviant sexual predilections. Brigid's secret was more arcane than the commission of petty crimes or manipulating the baronial system of government for personal aggrandizement.

Her secret was her photographic, or eidetic, memory. She could, after viewing an object or scanning a document, retain exceptionally vivid and detailed visual memories. When she was growing up, she feared she was a psi-mutie, but she later learned that the ability was relatively common among children and usually disappeared by adolescence. It was supposedly very rare among adults, but Brigid was one of the exceptions.

Due to her memory, everything she read or saw or even heard was impressed indelibly in her memory. Since her exile, Brigid had taken full advantage of the redoubt's vast database, and as an intellectual omnivore she grazed in all fields. Coupled with her memory, her profound knowledge of an extensive and eclectic number of topics made her something of an ambulatory encyclopedia. This trait often irritated Kane, but just as often it had tipped the scales between life and death, so he couldn't in good conscience become too annoyed with her.

Kane started walking, cradling the appropriated Calico in his arms. "Let's see what we've got here. Let's explore a little."

"What do you expect to find?" Grant demanded.

Kane shrugged. "How do I know? That's why I suggested we explore."

"Just about every time we explore one of these places, we end up having to run out of it as fast we can," Grant muttered.

At a cross corridor, they passed a small cafeteria-type dining room, equipped with two upright refrigerators and a large coffeemaker, but no one was seated at the long tables. On the opposite side of the passageway lay an office suite, furnished with a dozen desks, computer stations and file cabinets.

"Where is everybody?" Grant asked. "We saw them come in here, and the place can only be so big."

"Maybe there's a back way out," Brigid suggested.

The corridor turned to the left like an L. They passed a sign on the wall at the angle that read Los

Alamos Shuttle. An arrow pointed ahead, in the direction they walked.

Kane glanced around uneasily. "Maybe that's the back door they took."

"Could be," Brigid conceded. "But why?"

The hallway terminated in a door emblazoned with the warning No Unauthorized Admittance.

"That means us." Grant tried the knob and to his surprise, it turned easily.

Carefully, he pushed the door open and entered a narrow passage illuminated by naked light bulbs in ceiling fixtures. The three people navigated through a labyrinth of pipes, fuse boxes and cooling systems, all the machinery that kept the installation alive and self-sufficient.

Grant, Kane and Brigid became aware of a low hum ahead of them. It was almost like the bass register of a piano, which continued to vibrate long after a key had been struck. Their neck muscles tensed and their diaphragms contracted at the same time they became aware of a dull pain in their temples.

The passageway opened directly into a large circular room, the curving walls lined by consoles. The control surfaces flashed and glowed with various icons and indicator lights. A stainless-steel shaft mounted in a drum-shaped socket rose from the floor and continued through the domed roof.

"Here's where the tower is raised," Kane commented. "Whatever the hell it really is."

Three crystalline hoops surrounded the drum socket at the base of the shaft. The hoops turned slowly and emitted the deep drone. The sound seemed to tighten around their craniums, squeezing and compressing as if their heads were trapped in tightening vises.

Wincing, Kane said, "Let's get out of here. My head is really hurting."

"Yeah," Grant agreed. "Like my skull is being pinched against my brain or something."

"Just a second," Brigid replied absently as she inspected the control boards.

She noted the similarity of symbols and letters glowing on various monitor screens. The circle-and-ovoid combination representing the Greek letter theta was repeated over and over. The center screen showed a column of numbers, the digits clocking backward.

Suddenly, realization washed over her like a flood of icy water. She whirled toward her friends. "We definitely should get out of here before the pinching sensation gets any worse."

She moved swiftly toward the door. Grant and Kane fell into step behind her.

"What's the problem, Baptiste?" Kane asked.

"I think what we've got here is a theta-pinch transmitter," she said over a shoulder.

"A what?" Grant demanded, face drawn in a scowl.

"It's a form of experimental fusion physics," she

said, speaking quickly, ducking under a low-hanging pipe. "By magnetically compressing electrically conducting filaments, it creates an electromagnetic field that implodes rather than expands. They occur naturally in electrical discharges such as lightning bolts."

"What the hell is something like that for?" Kane asked.

"Research into the supergravity theory, from what I recall," Brigid replied, breathing hard. "I think it's set on a countdown to some sort of energy discharge. I'll explain when we're out of here."

"Looking forward to it," Grant said dourly.

They quickly retraced their steps, climbing back up the spiral staircase. As they ran toward the gate, Kane couldn't completely suppress a sigh of relief when he saw it still hung open.

A towering figure suddenly appeared on the other side of the gate, and Kane's sigh of relief turned into a curse. He snapped up the Calico, finger curling around the trigger.

Kane reflected grimly that they had been lucky so far—but now, typically, their luck had run out.

Chapter 6

Edwards frantically hurled his body to one side, shouting, "It's me!"

Kane gusted out a profanity-seasoned breath, feeling angry and ashamed. He, Brigid and Grant left the tunnel, slamming open the door. The other members of CAT Alpha stood in the crater, gazing at the spark-shedding and crackling metal transmission tower.

"What's going here?" Edwards asked. "Where the hell is everybody?"

"How'd you get here?" Grant asked.

"We followed your tracks."

Kane's eyebrows knitted at the bridge of his nose. "You didn't find a couple of consortium guys tied up?"

Edwards shook his head. "No, sir. Were we supposed to?"

Brigid eyed the dishes on either side of the metal tower apprehensively, noting the greenish aura shimmering around them. "I think we've been had. Let's double-time it out of here."

"We're going to leave this place unsecured?"

Edwards asked, gesturing with his rifle barrel to the tunnel entrance.

Brigid's lips compressed. "I don't think we have much choice. I think the consortium abandoned this place for a reason."

"Like what?" Kane inquired. "Besides headaches."

Edwards eyed him in surprise. "All of us have headaches…and I'm starting to feel sick to my stomach."

"What's causing this?" Grant asked. "Radiation?"

Glancing up at the indigo sky and the first emerging stars of the evening, Brigid answered bluntly, "I have no idea. But if they don't want the place, we probably wouldn't, either."

Kane opened his mouth to voice a question, but the muffled boom of a subterranean explosion made him jump. He bit back a curse. A second later they heard another explosion, followed by a third. The ground trembled under their feet.

Several sharp cracks burst from the disks mounted atop the metal tower. They sounded like huge sticks breaking simultaneously. From the mouth of the passageway gushed a billow of flame and smoke. Acrid black fumes grabbed everyone by the throat and set them to coughing.

A tremendous explosion cannonaded up from the throat of the tunnel, and a brutal column of concussive force slammed into them like an invisible tsunami, buffeting them backward.

A series of hammering blasts thundered up. The entire crater floor shook and trembled. Rifts split the ground. Rocks and dirt, shaken loose from the mesa, sifted down. A fissure opened up around the mouth of the tunnel with a clash of rending rock and a distant shriek of rupturing metal.

Boulders toppled down from above, blocking the entrance to the tunnel. The people moved away, staggering on the convulsing earth. They ran out in the center of the crater to avoid being crushed by rocks falling from the mesa.

The metal tower bent and with a prolonged creak, it sagged downward at a forty-five-degree angle. The crackling, popping pyrotechnic display around the metal mesh disks didn't ebb.

When the ground tremors ceased, Edwards demanded angrily, "What the fuck is going on?"

Brigid shook her head, fanning the dust-laced air away from her face. "The station was set to self-destruct. God knows why."

"We can tell you." The voice, amplified by a loud-hailer, was high-pitched but male.

The crater floor lit up with blinding rods of brightness. The searchlight beams stabbed through the night and intersected with the bodies of Cerberus Away Team Alpha, pinned like butterflies to a board. Squinting, Kane shielded his eyes, bringing up his Calico.

"Don't move," the voice said. "It's very important that you stay as motionless as possible."

"Fuck them," Edwards growled, finger crooking around the trigger of his rifle.

"If they meant to kill us," Grant muttered to him, "they'd have done it already, not threaten us."

"I think we're being warned," Brigid said, "not threatened. They didn't tell us to drop our weapons."

Trapped in the dazzling exposure of the light, Kane figured the Millennial Consortium really didn't care one way or the other if they were disarmed. They had other matters occupying them.

Beyond the blinding circle of the handheld spotlight, he could barely make out man-shaped shadows arrayed on the ridgeline. He asked, "Who are we talking to?"

"Shh!" came the reply. "Call me Mr. Blue, call me late for dinner, it doesn't matter. What does matter is that you don't move until we tell you to."

"Why?" Brigid asked.

"Shh!"

"Don't shush me," Brigid snapped irritably. "Are you responsible for blowing up the installation?"

"Shh! Don't make any noise. Be as quiet as you can and *don't* move. Stay in the light if you value your lives!"

Mystified, but feeling sweat form on his hairline, Kane cut his gaze over to Brigid. "Is he crazy or what?" he whispered.

She shook her head slightly. "For the time being, we probably should do as he says—until we can get a better idea of what's going on here."

"Nothing is going on around here," growled Higson, a CAT team member. "Except we're being set up to be slaughtered."

Kane considered Higson's words for a thoughtful second, then the sparks dancing along the rims of the disks suddenly faded away. He found the phenomenon worrisome, not comforting.

At the same time, the glare of the spotlight dimmed. He sensed it hadn't been done to spare their vision. Faintly, he heard a murmuring from the people on the ridgeline. Mr. Blue's voice whispered frantically, "Shut up! Be quiet!"

Kane blinked, trying to clear his vision of the amoeba-shaped floaters swimming over his eyes. His flesh suddenly prickled with a pins-and-needle sensation, almost as if a multitude of ants crawled over his skin. He felt rather than heard a feathery fluttering against his eardrums. His stomach surged with nausea.

Edwards shuddered and muttered, "Something is going on here."

The spotlight dimmed even more, becoming little more than a faint yellow halo.

"It's like the power is being drained," Brigid said wonderingly. "Localized ionization of the atmosphere, too."

Higson shifted his feet nervously and said in a guttural whisper, "What the fuck is that?"

Kane followed the man's gaze toward the smoke-occluded opening in the base of the mesa.

Movement shifted within the roiling vapors, and a green-hued light flickered in the haze. A faint, cold breeze touched his face, ruffling his hair, and he heard a distant hiss. The green light whirled, bathing the entire crater in an emerald glow. Then, slowly, the light contorted into the outline of a human figure.

Kane gazed, transfixed, his mind a whirl of bewilderment. He felt his throat constrict, and his heart began pounding in a sudden terror. The green figure twisted, stretching outward, growing broader. It split into another shape of identical size and dimension.

"Too late!" Mr. Blue bleated from the ridgeline. His voice thickened with horror and he screamed, "Run!"

Cerberus Away Team Alpha retreated from the ghostly, nebulous bodies, backing away toward the crater wall. The figures resembled cadavers glistening with a coating of green phosphorous. Their facial features were always in flux, sliding and re-forming, like smoke. Two more appeared, gliding over the ground toward them. Fingers like wisps of emerald smoke reached out at the end of skeletal arms, convulsing with grasping and clutching movements. The wraiths spread out in a horseshoe formation, clouds of fluorescent particles swarming around them.

Kane raised the appropriated Calico to his shoulder, sighted down its length and shouted, "Fire!"

He squeezed off a long rattling burst. Bright brass arced out of the smoking ejector port, tinkling down at his feet. Grant, Brigid and the other members of CAT Alpha triggered simultaneous full-auto fusillades.

The barrage ripped through the wraiths, punching holes, ripping them to shreds. The figures instantly re-formed, resolving into a dozen wavering, green ghostly shapes. Tiny pieces of green light floated over their heads, like a swarm of radioactive fireflies. The keening whines of ricochets reverberated and echoed all over the crater. The hailstorm of bullets struck bell-like chimes from the metal tower. The slugs bounced off with high-pitched whines.

Kane released his pressure on the Calico's trigger and shouted, "Cease fire! Fall back!"

CAT Alpha sprinted up the slope to the ridge surrounding the crater, causing miniature avalanches under their feet. Kane, Higson and Grant remained at the base of the crater wall, eyes and gun barrels fixed on the cluster of green ghosts less than ten yards away.

Higson snatched a round V-60 minigrenade from his combat webbing, and ran at an oblique angle away from the rest of the team. He shouted, "Keep going!"

"Get your ass back here!" Grant bellowed.

Higson paid no attention to the command. Swiftly he unpinned the grenade and hurled it overhead into the center of the glowing green wraiths, then he flung himself flat, covering up, face buried the cradle of his arms. The V-60 exploded in a ballooning ball of flame. The concussion slapped Kane and Grant backward a few paces. Dust sifted down and they impatiently waved it away.

Although they didn't see the ghostly figures, they saw the little swarm of orbs surrounding Higson. Howling, he leaped to his feet and flailed at them with the frame of his rifle, without making solid impact.

The cloud settled over the man's head and shoulders, spreading over his face. When he opened his mouth to scream, two of the orbs darted past his lips and his shriek turned into a gargling croak. Dropping his rifle, he ran in a blind panic across the crater, hands clapped over his eyes.

"Baptiste, get everybody back to the parallax point!" Kane snapped.

He didn't wait to find out if she obeyed his order or had even heard it. He and Grant kicked themselves into sprints as they chased after the frantically fleeing Higson.

The man stumbled over an irregularity in the ground and fell heavily. He writhed, crying out, limbs thrashing in wild spasms.

By the time Grant and Kane reached him, the swarm of green orbs had lifted from the man's body and circled high overhead. Higson lay sprawled on his back, saliva bubbling over swollen lips, his respiration shallow. A puff of gray-green vapor rose from his mouth.

Kane recoiled at the sight of his face—the blotched flesh leaking and suppurated as if suddenly exposed to a horrific blast of heat. Tiny blisters formed on his cheeks and burst with pops. The whites of his eyes showed only bloodshot streaks.

"He's still alive?" Grant rasped.

Stooping over the body, Kane pressed two fingers against the base of Higson's neck, timing the pulse. It beat fast and erratic. "Not for long."

When Kane removed his fingers, a layer of Higson's flesh peeled off. "It's like he's rotting from the inside out," he said quietly.

Grant shook his head. "Not so much rotting as disintegrating."

Even as he spoke, the left side of Higson's face went slack, sagging from the bone. With the moist sound like a wet rag dragged over a rock, the flesh completely fell away, revealing red-filmed cheekbone. The man shuddered violently for a moment, then died.

As Grant and Kane watched in stunned, shocked silence, Higson's body beneath his clothes collapsed in on itself, the flesh and bones dissolving into a foul-smelling green smoke. The cloud was shot through with tiny crackling flashes, like miniature versions of the pyrotechnics they had seen dancing on the tower's disks.

Kane backed away, feeling bile rise up his throat. "Let's get out of here."

"And leave Higson?"

"There's not much to take with us," Kane retorted flatly.

He eyed the witch-fire glow of the green orbs still hovering overhead. He said quietly, "We need go before we end up like Higson."

Grant's teeth bared in a silent snarl. "We don't know what was going on here!"

Kane nodded and backed away, keeping his gaze on the ghostly swarm. "Exactly. That's why we need to get the hell out of here as fast as we can."

Chapter 7

Grant and Kane scrambled down the rocky crater wall. The moon slowly rose ahead of them, casting a silver luminescence over the sand. The silence all around was ominous. They heard only the scuffling of their running feet as they sprinted in the direction of the village. As Edwards claimed, the bound and gagged millennialists were nowhere to be seen.

Kane resisted the urge to glance over his shoulder, looking for the swarm of green bees. He glimpsed them only once, whirling in the distance like jade-hued dust motes.

"I hate to say it," Grant half gasped, half growled, "but we've been skunked by the consortium again. I don't know what they were trying to pull, but they managed to do it."

"You don't really think they had anything to do with any of this, do you?" Kane panted.

The two men slowed their pace, noting the mess of footprints over a comber of sand. They stopped in order to catch their breath. Grant stared back toward Phantom Mesa. His face was beaded with sweat.

A thick plume of smoke coiled into the desert sky. Flames still erupted from some entrances to the complex, but the glowing orbs weren't visible.

"I think they decided we're not worth chasing after," Grant commented. "Maybe the consortium called them off."

"The Millennial Consortium isn't behind those things," Kane said flatly.

"What makes you so sure?"

"They wouldn't have warned us about attracting their attention."

Grant knuckled his chin thoughtfully. "Even so, I don't think they were worried about our safety."

Kane nodded in agreement. "Neither do I. But I have the distinct impression the millennialists bit off way more than they could chew."

Grant gusted out a sigh, then stiffened. He hissed, "Shit!"

Bobbing like a multitude of tiny bubbles on the surface of a stream, a cloud of green orbs circled overhead. An icy hand clenched around the base of Kane's spine. The orbs swirled in a clockwise direction, then back again. With each rotation, the glowing flecks sank lower and lower.

"What the hell are those things?" he demanded angrily. "Weapons? Tracking devices? Are they alive or what?"

Grant inhaled a deep breath, turned and started running again. "Let's ask questions when we're safe."

They ran toward an area of rock formations, dust spurting from beneath their boots. They jumped over a tumble of stones, turning toward a narrow cleft, wide and tall enough for a man to enter. Kane risked a misstep by looking over his shoulder. The green-glowing swarm darted after them. He heard a strange hissing noise, like static over a dead comm circuit.

The two men sprinted toward the cleft and squeezed into the crack, sidling through the deep shadows. After a few feet, they were in absolute blackness. They kept moving forward, wincing at the clink and crunch of stones beneath their feet.

The sandstone walls of the cleft would provide some protection from the swarm, since pursuit in a straight line was impossible. Kane and Grant threaded their way through a labyrinth of cracks, slamming their knees and banging their elbows against outthrusts of rock.

They swore between clenched teeth, but kept running, stumbling and lurching from wall to wall. The farther they penetrated into the cleft, the narrower the walls became. A stitch stabbed along Kane's left side, and the muscles of Grant's legs felt as if they were caught in a vise. Both men's vision became shot through with gray specks.

Even over the rasp and gasp of their own labored breathing, they heard the incessant hiss of their pursuers. It was like running on a conveyor belt and getting nowhere.

Then both men saw the wedge of relative brightness ahead of them and they struggled out of the cleft and into the cooling desert air. Looking behind them, they saw the green glowing swarm sliding around bends in the rock wall, like a stream of embers.

Panting, Grant snatched an M-33 fragmentation grenade from his combat webbing, slipping the spoon at the same time. "Enough of this shit."

He threw the grenade underhanded into the cleft. He and Kane dropped flat behind a tumble of low rocks. The grenade rolled only a few feet before detonating with a brutal thunderclap. A hell-flower bloomed, petals of flame curving outward. A rain of shrapnel spewed from the end of every petal, rattling violently against the rock walls. Loose shale showered down from above and crashed from the sides of the cleft. The rolling echoes of the explosion faded, replaced by clicks and clatters of falling rock.

Cautiously, Kane and Grant rose to their knees, spitting out grit and particles of sand. They saw only a thick, roiling haze of dust and smoke. Quickly they got to their feet, backed away, neither man wanting to voice the hope that the swarm of ghostly pursuers had been crushed and buried.

Suddenly a hiss of static filled their heads and both men jumped in startled reaction. Then Brigid Baptiste's voice filtered through their Commtacts. "Kane! Grant! Where are you?"

Glancing around, Kane saw the ridge of gravelly dunes that bracketed the settlement barely half a mile away. He said, "We're close. Be there soon."

"What was that explosion?"

"Our way of swatting bugs," Grant replied dryly. "When did the Commtacts start working again?"

"I don't know," Brigid replied. "The EM interference is still around, but it's not as pronounced. Brewster is still picking up an energy signature on the sensor. There's some sort of generalized power source around here, so I suggest you double-time back to us."

Brigid closed the channel and Grant said grimly, "I don't feel much like running anymore."

Kane shrugged. "Me, neither. But you heard the lady."

The two men sighed with weary exasperation and began jogging across the moonlight-splashed landscape. Both of them cast apprehensive glances over their shoulders, but saw no sign of anything small, glowing or green.

They reached the little settlement within ten minutes and found Brigid, Philboyd and CAT Alpha, tense, anxious and ready to move out. Two of the away team supported the man who called himself Mr. Gray between them. He looked pale and frightened. Brigid had already retrieved the interphaser's cushioned and waterproof carrying case from its hiding place in one of the abandoned dwellings.

"I thought I told you to wait for us at the parallax point," Kane said to her by way of a greeting.

Brigid lifted one shoulder in a dismissive shrug. "There wasn't enough time to get there. Besides, I didn't know that you weren't going to get yourselves lost out there."

Kane only smiled, not in the least offended by her mendacity, knowing it was her way of concealing her genuine concern and worry.

At the beginning of their relationship, it was very difficult for Kane and Brigid not to give offense to one another. Both people were gifted in their own way. Most of what was important to people in the early twenty-third century came easily to Kane—survival skills, prevailing in the face of adversity and cunning against enemies. But he could also be reckless, high-strung to the point of instability and given to fits of rage.

Brigid, on the other hand, was compulsively tidy and ordered, with a brilliant analytical mind. However, her clinical nature, the cool scientific detachment upon which she prided herself, sometimes blocked an understanding of the obvious human factor in any given situation. Accommodating their contrasting personalities, Kane and Brigid now worked very well as a team, playing off each other's strengths rather than magnifying their individual weaknesses.

Philboyd swept the sensor wand of the energy analyzer in the direction of the mesa. Despite his swollen lips, he frowned. "There's definitely a low-level pattern out there…it spikes, then flatlines, then spikes again."

"It's probably a good idea to get out of here during a flatline period," Grant said uneasily.

For once, Philboyd didn't seem inclined to argue. Turning on his heel, he said, "Let's do it, then. I'm looking forward to soaking in a hot bath."

Kane worked his right arm up and down, kneading his shoulder socket. "Me, too."

"What about me?" Gray asked hoarsely.

Kane regarded him bleakly. "If we leave you here, you could die of blood loss or exposure. Besides, we can always use a source of information."

Gray tried to tilt his head at a defiant angle. "You'll get nothing out of me."

Kane showed the edges of his teeth in a wolfish smile. "We'll see."

The Cerberus personnel marched out of the settlement, pretending not to notice a few locals peering at them from the windows of their hovels, their eyes gleaming like those of feral animals in the gloom. They were a small, dark people, furtive and apparently fleet of foot, since they had avoided being pressed into a work gang by the Millennial Consortium.

Kane made a rather exaggerated show of paying them no attention. It was always a chancy business communicating with Outlanders, particularly in settlements that had been isolated since the nukecaust of two centuries ago. He retained vividly unpleasant memories of the violent encounters in various Outland settlements over the years.

In the Outlands, people were divided into small, regional clans. Communications with other groups were stifled, education impeded and rivalries bred. The internecine struggles in the Outlands had not only been condoned by the baronies, but also encouraged to continue.

Outlanders, or anyone who chose or was forced to live outside ville society, were accustomed to living on the edge of death. Grim necessity had taught them the skills to survive, even thrive in the postnuke environment. They may have been the great-great-great-grandchildren of civilized men and women, but they had no choice but to embrace lives of semibarbarism.

The people who lived outside the direct influence of the villes, who worked the farms, toiled in the fields, or simply roamed from place to place, were reviled and hated. No one worried about an Outlander or even cared. They were the outcasts of the new feudalism, the cheap, expendable labor forces, even the cannon fodder when circumstances warranted. In return, they feared and hated anyone not of their clan.

Brigid moved forward to walk beside Kane. "It might not be a good idea to take Gray back to the redoubt."

"Why not? Aren't we always in need of intel about the Millennial Consortium?"

"Yes," she admitted. "But as far as we know, Gray may have a tracking transponder on him, much like ours."

"I think the consortium already knows where we live," Kane replied dryly. "But by the same token, we don't know anything about the central headquarters for their group. Or even if they have one."

Brigid considered his words for a silent few seconds, then nodded. "I suppose it's worth the risk to learn more about them."

The parallax point lay less than half a klick outside the settlement, marked by the circular ruins of a kiva, an adobe structure built centuries ago, according to Brigid, by the Hopi Indians.

In the center of the kiva lay a thick sandstone disk, its surface deeply engraved with elaborate geometric designs, a complex series of interlocking symbols that formed a spiral of concentric rings over twelve feet in diameter. The design cut into the stone was an ancient geodetic marker, carved into the naked rock as a two-dimensional representation of multidimensional space. The Cerberus exiles had seen similar markers in the past, in diverse places such as Iraq, China and even South America. Kane didn't completely understand the scientific principles of geomantic vortex points, but he respected their power, as had the ancient peoples who engraved the rock.

A few years before, during the investigation of the Operation Chronos installation on Thunder Isle, a special encoded program named Parallax Points was discovered. Lakesh learned that the Parallax

Points program was actually a map, a geodetic index, of all the vortex points on the planet. Each newly discovered set of coordinates was fed into the interphaser's targeting computer.

With the new data, the interphaser became more than a miniaturized version of a gateway unit, even though it employed much of the same hardware and operating principles. The mat-trans gateways functioned by tapping into the quantum stream, the invisible pathways that crisscrossed outside of perceived physical space and terminated in wormholes.

The interphaser interacted with the energy within a naturally occurring vortex and caused a temporary overlapping of two dimensions. The vortex then became an intersection point, a discontinuous quantum jump, beyond relativistic space-time.

Evidence indicated there were many vortex nodes, centers of intense energy, located in the same proximity on each of the planets of the solar system, and those points correlated to vortex centers on Earth. The power points of the planet, places that naturally generated specific types of energy, possessed positive and projective frequencies, while others were negative and receptive.

Brigid stepped into the center of the disk and kneeled down, unzipping and unsealing the interphaser's carrying case. Her movements were practiced and deliberate. When she lifted out the gleaming device, the shape of the interphaser resembled a very squat, broad-based pyramid made of smooth, gleaming alloy. Only one foot in overall height, its width did not exceed ten inches. From the base protruded a small blocky power unit and a keypad.

When making transits to and from the Cerberus redoubt, they always used the mat-trans chamber as the origin point because it could be hermetically sealed. The interphaser's targeting computer had been programmed with the precise coordinates of the mat-trans unit as Destination Zero. A touch of a single key on the interphaser's control pad would automatically return the device to the jump chamber, but sometimes the phase harmonics needed to be fine-tuned. The adjustments were normally within Brigid's purview.

Unlike the mat-trans gateway jumps, phasing along a hyperdimensional conduit was more akin to stepping from one room into another—if the rooms were thousands of miles apart.

A veil of light expanded from the apex of the pyramidion, stretching outward in a wavering parabola, giving the illusion of a Chinese hand fan spreading wide, with the interphaser acting as the centerpiece.

A faint hiss touched Kane's ears. Involuntarily, he reached up to adjust his Commtact. At the same time, Philboyd's shoulders stiffened as he stared at the LCD window on his energy. Dispassionately, he intoned, "Uh-oh."

Everyone looked up and saw the clot of green

glowing orbs lancing across the sky toward them. Kane's Sin Eater slid into his palm and he said with feigned indifference, "Get us out of here, Baptiste."

She cast him an irritated glance, then her gaze went beyond him to the swarm hovering overhead. Her fingers quickly tapped the inset activation toggles on the keypad, and a wavering funnel of waxy light fanned up from the apex of the pyramid. It looked like a veil of backlit fog, sparkling with tiny shimmering stars.

Eyeing the glowing fireflies overhead, Philboyd said nervously, "They seem to be attracted to the energy."

Grant unholstered his Sin Eater. "Everybody get on the marker. Be ready to make the transit."

As CAT Alpha moved to obey, the cloud of orbs dived downward. The Sin Eaters stuttered deafeningly, the slugs racing upward. The rounds fired by Kane and Grant seemed to tear a ragged hole in the flock of glowing orbs. The objects flew in a tightening circle around the sandstone disk like a cyclone cloud.

Kane didn't try to track any of the orbs individually. He maintained his finger's pressure on the trigger stud, bright brass arcing out of the pistol's ejector port.

Something hot stung his face and a flare of green blinded him. His skin burned, and the fine hairs in his nostrils seemed to vibrate. At the edges of his hearing he heard a whining buzz that quickly built to a high-pitched hiss.

Fire coursed along his nervous system as his entire body was engulfed by a wave of shock, followed by red-hued agony.

And black silence.

Chapter 8

Whenever he was either bored or restless, Mohandas Lakesh Singh made the evening internal security sweep, a practice that consisted of little more than checking the images displayed on various monitor screens.

Although Lakesh didn't feel particularly bored this evening, he felt distinctly restless as he strode down the main corridor of the Cerberus redoubt. Every time Brigid Baptiste, Kane, Grant or any Cerberus personnel were out on a mission, he tended to fret, but also felt slightly ridiculous about it. At one time he suspected his mother-hen tendencies stemmed from guilt, but lately he attributed them to control issues.

Still, despite their frequent disagreements and arguments, he felt that Kane, Brigid and Grant were his family. In most ways, the exiles of the Cerberus redoubt enjoyed emotional bonds that were stronger than those of blood kin.

A well-built man of medium height, with thick, glossy, black hair, an unlined dark olive complexion and a long, aquiline nose, Lakesh looked no older than fifty, despite a few strands of distinguished gray streaking his temples. He resembled a middle-aged man of East Indian extraction in reasonably good health. In reality, he had celebrated his 251st birthday several months earlier.

Lakesh quickly walked down the twenty-foot-wide passageway made of softly gleaming vanadium alloy and shaped like a square with an arch on top. Great curving ribs of metal and massive girders supported the high rock roof. He passed a few people who greeted him either with a deferential nod or with a respectful "Good evening, Dr. Singh."

He appreciated the respect. For many years he received very little of it, nor had he felt he deserved it. As a youthful genius, Lakesh had been drafted into the web of conspiracy the architects of the Totality Concept had spun during the last couple of decades of the twentieth century. A multidegreed physicist and cyberneticist, he served as the administrator for Project Cerberus, a position that ensured his survival during the global megacull of January 2001. Like the Manitius Moonbase refugees, he had spent most of the intervening two hundred years in cryostasis.

Lakesh reached the partially open sec door, which folded open like an accordion. Because the panels of vanadium were so heavy, only rarely was the door closed completely, since it required several minutes to open again.

Although the official designations of all Totality Concept-related redoubts were based on the phonetic alphabet, almost no one who had ever been stationed in the facility referred to the redoubt by its official code name of Bravo. The mixture of civilian scientists and military personnel simply called it Cerberus, and to commemorate that name, a large, luridly colored illustration of the triple-headed black hound was painted on the wall beneath the controls to the massive security door. A spiked metal collar bound the single muscular neck, fire and blood gushed out from between yellow fangs and the crimson eyes glared bright and baleful. Underneath the image, in overly ornate Gothic script was written Cerberus.

Although he couldn't be positive, Lakesh suspected that one of the original military personnel assigned to the redoubt, a certain Corporal James Mooney, was the artist. The exaggerated exuberance of the rendering seemed taken directly from the comic books the young man was obsessed with collecting.

Lakesh had never considered having the illustration removed. For one thing, the paints were indelible and for another, it was Corporal Mooney's form of immortality. Besides, the image of Cerberus, the guardian of the gates of hell, represented a visual symbol of the work to which Lakesh had devoted his life.

Constructed in the mid-1990s, no expense had

been spared to make the redoubt, the seat of Project Cerberus, a masterpiece of concealment and impenetrability. The Cerberus process, a subdivision of Overproject Whisper, had been a primary component of the Totality Concept. The researches to which Project Cerberus and its personnel had been devoted were locating and traveling hyperdimensional pathways through the quantum stream.

The thirty-acre, three-level installation had come through the nukecaust with its operating systems and radiation shielding in good condition. The redoubt contained two dozen self-contained apartments, a cafeteria, a frightfully well equipped armory, a medical infirmary, a gymnasium complete with a swimming pool and even holding cells on the bottom level.

When Lakesh had secretly reactivated the installation some thirty years earlier, the repairs he made had been minor, primarily cosmetic in nature. Over a period of time, he had installed an elaborate system of heat-sensing warning devices, night-vision vid cameras and motion-trigger alarms on the surrounding plateau.

He had been forced to work completely alone, so the upgrades had taken several years to complete. However, the remote location of the redoubt in Montana's Bitterroot Range had kept his work from being discovered by the baronial authorities.

In the generations since the nukecaust, a sinister mythology had been ascribed to the mountains, with their mysteriously shadowed forests and hell-deep, dangerous ravines. The wilderness area was virtually unpopulated. The nearest settlement was located in the flatlands and consisted of a small band of Indians led by a shaman named Sky Dog.

When Lakesh had been revived from stasis and drafted to serve the nine god-kings who assumed lordship over the Earth, he realized the horrific magnitude of their plan to conquer humanity.

Lakesh had tried many times since his resurrection to arrest the tide of extinction inexorably engulfing the human race. First had been his attempts to manipulate the human genetic samples in storage, preserved in vitro since before the nukecaust, to provide the hybridization program with a supply of the best DNA. He had hoped to create an underground resistance movement of superior human beings to oppose the barons. A revolutionary force needed a headquarters, and the Cerberus redoubt seemed the most serviceable.

Lakesh stepped over the threshold and onto the plateau, inhaling deeply of the chill mountain air and then repressing a shiver. The temperature was fairly mild for so late in the autumn, but he had been born in the tropical climate of Kashmir, India, and even after 250-plus years, his internal thermostat was still stuck there.

The emerging stars glittered in frosty wheels above the gray granite peak towering high overhead. The sprawling plateau was broad enough for the entire population of the redoubt to assemble without getting near the rusted remains of the chain-link fence enclosing it. The flat expanse of tarmac was bordered on one side by a grassy slope rising to rocky outcroppings and on the other by an abyss that plummeted vertically for nearly a thousand feet to the rushing waters of the Clark Fork River.

Lakesh tucked his hands into the pockets of his long coat and surveyed the plateau. Surrounded by a wilderness of trees, house-sized boulders and grass, a narrow road looped and curved away from it, twisting down like a path cut by a broken-backed snake writhing in its death throes. One side of the road butted up against the great, overhanging crags and the other bordered sheer cliffs.

The plateau still glistened with the residue of a late-afternoon sleet storm, making the uneven areas slippery underfoot as he crossed the plateau. The sleet had sifted in thin blankets over the grave sites on the slope of the far side of the plateau. The head-stones shone damply in the starlight. The fabricated markers bore only last names: Cotta, Dylan, Adrian and many more. Most of them were a little over two years old, inscribed with the names of the Moon-base émigrés who had died defending Cerberus from the assault staged by Overlord Enlil. The plateau itself was still pockmarked by the craters inflicted in that attack.

Lakesh saw Domi standing at the foot of one grave. The headstone read simply Quavell. A sprig of fresh wildflowers lay atop the marker. Judging by the color of the flowers, he figured Domi had gone down into the lower slopes, since the petals were still bright. Winter came early to the mountaintop concealing the Cerberus redoubt.

Domi didn't turn at the sound of his approach or when he said quietly, "Darlingest one, you're liable to catch a chill out here."

Domi chuckled briefly. "You know me better than that, Moe."

An albino by birth, the complexion of her limbs was as pale as creamed milk. Domi's spiky, bone-white hair was cropped short. The eyes on either side of her thin-bridged nose were the ruby color of fresh blood.

Every inch of five feet tall, Domi barely weighed one hundred pounds and at first glance, she gave the impression of being waiflike. But there was little of the waif about her compact body, lean and lithe, with small, pert breasts and flaring hips. Born a feral child of the Outlands, there was a primeval vibrancy, an animal-like intensity about her.

Lakesh grimaced at her use of the endearment "Moe." Recently she had fallen into the habit of addressing him by his first name of "Mohandas" rather than the more familiar "Lakesh." Then, because Outlanders tended to think and speak in shorthand, she had abbreviated even that to simply "Moe."

He had chided her about it, claiming only Jewish gangsters, surly bartenders and stooges with bowl-cut hairstyles went by such a name, but he suspected his objections only encouraged her.

"Why are you out here?" Lakesh asked.

Domi shrugged. "Just thinking about Quavell. Her baby is over two years old now and we haven't seen her since Balam took her away to Agartha. I wish we hadn't cut that deal with him. No need for it now."

"True," Lakesh said, sliding an arm around her shoulders. "The threat of the overlords seems to have passed, but Balam may not be aware of that."

He doubted the veracity of his own words. Balam had forged the truce between the overlords and the Cerberus exiles. Without him, the full wrath of Overlord Enlil would have been unleashed upon the redoubt. Only the fact that Balam held an infant as a hostage prevented such a catastrophe from coming to pass. The baby, carried to term by the hybrid female Quavell, had been bred to carry the memories and personality of Enlil's mate, Ninlil.

In actuality, Quavell had given birth to a blank slate, an empty vessel waiting to be filled. Although the child carried the Annunaki genetic profile, she was born in an intermediate state of development. Certain segments of her DNA, strands of her genetic material, were inactive and needed to be encoded aboard *Tiamat,* the ancient starship of the Annunaki named after the Sumerian goddess.

Once there, through a biotechnological interface, the child would have received the full mental and biological imprint of Ninlil. Then the Supreme Council would be as complete as it had been thousands of years before, and *Tiamat* could set into motion the rebirth of the entire Annunaki pantheon. However, *Tiamat* and all of the Supreme Council had apparently perished a few months before.

"We ought to contact Balam and tell him about the overlords," Domi said.

Lakesh nodded but said, "Balam made it quite clear that this was a case of 'don't call me, I'll you.'"

Domi glanced up at him, her ruby eyes flashing with anger. "We can take the Mantas to Tibet, find him and bring the baby back here to be raised like a human instead of a damn alien."

"Balam is not an alien," Lakesh pointed out. "He was born here on Earth."

"Mebbe," Domi conceded, stepping out from beneath the weight of Lakesh's arm. "Still not human, is he?"

After a thoughtful few seconds, Lakesh sighed, his breath pluming before his eyes. "No, I suppose he isn't. Not completely."

As Lakesh discovered in the waning years of the twentieth century, humankind's interaction with a nonhuman species had begun at the dawn of Earth's history. That relationship and communication had continued unbroken for thousands of years, cloaked by ritual, religion and mystical traditions.

The latest tradition dealt with a mysterious race known as the Archon Directorate, who allegedly influenced human affairs for many thousands of years. The nuclear apocalypse of 2001 was all part of the Archon Directorate's strategy. With the destruction of social structures and severe depopulation, the Archons established the nine barons and distributed predark technology among them to consolidate their power over Earth and its disenfranchised, spiritually beaten human inhabitants.

But over the past few years, the Cerberus exiles had learned that the elaborate back story was all a ruse, bits of truth mixed in with outrageous fiction. The Archon Directorate existed only as a vast cover story, created in the twentieth century and embellished with each succeeding generation. The only so-called Archon on Earth was Balam, the last of an extinct race that had once shared the planet with humankind.

After three years of imprisonment in the Cerberus redoubt, Balam finally revealed the truth behind the Archon Directorate and the hybridization program initiated centuries before.

Balam himself may have even coined the term "archon" to describe his people. In ancient Gnostic texts, "archon" was applied to a parahuman world-governing force that imprisoned the divine spark in human souls. Lakesh had often wondered over the past few months if Balam had indeed selected that appellation as a cryptic code to warn future generations.

Most shocking was Balam's assertion that he and his ancient folk were of human stock, not alien but alienated. The Cerberus personnel still didn't know how much to believe. But if nothing else, they no longer subscribed to the fatalistic belief that the human race had had its day and only extinction lay ahead. Balam had indicated that belief was but another control mechanism.

Beyond all of that, Domi's concern for Quavell's child sprang from a desire to be a mother. She and Lakesh had tried to conceive, but so far they had been unsuccessful. Lakesh didn't know whether to be relieved or saddened.

He reached for Domi, saying, "I agree with you, darlingest one. There's no need for Balam to keep Quavell's child any longer." He paused and added, "Apparently no need."

Domi canted her head at a challenging angle. "What do you mean?"

"I mean that we're not certain of the ultimate fates of the overlords. Yes, they could have all died aboard *Tiamat,* but they could have just as likely escaped. Some of them, anyway. Possibly even Enlil himself."

Domi snorted. "It's been months. If the snake-faces were still alive, we'd know about it by now."

Lakesh tacitly but silently agreed with her assessment. However, he knew that the Annunaki had laid plans a thousand years before to one day be resurrected and reign on Earth again. There was no reason to assume the Supreme Council could not have concocted another contingency plan.

The possibility chilled Lakesh far more than the mountain air. He shivered. "Let's go inside…I'm getting very cold."

"And shrunk up?" Domi inquired with a devilish half grin.

"Yes, I believe there has been significant shrinkage," Lakesh replied dryly.

She linked an arm through his. "Let's see if we can't do something about that."

The two people walked arm in arm across the plateau to the sec door. They had just stepped over the threshold when they heard the alarm Klaxons blaring discordantly, echoing all over the redoubt.

Bry's strident voice shouted over the PA system, "Internal incursion! CAT Beta to ops! Internal incursion!"

Domi's and Lakesh's relaxed stroll instantly became a flat-out sprint down the main corridor.

Chapter 9

The alarm Klaxon warbled, echoing throughout the redoubt like a choir of the damned. Personnel ran through the corridors to their assigned emergency red-alert stations.

Bry's voice continued to shout over the PA, "Internal incursion! Sealing ops in twenty seconds—mark! Internal incursion! CAT Beta to ops!"

Domi's legs pumped and she pulled ahead of Lakesh, darting among the people as she sprinted single-mindedly to the operations center. As she dodged, ducked and elbowed, Lakesh heard more than one person cry out in pain and anger. He forced more speed into his legs, silently enduring the spasms of pain in his knee joints. He glimpsed a pair of armed men forcing their way toward the entrance of the control complex and even over the blare of the alarm, he heard Domi shouting orders to her Beta team.

Lakesh had initially opposed the formation of the specialized Cerberus teams because he felt uncomfortable with the very concept of the redoubt's own version of the Magistrate Divisions—ironically composed of former Magistrates. But he knew that as the canvas of their operations broadened, the personnel situation at the installation also changed.

No longer could Kane, Grant, Brigid Baptiste and Domi undertake the majority of the missions and therefore shoulder the lion's share of the risks. Over the past year or so, Kane and Grant had set up Cerberus Away Teams Alpha, Beta and Delta. CAT Delta was semipermanently stationed at Redoubt Yankee on Thunder Isle, rotating duty shifts with the Tigers of Heaven. CAT Beta was charged with the responsibility of the redoubt and surrounding territory, and Domi served as Beta team's commander.

Lakesh ran into the central complex only a few seconds behind Domi and her two team members. The Klaxon continued howling, but the sound was underscored by the hissing of compressed air, the squeak of gears and a sequence of heavy, booming thuds resounding from the corridor.

Four-inch-thick vanadium-alloy bulkheads dropped from the ceiling to seal off the living quarters, engineering level and main sec door from the operations center, completely isolating it from the rest of the redoubt. A set of double doors slid shut behind Lakesh. He was a fraction of a second too slow, and one of the panels painfully clipped his left heel. He staggered, grabbing the back of a chair to keep from falling.

The central command complex served as the brains of the installation. Two aisles of computer stations divided the long, high-ceilinged room. A half-dozen people sat before the terminals. Monitor screens flashed images and streams of code.

The operations center had five dedicated and eight shared subprocessors, all linked to the mainframe computer concealed behind a shielded far wall.

A huge Mercator-relief map of the world spanned the entire wall above the door. Pinpoints of light shone steadily in almost every country, connected by a thin, glowing pattern of lines. They represented the Cerberus network, the locations of all functioning gateway units across the planet.

Lakesh pushed himself away from the chair and demanded loudly, "Report!"

Donald Bry glanced over his shoulder. He acted as Lakesh's lieutenant and apprentice in matters technological. A round-shouldered man with curly, copper-colored hair, his expression was always one of consternation, no matter his true mood. His face appeared strangely composed.

"Problems in the jump room," he said. "An incursion of some sort."

Lakesh frowned. "An incursion? By whom?"

"CAT Alpha brought something back. Don't know what, but—"

"Turn off that damn noise!" Domi shouted as she jogged down the aisle.

Farrell, a shaved-headed man who affected a goatee and a gold hoop earring, slapped a button and the Klaxon fell silent. "We don't know what's going on," he said querulously. "It's bad, whatever it is."

Farrell's words sent a prickle of icy dread up Lakesh's spine. He retained vivid and horrifying memories of the mad Maccan's assault on Cerberus, gating in through the mat-trans unit.

On the opposite side of the operations center, an anteroom held the eight-foot-tall gateway unit, rising from an elevated platform. Six upright slabs of brown-hued armaglass formed a translucent wall around it. Manufactured in the last decade of the twentieth century, armaglass was formed of a special compound that plasticized and combined the properties of steel and glass.

It was used as walls in the jump chambers to confine quantum-energy overspills. The redoubt's particular unit was the first fully debugged matter-transfer inducer built after the prototypes. It served as the template for all the others that followed, and Lakesh still felt a strong degree of fondness for it.

Now a cacophony of voices rose from the jump room in an nearly incomprehensible babble, but Lakesh heard Brigid Baptiste shouting in an uncharacteristically agitated tone, "Are we locked down yet? Somebody answer me!"

"Yes!" called Domi, pausing in the doorway and gesturing to the two Beta team members to assume cross-fire positions on either side of her. "We're secure. Now, what's going on?"

"Don't come in here!" Brigid ordered, gesturing with one arm.

Breathing hard and limping slightly, Lakesh joined Domi in the doorway. He glimpsed CAT Alpha arranged around the metal platform that supported the gateway unit. Their weapons were out and trained toward the ceiling. The confusion and fear filling him became a sharp pang of panic when he saw Brigid and Grant kneeling over the motionless body of Kane, lying sprawled on the floor. He also saw a man clad in a dun-colored coverall sitting nearby, a bloody bandage wrapping his left ankle. His eyes bulged in terror.

Domi shouted, "Grant! What the hell is happening?"

Grant didn't look at her but he bellowed, "Duck!"

Without hesitation, Domi bent double. A green-glowing bead shot over her head, missing the tip of Lakesh's nose by the thickness of a sheet of paper. He felt a brief sear of heat before he threw himself to one side, crying out.

Philboyd's voice rose in a yell. "Everybody take cover! Nobody touch it!"

He appeared in the doorway, pushing past Domi. "And don't let it touch you!"

Straightening up, Domi latched on to his arm and spun him around to face her. "Don't let what touch us?"

The little orb flew around the big room, pirouetting, twirling and circling. It dived down toward people sitting at the computer stations, and with cries of fright, they slid from their chairs and took refuge beneath the desks. As the green ball arrowed past the monitor screens, the images on them flickered and broke up into patterns of jagged pixels.

Panting, Brigid joined Lakesh, Domi and Bry at the doorway. Her expression was stark and drawn, her complexion very pale. "We were attacked by a swarm of those things. They killed Higson. One of them stung Kane right as we were phasing back here. It must have been caught in the transit field and came along with us. The thing seemed attracted to the interphaser's energy."

"Stung?" Lakesh echoed, gazing toward the fallen Kane. "Stung him how?"

"Or shocked him," Brigid said tersely. "All we know is, he's unconscious."

"Why didn't you keep the whatever it is locked up in the mat-trans chamber?" Domi demanded.

Philboyd's eyes flitted back and forth as he tried to follow the darting orb as it flew through the ops center. "We didn't know it came back with us until we opened the door. Then it bolted."

"Besides," Brigid interjected grimly, "our priority was getting Kane medical attention."

"That's not going to happen until we contain whatever it is," Domi declared. She turned toward Cohen, one of the Beta team. "Give me your weapon."

The man handed her his Copperhead, and she settled the stock of the subgun in the hollow of her right shoulder. All of the Cerberus personnel were required to become reasonably proficient with small arms, and the lightweight point-and-shoot subguns were the easiest for the novice to handle.

Grant rose and came to the doorway, fisting his Sin Eater. "You don't mean to shoot it down, do you?"

"Why not?" she countered, sighting down the weapon's short length.

"Firstly," Lakesh said, his voice hitting a high note of fear, "there is a lot of valuable and irreplaceable equipment in here, including the mainframe. If the hardware is damaged, our work at Cerberus comes to an end."

Two centuries before, the computer had been one of the most advanced models ever built, carrying experimental, error-correcting microchips of such a tiny size that they even reacted to quantum fluctuations. Biochip technology had been employed when it was built, protein molecules sandwiched between microscopic glass-and-metal circuits.

The information contained in the main database may not have been the sum total of all humankind's knowledge, but not for lack of trying. Any bit, byte or shred of intelligence that had ever been digitized was only a few keystrokes and mouse clicks away.

"I'll be careful," Domi retorted, following the movements of the orb with the barrel of the Copperhead.

"Also," Philboyd said, "that thing is made of energy, probably along the lines of a plasmoid. It would be like trying to shoot down ball lightning."

"What's a plasmoid?" Domi asked, her eyes flickering in momentary uncertainty.

"A ball of plasma…a quantity of gas that has been heated to a point where the atomic particles ionize into a median state."

"That doesn't tell me anything," Domi snapped irritably.

"It's a moving electrical charge that generates a self-sustaining magnetic field by spinning clockwise," Lakesh explained. "The field maintains its cohesion until something stops its motion."

"Couldn't bullets do that?" Grant inquired.

The orb swooped down from the ceiling and struck the double sec doors, bouncing away with a flash of energy. The green bee spiraled upward, giving the distinct impression of frustration, if not anger.

"If vanadium alloy couldn't stop its motion," Brigid declared, "I don't think lead will, either."

"It acts almost intelligent," Lakesh commented, "as if it's being guided by remote control."

"Unlikely," Philboyd said.

"Don't be so sure," said a voice from the anteroom.

Lakesh cast a glance over his shoulder at the man in the coveralls. "Who is that, pray tell?"

"He calls himself Mr. Gray," Grant said dourly. "He's a millennialist."

"Yes, I deduced that by his identifying button. What is he doing here?"

"Information," Brigid said brusquely. "His crew deserted him."

Domi gestured with the barrel of the Copperhead toward the green bee. "Does he have useful information about that goddamn thing?"

"No," Gray answered. "I wish I did. All I know is that when they show up, men die—"

"Shut up," Domi broke in.

The albino girl took a deep breath, held it, squinted through the autotargeter and squeezed the trigger, firing off a stuttering triburst. The bullets struck chimes and flares of sparks from the vanadium-sheathed ceiling. The orb danced and curved away from the brief barrage. The ricocheting bullets hit desks and chairs, drawing outraged cries from the people cowering beneath them.

"You'll never hit the fucking thing that way," Grant growled.

Domi glared at him, lowering the weapon. "Think you can do better?"

"I think I can come up with a better plan...and we

need to do it fast so we can get Kane to the infirmary."

Lakesh tugged at his nose, an absent gesture that meant he was deep in thought. "You said it seemed attracted to the energy output of the interphaser?"

Brigid nodded. "Yes. Drawn to the EM field, I think."

"Makes sense if the thing is basically a plasmoid," Philboyd said. "Tapping into another source of electromagnetic energy would be a way of sustaining itself."

"You make it sound intelligent," Domi stated, her eyes boring in on the astrophysicist.

The man lifted a knobby shoulder in a shrug. "Not so much intelligent as one form of magnetic energy being drawn to another."

Lakesh turned toward the anteroom. "Friend Edwards, would you be so kind as to fetch the interphaser for me, please?"

The big man stared at him, perplexed for a silent second, and then did as he was asked. Swiftly he entered the mat-trans chamber and returned a moment later balancing the metal-walled pyramid on the palms of his hands. He walked with exaggerated care, as if the device were extremely fragile or unstable.

Lakesh took it from impatiently, saying, "It's not full of nitroglycerin."

"What do you plan to do?" Brigid asked, a line of worry appearing above the bridge of her nose.

"Lay out some bait."

Lakesh strode up the aisle between the computer stations. Bry poked his curly head out from beneath a desk. "Anything I can do to help?"

"As you were, Mr. Bry. Let's not make this any more complicated."

When Lakesh reached a wide, open space between a desk and the far wall, he placed the interphaser on the floor. Bending over, he pressed a pair of keys on the pad, then stepped back. With a faint whine, the device juiced up. A faint white aura played along the gleaming sides.

"What good will that do?" Philboyd demanded skeptically. "The interphaser doesn't function unless it's engaged with a parallax point."

Lakesh didn't answer. Silently he watched the thread-thin static discharges crackle up from the apex of the pyramid.

"He's just turning on the power," Brigid murmured.

"Why?" Domi asked.

Before anyone could answer, the little green orb lanced down from the ceiling and rapidly began orbiting the veil of light shimmering around the interphaser. It inscribed tighter and tighter circles, rotating so fast the bee was barely a jade-hued blur.

Then, moving with calm deliberation, Lakesh picked up a metal wastepaper basket, upended it, dumped out its contents and very calmly slammed it down over both the interphaser and the glowing bee. They heard a frantic series of muffled taps as the orb hammered against the inner walls of the basket, trying to break through.

Planting his foot atop the canister to hold it in place, Lakesh announced, "Mr. Bry, unseal the doors, raise the shields and get Dr. DeFore and a medical team in here, stat!"

Chapter 10

Erica van Sloan was sound asleep in her quarters when the insistent buzz from the comm unit on her bedside table prodded her awake. She fumbled for it, reaching over Mickey, who lay on her right. Snuggled up to her back on her left, Minnie murmured petulantly.

Erica squinted with one eye at the early-morning sunshine slicing painfully into her bedroom through the venetian blinds. Picking up the small radiophone, she flipped open the cover with a thumb, engaging the circuit at the same time.

"What is it?" She tried but failed to sound wide-awake and perfectly in control.

A dispassionate male voice said, "This is Brown. Call from central clearing. A blue message came through from the Phantom Mesa site. Not promising. Central clearing has called a conference."

"When?"

"In fifteen minutes with Mr. Vermilion."

"Have some breakfast ready for me."

Erica folded the cover of the comm back down,

and then jammed an elbow hard into Mickey's ribs. "Move your ass. I have to get up."

Grunting, the big man rolled out of bed, digging his knuckles into his eye sockets. "What time is it?"

"Time for you to leave."

"You sure were a lot friendlier last night."

Mickey's high-pitched contralto was at complete variance with his appearance—a tall man well over six feet in height with short blond hair and built with a heavy musculature that could easily turn to fat if he didn't exercise. His hands were strong, his cock sturdy, and he was equally adept at manipulating both to quickly bring Erica to orgasm.

She didn't know his real name, but she addressed him as Mickey because his voice reminded her of a cartoon mouse she had been fond of as a child.

"Wha's goin' on?" Minnie asked in a drowsy little-girl voice, stirring restlessly beneath the white silk sheets.

Erica turned to smile at the girl with the long, straight, strawberry-blond hair spread out on the pillow. Her breasts stood up like two small hills under snow.

"Go back to sleep, sweetheart," Erica told her. "I have business."

"How come she can go back to sleep and I got to go?" Mickey demanded, making an exaggerated show of fondling his large genitals. "I can make business, too."

Erica stood up in a rush, her raven's-wing-black

hair falling over the right side of her face. "That you do—with the plumbing system. Get to it or I'll report you for insubordination."

Mickey's mouth fell open in dismay, then he ducked his head deferentially. "Yes, ma'am."

Without another word, he picked up the olive-drab jumpsuit from the back of a chair and pulled it on, zipping it up to his throat. He left Erica's bedroom quickly, carrying his heavy-soled work shoes. She waited until she heard the closing of the front door before going into the bathroom and turning on the shower.

She felt a bit sore from the activities of the night before, but she was used to far greater pain, without any accompanying pleasure. When she felt sufficiently clean, she stepped out of the stall and dried herself in front of the full-length mirror affixed to the back of the door. She saw what she expected—and always hoped to see.

She gazed at the reflection of a tall and beautiful woman with a flawless complexion the hue of fine honey. Her long, straight hair, swept back from a high forehead and pronounced widow's peak, tumbled artlessly about her shoulders. It was so black as to be blue when the light caught it. The large, feline-slanted eyes above high, regal cheekbones looked almost the same color, but glints of violet swam in them.

The mark of an aristocrat showed in her delicate features, with the arch of brows and her thin-bridged nose. A graceful, swanlike neck led to a slender body with full breasts, a narrow waist and a jet-black smudge at the juncture of her thighs.

Although no new lines marred the sculpted smoothness of her face, the flesh surrounding her right eye socket was still wealed and reddened, even more than a year after Wei Qiang had plucked out her eye.

Still, Erica van Sloan was adaptable and had fashioned a black leather patch to cover it. She put it on, adjusting it above her cheekbone, liking the piratical effect. She had vainly hoped that the nano-machines injected into her body several years before by Sam would restore the eye, but they had not and so she had assumed they had become inert.

Quickly, she put on a dab of lipstick, pursing her lips at her reflection, once again reminded of marble statues of goddesses she had seen in museums. For over thirty years following her revival from stasis, Erica van Sloan had almost never looked at herself in a mirror. There had been nothing to see but a withered old hag confined to a wheelchair. She had avoided her reflection with a diligence that would have made Dorian Gray proud. As far as she was concerned, her identity had died during her century and half in cryostasis.

Born in 1974, Dr. Erica van Sloan was half Latino and half British. She had inherited her dark hair and eyes from her Brazilian mother, but she possessed her father's tall frame and long, solid legs. God only knew from which side of her family her two-hundred-point IQ derived, but she knew she received her beautiful singing voice from her mother.

At eighteen years of age, the haughty, beautiful and more than a trifle arrogant Erica earned her Ph.D. in cybernetics and computer science. She wanted to pursue a singing career, but within days of her graduation from Cal Tech she went to work for a major Silicon Valley hardware producer as a models and systems analyst.

Less than a year later, she left her six-figure salary to accept a position with a government-sponsored ultra-top-secret undertaking known as Overproject Whisper. Only much later did she realize Whisper was a major division of something called the Totality Concept, and she was assigned to one of its subdivisions, Operation Chronos. In the vast installation beneath a mesa in Dulce, New Mexico, she served as the subordinate, lover and occasional victim of a man who made her own officious personality seem mousy and shy by comparison.

Torrance Silas Burr was brilliant, stylish, waspish and nasty. He excelled at using his enormous intellect and equally enormous ego to fuel his cruel sense of humor. He delighted in belittling and degrading not just her, but other scientists assigned to Overproject Whisper. The one scientist he could not deride was Mohandas Lakesh Singh, the genius responsible for the final technological breakthrough of Project Cerberus, which permitted Operation Chronos to finally make some headway.

With the advent of the Cerberus success, the new installations were linked to each other by gateway units. Though the COG facilities and the redoubt scientific enclaves were not part of the same program, there was an almost continuous trade-off of design specifications, technology and personnel. Many of the Totality Concept's subdivisions and spin-off researches were relocated to these redoubts. Operation Chronos was moved to Chicago, and Cerberus was moved to Montana.

The most ambitious COG facility was code-named the Anthill because of its resemblance in layout to an ant colony. It was a vast complex, with a railway, stores, theaters and even a sports arena. Supplies of foodstuffs, weapons and anything of value were stockpiled, often times in triplicate. The Anthill was built inside Mount Rushmore, using tunneling and digging machines. The entire mountain was honeycombed with interconnected levels, passageways and chambers.

Erica learned that once construction on the Anthill was completed, the entire Totality Concept program would be moved into it and she was ordered to come along. She couldn't understand why exactly and complained bitterly. When the world blew out on noon of January 20, 2001, she ceased to complain. She would be part of the new world order that would emerge from the radioactive ashes of the old.

The prolonged nuclear winter changed ideas about a new world order. Even if the Anthill personnel managed to outlast the big freeze, the skydark, they would still sicken and die, either from radiation sickness or simply old age.

So they embarked on a radical and daring plan. Cybernetic technology had made great leaps in the latter part of the twentieth century, and Erica herself had made some small contributions to those advances. General Kettridge, the self-styled commander of the Anthill, ordered operations to be performed on everyone living in the Anthill, making use of the new techniques in organ transplants and medical technology, as well in cybernetics.

Over a period of years, all the Anthill personnel were turned into hybrids of human and machine. Since the main difficulty in constructing interfaces between organic and mechanical-electric systems was the wiring, Erica oversaw the implantation of SQUIDs directly into the brain. The superconducting quantum interface devices, one-hundredth of a micron across, facilitated the subjects' control over their new prostheses.

Although Erica herself had designed the implants and oversaw the early operations, she certainly didn't care for the process being performed on her. She knew the SQUIDs could be used to electronically control the personnel, and she wasn't fond of being turned into a biomechanical drone. However, she was even less fond of the alternative—euthanasia.

Of course, the transformations didn't solve all of the Anthill's survival issues. Compensation for the natural aging process of organs and tissues had to be taken into account. The Anthill personnel needed a supply of fresh organs, preferably those of young people, but obviously the supply was severely limited. So General Kettridge, now calling himself the commander in chief, offered cryogenics as a solution. He ordered the internal temperatures inside the installation to be lowered just enough to preserve the tissues but not low enough to damage the organs.

However, even those measures were temporary. Erica volunteered to enter a stasis canister for a period of time, to be resurrected at some future date when the sun shone again and the world was secure.

When Erica awakened, over 122 years had passed. During her long slumber, the Anthill installation suffered near catastrophic damage. General Kettridge was killed and a number of stasis units malfunctioned, including hers.

Due to that malfunction, her SQUIDs interface had inflicted neurological damage on her body and she was resurrected as a cripple. Worse than finding out her long, shapely legs were little more than withered, atrophied sticks was learning the plans made for her while she slept.

Erica was briefed on the unification program, the baronial oligarchy and the Archons. She was told that to be of optimal use to the Archon Directorate and their hybrid plenipotentiaries, she needed to be as fit as it was possible for a human in her physical condition and chronological age. She was to concentrate only on what her technological skills could contribute to the furtherance of the Program of Unification. Otherwise, she would be put out of her misery.

Erica learned quickly not to question. Over the years of her long life, due to the creativity and skills of her intellect, she had undergone many organ transplants so as to extend her value to the united baronies. Despite the pain and suffering that had gone with each successive operation, Erica never regained the use of her legs, and the neurological degeneration grew so acute she became a complete cripple.

But the entity she had first known as Sam had not only put life back into her legs again, but also he restored her youth. She had dedicated her life to helping him build a new, productive society on the framework of the ville system.

Then Sam had betrayed her so thoroughly she could not even whisper his name for a long time. But since that day, when she learned she had been duped and manipulated as part of an ancient conspiracy, Erica van Sloan had vowed to never be a pawn again—a knight, perhaps, even a rook, but always with the overarching ambition of being a queen.

Erica left the bathroom and took one her dun-colored bodysuits from a closet. She despised the color, but she was glad it had been tailored to fit the thrust of her breasts and the flare of her hips.

Zipping it up, she stepped to a bedroom window and tugged on the cord, raising the venetian blinds. Sunlight washed over the walls of the keep of Front Royal, giving it the fairy-tale appearance of a medieval fortress. She couldn't help but smile slightly.

Every queen should live in a castle.

Chapter 11

Erica gently closed the door of her quarters so as not to disturb Minnie. Like her male counterpart, Erica didn't know the girl's real name but she didn't think it was important, either. The girl was there to pleasure her and so answered to anything Erica cared to call her.

She walked along the carpeted hallway, glancing out the windows at the familiar sight of the keep. Front Royal was not greatly changed since the time of the inaugural Council of the Nine, almost a century before. The towers and turrets and observation eyries overlooked a wide, green valley. The weathered stone blocks were clean of vines and lichens. The main building in which she kept her quarters rose above the protective walls in a defiant thrust of chiseled stone, stained-glass windows and forged steel.

The fortress and the little village were enclosed by walls nearly fifty feet tall, and they in turn were surrounded by a river with only a single bridge crossing it.

Powerful halogen spotlights were mounted both

on the walls and atop the turrets. Projecting from each corner were Vulcan-Phalanx gun emplacements.

Front Royal had never been part of the baronial ville system. Rather it was more of a neutral zone, a place where the barons could meet on equal terms. It held historical significance because it was the birthplace of the Program of Unification, when the nine most powerful barons put aside their differences and regional jealousies in order to consolidate their collective strength and unite the nation under their control.

Erica was revived from cyrostasis to help further the Program of Unification. Her background in cybernetics was viewed as helpful. Since cybernetic principles were applied to management and organizational theory, she always had much to offer in the way of streamlining ville government. Just as everything that occurred in the universe could be analyzed into cause-and-effect chains, the chains themselves could be used to build organizational models.

In those early, postresurrection years, Erica was not assigned to any particular ville for any length of time. She was given quarters in Front Royal, and from there she traveled from barony to barony, setting up their computer systems, training personnel in their operation and in troubleshooting procedures. The systems, although in absolutely pristine order, were not state-of-the-art, certainly not by the standards of the first year of the twenty-first century.

None of the mainframes employed the biochip developments that would have been commonplace if the nukecaust had been averted. Most of the software, hardware and support systems were fairly basic, as well. Erica always suspected that the truly advanced predark tech was being deliberately suppressed. She could only assume it was done out of fear of the new postnuke society becoming just as dependent on technology as the old one.

The elevator deposited her in the main hall of the keep, wryly smiling as she always did at the fake old-world architecture meant to suggest a much older and grander day. The hall was immense, its heavy-beamed ceiling and waxed, oak-paneled walls dancing with the light of a hundred electric candles shining in a wrought-iron chandelier.

The polished marble floor swirled with complex patterns. At far end of the hall rose a hearth big enough to comfortably sleep three men the size of Mickey. A yard-long electric log always glowed there.

Despite its tasteful furnishings, the place was so obviously faux it almost reached the point of being a parody. Eric van Sloan could not help but be reminded of theme parks built to emulate King Arthur's Camelot or some other fanciful place that never existed outside of the imagination.

However, there had been a few additions to the fortress in the past few years, including a mat-trans unit within a shielded cubicle and a video comm system. The modular gateway unit had been installed shortly after the first baronial council and the comm system was set up over the past few months, after the Millennial Consortium claimed Front Royal as its East Coast headquarters.

Erica van Sloan walked across the hall and entered a room that seemed to stretch for a mile. The walls, the floor, the ceiling all were composed of a slick, slightly reflective vanadium alloy. Not only was the sheathing for security purposes, but it also provided protection from attack.

At the far end was a rare and expensive teak conference table, highly polished and twelve-feet in diameter. The man she knew as Brown set a place for her, right beneath a huge flat-screen vid monitor.

She smelled the aroma of fresh coffee and toast. She never knew where the Millennial Consortium found the coffee, and she never asked. She assumed it was a rare commodity, shared only with section chiefs, like her.

Erica nodded to Brown as he handed her the steaming mug. A slightly built man with overlarge ears and a perennially grave expression, Brown acted as her clerk and secretary.

"The call should be coming through momentarily, ma'am," he said.

She sat down at the table and picked up a wedge of buttered toast. "Thank you, Brown."

He inclined his head in a deferential bow. "Ma'am."

The first representative of the Millennial Consortium Erica had met was anything but deferential. In fact, he had been instrumental in usurping her position as Tui Chui Jian, the Dragon Mother, in China.

After that encounter, with no place to go, Erica van Sloan sent out feelers to the consortium. Although her first experience with the organization had been decidedly adversarial, she hoped the people in charge would be pragmatic enough to realize she made a far more reliable ally than an enemy.

When she learned that the consortium did not have a headquarters on the Eastern Seaboard, she traded her knowledge of Front Royal for a high rank. The millennialists easily displaced the ragtag band of former Magistrates who had occupied the keep since the fall of the baronies, and now Erica was back where she had started—without the wheelchair this time around.

The monitor screen suddenly lit up with flashing pixels, dividing into four small square sections. One squares showed the interior of the conference room and part of Erica's left elbow. Brown moved forward to adjust the video feed, focusing it on Erica's head and shoulders.

The image of a middle-aged man wearing the

standard dun-colored coverall appeared on the screen. "Good morning."

Mr. Vermilion's face was flat and unmemorable, and he spoke in a flat, fluid voice unmarred by any trace of accent. His hair looked like a steel-colored skullcap, and his eyes were no particular color. His tone was sterile, with a lack of inflection. Erica had never met the man in person and she wondered if he was a computer-generated hologram or an android.

"Good morning," Erica replied. "It's rather early here."

"It's early everywhere," Vermilion replied. "I speak for central clearing. A sudden situation has arisen. You are familiar with Section Chief Breech, are you not?"

"I replaced him," Erica replied, sipping at her coffee to hide her smile. "After he disappeared."

"Yes. When we dispatched him to investigate an opportunity you brought to the consortium."

"Has he reappeared?"

"Not as such. However, we received a report from your subordinate, Mr. Blue."

A blank square on the screen flickered and then displayed the head and shoulders of the man Erica knew as Blue. In many ways, he could have been the brother of Mr. Brown.

"Report," Erica ordered.

Blue shifted uncomfortably. "The station was exactly where you said it would be, Chief van

Sloan, right at the base of the mesa. But Breech had been there long before us and he must have done something to the database. It was inoperable. We stayed there for two full days, trying to track Breech and his crew and download the files in the computer system."

He paused, licked his lips nervously and added, "We were unsuccessful."

"There is more," Vermilion stated. He did not ask a question.

Blue inhaled deeply, then blurted, "The ghost-walkers came back."

Erica sat up straight in her chair and placed her coffee mug down on the table with a clatter. "How can that be? Explain!"

"It was like the last time, Chief van Sloan. We activated the Theta-pinch transmitter the way you indicated, but the ghost-walkers still returned. Then there was another complication."

"Which was?" Erica inquired.

"Cerberus."

Erica nodded as if she had expected the one-word response. "Go on."

"We set the transmitter to overload as per your instructions. The entire station self-destructed, but the theta circuit wasn't broken. The ghost-walkers seemed unaffected. They killed one of the Cerberus people."

"And there is more to tell yet," Vermilion said quietly.

Blue's lips compressed as if he was in pain. "I'm afraid so. Gray was apparently apprehended by Cerberus. We should assume he is their prisoner and taken to their base in Montana."

Addressing Vermilion, Erica said curtly, "Gray knows very little. His apprehension is not dire."

"Any information in the possession of an enemy is potentially dire," Vermilion intoned. "Resourceful enemies like Cerberus can use that information to our disadvantage."

"I am familiar with the Cerberus personnel," Erica said, flicking a crumb from the front of her bodysuit.

"Yes," Vermilion replied. "And you probably would agree with me that if one of their people was killed by these so-called ghost-walkers, they will most certainly investigate further."

"I agree with that assessment."

"We have enough different projects under way that Cerberus could interfere with in their efforts to find the culprits behind the death of one of their own. I do not care to shift schedules and remake our rosters. Therefore our primary efforts must be directed toward distracting Cerberus from learning our objectives."

"Unless," Erica van Sloan declared, "we do the opposite."

For the first time, Vermilion's face registered emotion. "Elucidate, please," he said.

"I think we should draw more of the attention of

Cerberus to our project and enlist their aid—turning enemies into allies."

"A very risky proposition, Section Chief, without a clearly defined reward."

"You know that Cerberus has access to resources that could be very useful to the consortium. That is why we have never staged a full-scale assault upon their base, true?"

Vermilion inclined his head a quarter of an inch. "True. The potential losses outweighed the gains."

"In this instance," Erica continued, "their resources can help the consortium complete our project with the Theta-pinch transmitter. If left unchecked, Breech will achieve controlled thermonuclear fusion and pose a threat not to just us, but the entire world."

"We know Breech is in Area 51," Vermilion droned. "But we have neither the resources nor manpower to search for him there. That is why we approved your plan to draw him out at the experimental station in Phantom Mesa."

"It worked, but not sufficiently."

Vermilion said, "We cannot try it again. The station and the transmitter are destroyed. Our only chance, as slim as it may be, is to corner Breech in Area 51. I fail to see how inveighing upon Cerberus will help us flush him out."

Erica smiled. "I have a history with Cerberus. I know far more about them than Millennial Consortium has been able to learn. For example—"

She paused, both for dramatic effect and to collect her thoughts. Calmly, she said, "Kane was held prisoner in Area 51 for several weeks. He has intimate knowledge of the place and its layout that would prove invaluable to us."

Vermilion's lips barely stirred. "A very audacious undertaking."

"But necessary…if we ever to hope to locate Breech and break the theta circuit. We will use one enemy to destroy another. If we are fortunate, both of the consortium's enemies will perish."

Vermilion's image gazed at her unblinkingly. She met his gaze stolidly. Then, at length he said softly, "As I indicated…an audacious plan. But it is approved. Implement it immediately."

Chapter 12

Overlord Enlil and Sindri had converted the Cobalt-ville Administrative Monolith into a gaudyhouse. Enlil wanted Kane to play the roulette table and he agreed before he remembered that he was scheduled to lead a Magistrate squad on a hard-contact probe down in the Tartarus Pits.

So Kane ran through the cavernous halls of the monolith, looking for the Magistrate Division. Instead he turned a corner and found himself sitting at a ringside table in the Dai Jia Lou nightclub, watching Lilitu perform the Annunaki mating dance.

Surrounded by the pale green halo cast by a spotlight, Lilitu's arms weaved back and forth like cobras awakening from a nap. Her hips rolled in tempo with the drumbeats. The gems encrusting her gilded headpiece glittered and gleamed with every sinuous undulation. Tiny finger cymbals chimed in a clashing rhythm.

Her and arms and legs flashed in intricate movements within the aura of hazy light. Her body curved, bending forward and backward as if her spine were made of rubber. Her dance was a dervish whirl of primal, maddening passions.

Kane watched as she writhed in rhythm with the music, feeling trickles of sweat flowing down his face from his hairline.

Lilitu whirled on the balls of her bare feet, and glared directly at him, her eyes blazing with contempt and accusation. She opened her lipless mouth and demanded, "Are you going to sleep all day or what?"

KANE CAME UP out of a sedative slumber for the second time that day and wondered if he should have bothered. Reba DeFore leaned over him, a smile on her full lips but her brown eyes full of worry. A sturdily built woman with deep bronze skin and ash-blond hair, DeFore served as the Cerberus redoubt's chief medical officer. She dabbed at his face with a wet washcloth.

Kane squinted up at her, then down at himself, a little disturbed to see he wore a cotton shift and lay on a bed in the infirmary. DeFore's face darkened around the edges and he felt his eyelids closing.

A hard prod on his shoulder forced his eyes open again. DeFore said loudly, "Don't go back to sleep, Kane. I want to make sure you're not suffering from a concussion. If you are, you know what that means."

"I do?" he whispered, his throat feeling raw and

abraded, his tongue dried out. "I need a drink… haven't so much as a sip of anything wet since last night."

DeFore handed him a bottle of water with a flexible straw extending from the neck. "It wasn't last night, Kane. You've been unconscious for over a day. You woke up for a minute early this morning. Now it's nearly noon. I thought you might be catatonic, but you were only reacting to the painkillers and sedatives. They should be out of your system now."

Kane sipped at the water, swallowed and then propped himself up on his elbows. He almost immediately collapsed under the wave of pain that burst in his head. He clenched his teeth, squeezed his eyes shut and muttered, "Ow."

DeFore took away the water bottle. "Let that be a lesson to you."

"Is it a concussion?" he managed to husk out between clenched teeth. Slowly the pain abated.

"No," DeFore answered, "I don't think so. As best as I can diagnose, you're suffering from acute but external electromagnetic irradiation as the result of a shock."

She peeled back Kane's left eyelid, and the narrow beam of a penlight caused him to wince and flinch. "Your pupils dilate and contract normally. Is your vision blurry?"

Kane carefully opened his right eye, then the other. It required several seconds for DeFore to come into focus. "Yeah, a little."

The medic nodded. "The eyes are particularly vulnerable to EM radiation. Prolonged exposure can lead to cataracts and blindness."

An icy hand clutched Kane around the heart. "Blindness?"

"Relax. According to Brigid and Grant, you got zapped by one of those little plasma bugs. It was like you were subjected to an electric shock of considerable voltage. It temporarily affected your nervous system and even parts of your brain."

Kane massaged his throbbing temples with his fingers. "My second-favorite organ. Where is everybody? Are they all right? Brewster got smacked around."

"He's fine. He didn't even need stitches, which is more than I can say for the millennialist you brought back. I had to perform surgery on his foot."

"Brigid? Grant?"

"I'm keeping them apprised of your condition. Brigid is busy."

"Busy with what?"

"She's studying that little energy bee that stung you. It came back to Cerberus with you. Caused us some excitement for a few minutes."

Kane struggled to sit up. "Where the hell is it now?"

DeFore lay a restraining on his shoulder. "Calm down. It's been contained."

Kane sagged back against the mattress. "Call Grant or somebody, will you? I want to check out of here."

DeFore frowned. "That may not be wise until I give you a complete physical."

Kane bit back the profane retort that leaped to his tongue. "A physical won't tell you anything other than what you see right here. I don't feel great, but I don't feel terrible. If I start feeling worse, I'll just come back."

DeFore hesitated, her frown deepening. Kane smiled at her, waiting. At one time, the medic had been openly antagonistic toward him—or rather what he represented. As a former Magistrate, Kane embodied the totalitarianism of the villes, glorying in his baron-sanctioned powers to dispense justice and death.

For a couple of years, Reba DeFore had believed that due to his Mag conditioning he was psychologically conflicted and therefore couldn't be trusted. Although she had reevaluated her attitude, DeFore was still quick to take offense at what she interpreted as disrespect directed toward her position in the redoubt.

DeFore laid a cool hand on his forehead. "You don't feel feverish."

"I'm not," he replied. "I don't intend to do anything more strenuous than walk around a little and maybe go take a shower. There's nothing wrong with my legs, is there?"

"No," DeFore answered. "But your coordination and balance could be adversely affected."

"There's no better way to find out than if I'm ambulatory, is there? Call Grant and let him take the responsibility."

DeFore nodded and walked into the adjacent room. Kane heard her make a comm. call to Grant's quarters. Kane experimentally moved his arms and legs, wiggling his fingers and toes. Aside from varied degrees of stiffness in different parts of his body, he didn't feel too badly. His head still throbbed and his eyes burned, but he figured those symptoms would disappear in time.

Carefully he pushed himself into a sitting position, silently endured a brief spasm of vertigo and then swung his legs over the side of the bed. He saw his clothes folded atop a nightstand and he quickly dressed. Just as he laced up his boots, Grant sauntered in wearing his usual redoubt ensemble of black T-shirt, camo pants and combat boots.

"Reba has put you in my custody," he rumbled. "So if you fall down and break your head open, I'll be blamed."

Kane took a tentative step. "Appropriate. Where's the plasma bug being studied?"

Grant pointed to the floor with his thumb. "Way below, in the sec area."

Kane nodded in understanding, running a hand first over his unshaved jaw, then his disarrayed hair. "I'll take a shower after I see this thing."

Grant angled an eyebrow at him, then sniffed. "You sure you want to do it in that order?"

It took Kane a moment to grasp the meaning of

Grant's query. Crossly, he asked "Why do you care? You couldn't smell a dead stickie's skin if you were wearing it."

Grant's nose had been broken three times in the past and always poorly reset. Unless an odor was remarkably pleasant or violently repulsive, he was incapable of catching subtle smells, unless they were right under his nostrils. A running joke during his Mag days had been that Grant could eat a hearty dinner with a decomposing skunk lying on the table next to his plate.

Kane took a few cautious steps toward the exit, testing his knee joints. When his legs didn't buckle and he wasn't assailed by dizziness, he moved out into the corridor. Grant strode beside him, ready to grab him by the collar of his shirt if he stumbled.

Although he didn't express his gratitude, Kane felt thankful that Grant was around when he was needed. It wasn't always easy being the man's friend, but then again, Kane reflected, he wasn't the easiest person to get along with, either.

As Magistrates, he and Grant had served together for a dozen years, and as Cerberus warriors they had fought shoulder to shoulder in battles around half the planet, and even off the planet. Through all of it Grant had covered Kane's back, patching up his wounds and on more than one occasion literally carrying him out of hellzones.

At one time, both men enjoyed the lure of danger, the risk of courting death to deal death. But now it was no longer enough for them to wish for a glorious death as a payoff for all their struggles. They had finally accepted a fact they had known for years but never admitted to themselves—when death came, it was usually unexpected and almost never glorious.

All Magistrates followed a patrilineal tradition, assuming the duties and positions of their fathers. They did not have given names, each taking the surname of the father, as though the first Magistrate to bear the name were the same man as the last.

The originators of the Magistrate Divisions had believed that only surnames, family names, engendered a sense of obligation to the duties of their ancestors' office, insuring that subsequent generations never lost touch with their hereditary roles as enforcers. Last names became badges of social distinction, almost titles.

The bottom level of the Cerberus redoubt lay some 150 feet below solid, shielded rock. It held the nuclear generators, various maintenance and machine rooms and the air-conditioning core, as well as the water-filtration system. A semidetached wing contained ten detention cubicles and a vault where dangerous and stable substances were stored.

The two men took the elevator down rather than the stairs. Kane tapped in the sec code on the door leading to the security wing. They walked down a dimly lit corridor that had once been bisected by a wire-mesh security checkpoint and turnstile. Only the frame remained.

"Has anybody interrogated Gray?" Kane asked.

Grant lifted the broad yoke of his shoulders in a shrug. "Both Domi and I had a go at him this morning, playing bad cop and worse cop. We didn't get anything out of him, but I think that's because he doesn't know much of anything. I think he's exactly what he claimed to be—a grunt."

They walked past an open cell door, guarded by one of Beta team, a burly ex-Mag from Mandeville named Crosco. Glancing in, Kane saw Gray sitting huddled in a corner, his left foot very professionally bandaged. He smiled around a mouthful of ham sandwich.

He called, "Hey, Kane, glad to see you're up and around. How are you feeling?"

Kane paused, glaring at him. "Not so good. Who gave you that food?"

Crosco cleared his throat and said contritely, "Miss Baptiste told us to feed him."

Kane continued glaring. "Mebbe once your belly is full, you'll feel more like cooperating?"

Gray took a swig of water from a cup. "I'd cooperate if I could. I just don't know that much."

Kane began walking again. "We'll find that out for sure, Gray."

A side corridor terminated in a disk sheathed in gleaming metal surrounded by three concentric steel collars. A sec-code keypad was affixed to the wall beside it.

Grant punched in the three-digit entry code. With a rumble and hiss of pneumatics, the metal disk rolled into a slot on the right.

Fluorescent light fixtures cast a yellowish light over three people standing around a trestle table loaded with a complicated network of electronics. Lakesh, Brigid and Philboyd all glanced toward him, but none of them seemed particularly surprised that he was up and on foot.

"Friend Kane," Lakesh said casually. "We were wondering when you'd wake up."

"Were you now." Kane joined them at the table. "What a coincidence. I was wondering when I'd receive my get-well-soon bouquet."

"We were getting around to it." Brigid peered at him over the rims of her former badge of office, a pair of wire-framed, rectangular-lensed eyeglasses. They were the only memento of the many years she had spent as an archivist in Cobaltville's Historical Division. She wore a black T-shirt and jeans that accentuated her full-breasted, willowy figure.

"Yeah," Philboyd said. "But we got so wrapped in bug-watching—"

From the center of the table rose a long glass cylinder, capped on both ends with heavy layers of rubber. A little green ball hovered in the center of the tube, bobbing up and down very slightly, as if stirred by air currents. Its glow was a barely discernible aura. A faint steady buzz emanated from the cylinder.

Kane stepped beside Brigid, ignoring the way she wrinkled her nose and leaned away from him. "Why do you call it a plasma bug?" he asked.

"Because that's what we figure it's made of," Brigid said. "It's a ball of ionized gas where the atoms are separate from the nucleus. The fourth state of matter. It's held together by a self-generating cohesive magnetic field. Did you come straight here from the infirmary?"

"Yeah. Why?"

She fingered her nose. "No reason."

Kane knew to what she was referring but he refused to be baited. "Was it hard to capture?"

Grant snorted. "Lakesh just slapped a wastepaper basket over it…if you can call that hard."

Lakesh chuckled self-consciously. "At least it was direct. And then friend Brewster rigged up this magnetic bottle with a field configuration that bounces back the bug's charged particles to keep it more or less motionless inside the bottle."

Kane narrowed his eyes. "Have you made up your mind about what the hell it really is?"

"What do you mean?" Philboyd asked impatiently. "It's a form of plasma, like Brigid said."

"If it was just a ball of plasma, wouldn't it have dissipated by now? It's got to be drawing energy from someplace, right?"

Brigid nodded. "Right."

"How was it made?"

She shook her head. "We're still working on that. I'm positive its existence has something to do with the theta-pinch transmitter we found."

"Yeah, we figured that out ourselves," Grant said dryly. "But something to do with how, what and why?"

Lakesh cleared his throat, as if preparing to deliver a scientific treatise. "First we must determine the frequencies of energy the orbs can manipulate and the waveforms they take."

"I'm more interested in how the things are able to sting people and kill them," Kane declared, leaning down to stare at the little glowing shape within the cylinder. "Or transform them."

Before Lakesh could reply, the green aura around the orb deepened, taking on a jade hue. The bug began inscribing a circular pattern within the tube, following the curvature of the walls. The buzzing sound grew louder.

"Interesting reaction," Brigid commented.

"What is?" Kane asked, not caring for her tone of voice.

She nodded toward the firefly flicker contained within the magnetic bottle. "I'd swear it recognizes you, Kane."

A chill crept up his spine and he straightened up quickly. "That's ridiculous."

Lakesh tugged at his nose. "Not necessarily, friend Kane. From what I gathered from the debrief, those orbs of plasma suck the life energy out of a human being and quite possibly transform the organic material into a flux state, much like plasma. Perhaps when this particular one stung you, it also marked you in some fashion. It's responding to that."

"Marked him for what?" Grant asked.

"Conceivably to be transformed into one of those ghost-walkers you told me about."

"How could something like that work?" Brigid asked, her tone rich with skepticism.

"Perhaps the plasma bug acts like a viral carrier…and when it stings its victims, it also infects them."

Kane felt his breath catch in his throat. "You mean I'll become a green ghost-man?"

No one answered. The dancing orb cast a sickly green light over everyone's faces.

Then the PA system emitted a warning buzz and Bry's voice blared, "Unscheduled jumper!"

Chapter 13

With the wailing alarm Klaxons reverberating throughout the redoubt, Kane decided to take the stairs back up to the main level. Lakesh took the elevator, while Philboyd chose to remain behind with the plasma bug.

Brigid ran ahead of Kane, and Grant brought up the rear. The three people pounded up the steps, taking the risers two at a time.

"This is getting old," Brigid declared.

"What is?" Kane wheezed, hauling himself along by the handrail. His vision swam with gray specks.

"All these red alerts," Brigid answered. "Not to mention the unannounced drop-ins by various and sundry friends and foes."

The stairwell led to the main corridor only a few yards from the ops center. When they rushed in, they found Lakesh already bending over Bry's shoulder staring at the screen of the mat-trans control console. Legs aching, lungs burning, Kane cast a glance over his shoulder at the Mercator-relief map on the wall. A tiny light situated on the American seaboard flashed, indicating Cerberus network activity.

Before he could identify the geographical location of the jump point, Lakesh exclaimed, "Front Royal! The carrier wave originates from Front Royal."

Brigid, Kane and Grant all exchanged swift, puzzled glances. "*The* Front Royal?" Brigid inquired.

"Yes, the very same," Lakesh replied. "One of the modular gateway chambers was installed there quite a few years ago. I can't imagine who would be using it to transport here. They would have to know our unit's code."

"Got it covered!" Domi's voice called from the gateway room. She and a Beta team member named Halliday were positioned at opposite walls, Copperheads trained on the chamber.

From the emitter array of the gateway unit emanated a sound much like the distant howling of a gale-force wind, rising in pitch. Bright flares showed like bursts of heat lightning on the other side of the brown-hued armaglass walls, but they were safely contained.

Bry nodded to the screen. "That's definitely the origin point—the indexed unit in Front Royal, all right. Only a single biosign, though."

Kane and Brigid leaned forward, scrutinizing the drop-down window on the monitor screen. A jagged wave slid back and forth across a CGI scale. In a perplexed tone, Brigid said, "The system is allowing the materialization."

Eyeing the jump chamber distrustfully, Grant growled, "We don't know anybody in Front Royal, do we? So who the hell could it be?"

No one answered, assuming Grant's question to be rhetorical. However, they did know that every piece of matter, whether organic or inorganic, that had been ever been transported to or from the Cerberus gateway imprinted a computer record in the database. The image processor scanned for patterns corresponding with those in the record and permitted materialization unless the pattern was locked out, redirecting it to a holding buffer.

"All we know," Lakesh said, "is that whoever is coming into phase has been here before."

Kane nodded. "There are only a handful of people with the destination code for this unit, so that narrows down our list of suspects."

From the security board, Farrell said, "To be on the safe side, I think we should go on lockdown again."

With a weary sigh, Lakesh said, "Do it."

Farrell pressed the appropriate buttons, and the bulkheads began thudding into place. After the op center was sealed, Kane said, "We can do without the noise now, Farrell."

Obligingly, the man turned off the alarm. Kane, Grant and Brigid moved quickly into the anteroom. They took Copperheads from the weapons locker and assumed positions at equidistant points around the gateway unit, aiming the weapons so as to make the door of the chamber the apex of a triangulated cross fire. They waited as the unit droned through the final stage of the materialization cycle. Within seconds, the stuttering electronic whine melded into a smooth hum that faded into inaudibility.

Because of the translucent quality of the armaglass shielding, they could see nothing within it except vague, shifting shapes without form or apparent solidity.

"We're all set here," Domi called over her shoulder. "Unbutton it!"

"Unbuttoning!" Lakesh activated the remote control from the console.

Solenoids clicked and the heavy armaglass door swung open on its counterbalanced hinges. Mist swirled and thread-thin static-electricity discharges arced within the billowing mass. The chamber was full of the plasma bleed-off, a byproduct of the ionized waveforms that resembled mist.

The laser autotargeters mounted atop the subguns pierced the thinning planes of vapor with bright red threads and cast killdots on a dark shape at the rear of the chamber.

"Come on out," Domi ordered. "Very slowly and very carefully. Hands where we can see them."

Looking like a backlit shadow emerging from a fogbank, a figure appeared in the doorway and fearlessly stepped off the platform and into the ready room.

For a few confused seconds, Kane had difficulty

recognizing the tall, dark-haired woman in the formfitting, dun-colored bodysuit. Then, despite the black patch covering her right eye, he realized who she was.

Forcing a studied indifference into his voice, he said, "Erica. It's about time you came calling…but I can see by your outfit, you've been otherwise occupied."

Erica smiled at him and then nodded to everyone in turn. "Kane. Brigid. Grant. Little bleached-out bitch."

Domi's lips curled first in a snarl, then a contemptuous smirk. "Halliday, search Dr. van Slut here. The strip kind."

Erica's superior smile did not falter. "Where is Mohandas?"

"Right here," Lakesh said, hurrying through the doorway. "I think we can pass on the strip search for the nonce."

"I'm willing to cooperate with your security protocols," Erica replied. "But I can assure you that I'm unarmed. All I'm carrying is a DVD in my pocket."

Stepping forward, Halliday carefully patted her hips, then slid a hand into the slit pocket of her bodysuit and removed a disk inside a protective sleeve. He handed it to Lakesh, who eyed it carefully.

Brigid regarded Erica with a cold glare. "The last time we saw you was in China. You were still Tui Chui Jian, the Dragon Mother. Joining the Millennial Consortium is a little bit of a comedown for you, isn't it?"

Erica shrugged, her hands still held at shoulder level. "I didn't have anything to go back to. Wei Qiang's forces still occupied the Xian pyramid. Even without him around to give orders, they weren't about to move out on my say-so…and none of you were inclined to help me reclaim it."

Lakesh scowled. "The pyramid wasn't yours *or* ours to claim in the first place and you know it."

The two people referred to the ancient immense structure in the province of Xian. Composed of countless blocks of seamlessly fitted stone, the pyramid was painted black on the north side, blue-gray on the east, red on the south and white on the west.

In predark days, archaeologists had theorized the Great Pyramid of China was part of the tomb complex of Emperor Shih Huang. The purpose of the pyramid or tomb was never known, though Taoist tradition attributed its construction to a very powerful race called the Celestials, one of whom was reputed to be the first emperor of China, the legendary Huang-di.

Although the Cerberus warriors and Erica van Sloan had learned that Huang-di had been involved in the pyramid's construction, they also discovered the huge structure represented a cardinal point in the global harmonics grid, a network of pyramids built at key places around the globe to tap the

Earth's natural geomantic energies. That aspect of the structure's design was not conjecture.

It had been built over a hub over geomantic energy, known as the Heart of the World. Similar hubs were found throughout Asia, such as Angkor Watt in Cambodia and Cooling in Tibet, but none had the concentration of sheer power that lay beneath the Xian pyramid.

Erica van Sloan's last act before abandoning the pyramid only minutes before Weir Qiang's army occupied the place was to bury the Heart of the World by setting off explosives.

"So you moved back into your old digs at Front Royal?" Kane asked.

Erica nodded. "With the consortium's help, yes. They dispossessed some squatters."

"Didn't the consortium supply old Wei Qiang?" Grant inquired. "It's basically *their* fault you got dispossessed from Xian, right?"

"Yeah," Kane said, tone heavy with suspicion. "So how'd you end up joining them?"

"Because she's a mercenary slut," Domi interposed. "How else?"

Erica's one violet eye flashed with a sudden anger, but she quickly veiled her reaction with another taunting smile. "Unlike some people here, when I'm presented with an opportunity, I examine it before rejecting it out of hand. The consortium reached out to me with an opportunity. I met them halfway. It's nothing more complicated than that."

"I'll bet," Brigid drawled sardonically.

"Boss Bitch," Kane stated matter-of-factly.

Erica swiveled her head toward him, the smile fleeing from her lips. "Excuse me?"

"You're Boss Bitch, the section chief Gray talked about."

Her smile returned. "Is he here?"

Lakesh tapped the DVD against the palm of a hand. "He is. The main question is why are *you?*"

"You supplied me with the destination code for this unit, Mohandas—"

"I didn't ask how," he broke in harshly. "I asked why."

Erica took a deep breath, her bosom straining at the fabric of her bodysuit. "May I put my hands down?"

Lakesh nodded. "You may."

Dropping her hands to her hips, she swept everyone in the room with a challenging stare. "I'm here to offer you an opportunity, not just on the part of the Millennial Consortium but from me, as well. You need to examine it very closely before reaching the decision to reject it."

"What kind of opportunity?" Brigid challenged. "What does the consortium offer that we would be interested in?"

"Area 51." Erica van Sloan's tone was flat, matter-of-fact.

Kane's eyebrows rose toward his hairline, then angled down to the bridge of his nose. "The Millennial Consortium is offering us Area 51?"

"The consortium is offering you the opportunity to help them lay claim to it or to see it destroyed."

Grant nodded. "Ah. Well, all things being equal, I vote we see it destroyed."

"Me, too," Domi chimed in fervently. "Now that's been settled, you can gate your ass back to where it came from and stop bothering us, Erica."

Erica gestured toward the DVD in Lakesh's hand. "I'm very tempted to do that, but first I think it would behoove all of you to take a look at that so you'll have an informed opinion. Agreed?"

Lakesh hesitated, then met Erica's steady gaze and said quietly, "Agreed."

Chapter 14

The alert level was downgraded and the security shields lifted. Brigid, Erica, Grant, Kane and Lakesh stepped over to a vacant computer station. Domi did not care to linger and left the ops center in something of a huff as soon as the bulkheads were raised.

She resented the connection, if not the bond, shared by Erica van Sloan and Lakesh. Other than the fact they were both exiles from the twentieth century and scientists by trade and training, both people owed their apparent youth and vibrancy to the entity they had known as Sam the imperator.

A few years before, Sam had restored Lakesh's physical condition to that of a man in his mid-forties by what seemed to be a miraculous laying on of hands. At that time, Lakesh's eyes had been covered by thick lenses, a hearing aid inserted in one ear, and he resembled a hunched, spindly old scarecrow fighting the grave for every hour he remained on the planet.

Sam claimed he had increased Lakesh's production of two antioxidant enzymes, catalase and

superoxide dismutase, and boosted his alkyglyce-
rol level to the point where the aging process was
for all intents and purposes reversed.

Sam had indeed accomplished all of that, but
only much later did Lakesh learn the precise meth-
odology—when he laid his hands on both him and
Erica, Sam had injected nanomachines into their
bodies.

The nanites were programmed to recognize and
destroy the dangerous replicators, whether they
were bacteria, cancer cells or viruses. Sam's nanites
performed selective destruction on the genes of
DNA cells, removing the part that caused aging.
But with the transformation of Sam into his true
form of Overlord Enlil, what control he exerted
over the nanomachines vanished. Both Lakesh and
Erica now aged at a normal rate.

Lakesh slid the DVD into the tray and an image
flashed onto the screen: a thick-walled red triangle
enclosing and partially bisected by three elongated
but reversed triangles. Small disks topped each one,
lending them a resemblance to round-hilted dag-
gers.

Kane immediately recognized the insignia as the
unifying symbol of the Archon Directorate. His belly
fluttered in a cold reaction. He knew the emblem was
supposed to represent some kind of pseudomystical
triad functioning within a greater, all-embracing
body. To him, all it represented was the deception, the
co-opting and deliberate extinction of the human race.

A colorless male voice intoned, "Project Theta Pinch update. Authorized Mission Snowbird and Project Sigma personnel only. MJ-Ultra clearance required."

The image of the triangle disappeared to be replaced by a date stamp: "10-20-00." Kane absently noted the date as being three months before the first mushroom cloud swallowed Washington, D.C.

On the screen appeared the head and shoulders of a heavyset, coarse-featured man. Completely bald, his brown eyes stared unblinkingly from behind the round lenses of steel-rimmed spectacles. Visible behind him were people in white coats and coveralls, bustling around a raised platform on which machine parts were scattered.

Lakesh stiffened in his chair. "Is that—?"

"My name is Dr. Spiros Marcuse," the man stated in a voice that held an indefinable accent.

Both Kane and Brigid recognized the man's name and his face. In the disastrous mission to the twentieth century, they had briefly seen Spiros Marcuse in Lakesh's company on New Year's Eve 2000. But that had only been a version of this particular man, in an alternate temporal plane.

"Thank you for your attention," Marcuse said with a bland insincerity. "Rather than launch into a defense of our cost overruns and blown timetables, I shall say up front that Project Theta Pinch has no current practical uses. In fact, we have found that it is absolutely deadly to human subjects—both the willing and the unwilling."

"I like a man who doesn't beat around the bush," Grant muttered, folding his arms over his chest. "Unlike most whitecoats I've ever met."

"Hush," Lakesh said, casting him an annoyed glare. He knew "whitecoat" was postnuke slang for a scientist.

"As you know," Marcuse went on, "pinch-plasma, or Z physics, deals with the compression of electrically conducting filaments by magnetic forces. The conductor is plasma and in a Z-pinch operation, the electrical current flows in an axial direction. The magnetic field itself is azimuthal. In a theta pinch, the current is azimuthal and the magnetic field is axial. We have achieved a balance between theta and Z."

The scene on the screen shifted, displaying various shots of lightning bolts streaking across the sky, accompanied by sizzles and the booms of thunder.

Marcuse said, "The phenomenon occurs naturally in electrical discharges, particularly ball lightning. The plasma pinches created in the laboratory are related to nuclear fusion. High-energy-plasma physics have been experimented with for years, primarily by the scientists of Nazi Germany employed by their Totalitat Konzept."

Kane, Grant and Brigid exchanged sour glances. "Figures," Kane murmured.

They had come across the residue of Nazi Germany on more than one occasion. A few years before, they had found a subterranean installation beneath the Antarctic ice, occupied by a crazed German officer they had found in the base.

"The Third Reich's experiments were driven by fusion-power research," Marcuse said. "If they had been even marginally successful, Germany would have tapped into an energy source that might have made them invincible."

"And so," Erica said with a hint of bitterness in her tone, "the American version of the Totality Concept just picked up where the Nazis left off. Very typical."

A diagram appeared, a jumble of cylinders, ellipses and hexagons. All the pieces of hardware were labeled: coils, capacitors, current conduits, spark gap switches and influx-outflux diodes. A column of numbers glowed beside the schematic.

Marcuse said, "We built the theta-pinch transmitter so it would generate force-free magnetic fields, gravitationally balanced magnetic pressures with a continuous transition between these states. The theory is applied to electric currents in the magnetosphere, in the solar atmosphere and in the interstellar medium. Electromagnetic currents in the solar atmosphere and in the interstellar medium may lead to pinches that are of vital importance to our understanding of star formation."

The schematic faded away, followed by a sequence filmed within a windowless room. A big wire cage holding a brown-furred monkey sat in the center of the floor. The monkey was engrossed in eating a piece of fruit.

"Once the transmitter was completed, we directed a cylindrical column of fully ionized plasma, with an axial electric field, that produced an axial current density into the test chamber," Marcuse announced, his voice studiedly indifferent. "You can see the plasma waveforms as a mist."

A pale green vapor spread across the room, creeping toward the cage. When it touched the metal, there came a green flash, as of embers blazing in a fire. The monkey suddenly dropped the fruit and began rushing from one side of the cage to the other, its teeth bared in terror. The glow reddened, coating the cage and spreading wider and wider. The monkey's face distorted in agony, its body quaking with fear. The green glow of its eyes reflected madness.

It made one convulsive lunge toward the left-hand side of the cage—then it burst into emerald-hued flame and disappeared, leaving a swirl of little motes in its wake. The cage itself collapsed, as if it were crushed by a giant invisible hand. It did not so much compress as implode into a fist-sized, irregularly shaped cube.

"Oh, my god," Brigid said under her breath.

"As you can see, the associated azimuthal magnetic field generated a pinch with an inward-radial-force density of approximately one million milli-bars," Marcuse intoned.

The scene switched to a desolate, windswept landscape, with clouds of dust gusting over a flat terrain. Grant, Kane and Brigid recognized the crater at the base of Phantom Mesa. A time stamp appeared on the lower-right corner of the screen: "Test 8, day 4."

"We chose an inaccessible site on the outskirts of the Los Alamos testing range for further tests of the Project Theta Pinch transmitter," Marcuse said. "Of course, our ultimate objective was to refine a sustainable form of fusion-energy generation that could be controlled—which has always been the drawback of all pinch-plasma researches."

In the center of the crater stood a small, naked man bound hand and foot to a wooden post planted deeply in the ground. He looked like a Mexican laborer, his black hair bowl-cut in a ragged peon style. Fine wires twined all about him. He hung his head as if unconscious, but his eyes were open.

"We proceeded to our first human trial," Marcuse declared. "Even at a substantially reduced power output, the results were not encouraging."

When a pale green fog covered the man, the sequence of film jumped, as if the surroundings vibrated violently. The bound man blurred. His body twisted to and fro as though he fought his restraints. He writhed and threw back his head, mouth opening in a scream. Shimmering green light covered him completely, and little pieces of his body flew away, floating up from his shoulders and skull. Suddenly he vaporized, turning into an emerald cloud.

Lakesh swallowed hard and murmured something in Hindi.

"Horrible," Brigid husked out. "He disintegrated."

"Keep watching," Erica said.

As the haze faded away, they saw a sparkle in the air, as evanescent as the reflection of sunlight on dancing soap bubbles. A swarm of little green orbs darted all around the post to which the man had been tied.

"The fundamental law of conservation of mass and matter," Spiros Marcuse said, "is quite clear that matter can neither be created nor destroyed, only rearranged. The theta-pinch transmitter enhances the mass defect of matter and exceeds the limit of the binding energy. However, it does not just convert mass into energy, but actually transforms it into a new form of life."

Lakesh sat up straight in his chair. "Impossible."

"I know some of you think such a transformation is impossible," Marcuse droned on, "but we have the evidence before us."

The dancing pattern of light darted back and forth, giving the impression of a flock of birds exploring a new roost. The swarm moved swiftly forward toward the edge of the crater before it came to a stop.

"However, the form of life created as a byproduct of the plasma pinch was not organic," Marcuse continued, "but more akin to an electric viral phenomenon that can replicate itself and convert other objects into copies of itself."

Slowly, the little orbs coalesced and took on the outline of a human being made of a swirling cloud of fog. A translucent green ghost, the shape swirled and undulated. Arms waving, it came swaying toward the camera, a wraithlike monstrosity.

"That thing is a disease?" Grant demanded.

"Not exactly," Erica replied. "The concept of something other than a biological entity behaving as a virus became common in the late 1990s. An object, even a nonmaterial object, is considered to be viral when it has the ability to spread copies of itself or change other, similar objects to become more like itself."

Marcuse declared matter-of-factly, "All I can say is that although the byproduct is a form of viral life, it is composed of plasma and electrical impulses contained in a cohesive binding field. We still don't know about their method of reproduction or how they transform organic matter into copies of themselves. I can only speculate. A human being is partly chemical, partly electrical and a partly mechanical creature."

"Mechanical?" Kane muttered, brow furrowing.

"Our muscle system and skeletal structure act as a system of weights and pulleys," Brigid said. "That's mechanical."

"Oh."

"However," Marcuse continued, "a human being also uses electrical energy at many frequencies for many different tasks, even though our bodies are designed to function in a completely physical, material universe. We see physical objects, we are aware of them with our tactile senses and we hear them if they are vibrating in a certain aural range and smell them if they are vibrating in another particular range. We can even taste them under certain conditions.

"These are the senses by which we humans are aware of and interact with our environment. We guide ourselves through our world by our senses. So, out of a combination of all these chemicals, electrical impulses and even our senses, the theta-pinch transmitter brought the viral form to life."

Spiros Marcuse paused, frowned and added, "*Life* is not the proper term. *Existence* is better and more appropriate, even though we are dealing with the life principle itself, the organizing, energizing function that births all organisms."

"Is he claiming the plasma bug is actually a sentient life-form?" Brigid asked. "Some sort of mutation?"

"More than an adaptation of a preexisting form," Erica replied. "Listen."

"As you can see," Marcuse said, "the viral employs a type of high-frequency radiation across the electromagnetic spectrum."

The scene switched, showing a glass-walled booth. Networks of fine wires could be seen sandwiched between the panes. Inside the booth, the air shifted and twisted with hundreds of tiny green orbs. They bobbed, weaved, danced and spun. If one touched the glass, it flared and then vanished, like a candle flame.

"So they trapped them in that?" Lakesh inquired. "A containment unit?"

Spiros Marcuse said, "What you see here might be described as both a nursery and an abortion clinic. There we managed to control the birth of the virals and make them sterile, so they could no longer reproduce by making copies of themselves."

Kane said, "So the bugs are mortal. Where is the containment unit?"

Erica cast him a wan smile, but there was no humor in it. "Where do you think?"

With a sudden sinking sensation in the pit of his stomach, Kane could only sigh. "Let me guess. Area 51."

Chapter 15

A series of unsteady flickering shapes flashed over the screen. Gray-and-white figures moved jerkily about the dimly lit circular chamber, the curving walls lined by consoles. A metal shaft mounted in a drum-shaped socket rose from the floor.

"That's the control room of the theta-pinch transmitter," Brigid said.

"It is," Erica van Sloan conceded. "Inside Phantom Mesa. This sequence was copied from the installation's security cameras. The quality isn't the best, but considering the video equipment was installed over two hundred years ago, I'm surprised anything at all was recorded."

"Why show us this?" Lakesh asked impatiently.

"This is the first consortium team to enter Phantom Mesa Theta-Z Research Station. When the power was restored, the cameras began recording automatically. It was filmed about three months ago."

"How did the consortium find the place?" Kane wanted to know.

"I'd think you'd be able to guess," Erica replied

dryly. "I told them, of course. I was aware of the researches into theta fusion. It was one way of establishing my bona fides."

"The work of many divisions of the Totality
Concept overlapped from time to time," Lakesh
interposed.

Erica nodded. "Exactly. Now pay attention."

On the screen a slender dark-skinned man came
into view. He was attired in the standard bodysuit
of the Millennial Consortium operative, but it fit
him very well.

"There he is," Erica stated, touching a button on
the keyboard and freezing the image. "The quintes-
sential devil in this situation. Section Chief Quintus Breech."

He was tall, with dark brown skin. His face was
youthful, unlined and slightly rounded. The man's
hair was short and black, a cap of tight curls. There
was about him an air of childlike enthusiasm, but
the posture of his body and the tilt of his head suggested absolute authority.

"Gray mentioned that name," Brigid commented. "He was your predecessor."

"Yes," Erica said simply.

The man seemed to stare aggressively out at the
screen at her, and she averted her face, turning her
gaze on Brigid.

"Breech was recruited into the consortium from
the Mandeville Historical Division three years ago,"
Erica declared. "He was considered quite a wunder-

kind with a very impressive degree of knowledge about predark technology. He obviously had been tapping into archived, classified files. But unlike you, Brigid, he was never found out. He joined the consortium and swiftly rose through the ranks."

"Ranks," Grant repeated. "Is the Millennial Consortium set up like the old ville hierarchy?"

"Not exactly. You might look at the consortium as more of a franchise with semi-independent operations going within it. The range of activities is very broad."

"There's some sort of oversight council or committee, isn't there?" Kane asked.

"There is," Erica answered reluctantly. "Which basically makes sure all the operations are geared to the same ultimate end."

"I'm sure I can guess this one," Kane said sarcastically. "The conquest of the world and the institution of a technocratic rule."

Erica shrugged negligently. "Something like that. Anyway—"

"Anyway," Brigid broke in, a hard edge to her tone, "you don't believe in the consortium's philosophy any more than we do."

Erica regarded her with a calm violet eye. "What difference does it make if I do or not? Technocracy is as serviceable a set of ideals as any. Technocrats are primarily driven by problem-solution mind-sets. If technocracy had been adopted as the form of government in the twentieth century when it was first proposed, there would not have been a nuclear holocaust."

"Perhaps not," Lakesh retorted, "because we would have had, for all intents and purposes, a dictatorship. At the heart of technocracy is de facto elitism, whereby the concepts of the most qualified and the ruling elite are the same. The elite are selected through a bureaucratic process on the basis of specialized knowledge rather than through democratic elections. However, they do abide by the old two-party political system—masters and slaves."

Erica did not seem particularly interested in Lakesh's opinion. She brushed a strand of hair away from her face and said, "The Millennial Consortium operates on the big-business principle, and I can at least relate to that."

"How so?" Grant inquired.

"The price of any commodity can be gauged by supply and demand. Any glut on the market reduces the value of the commodity, and at this point in time, human life is about the cheapest commodity available. The consortium understands this. So do I."

"I understand you're a cold-blooded bitch," Grant said flatly.

"I really don't care one way or the other what any of you think of me, as long you realize you're in as much danger from Quintus Breech as the Millennial Consortium is."

Lakesh swiveled his head swiftly toward her, eyebrows raised. "Indeed? Why does he pose a threat to us—or to you, for that matter?"

Erica gestured to the image of Breech. "He managed to activate the theta-pinch transmitter in the Phantom Mesa station. He transformed his own men into the plasma virals. That's who—or what— you encountered there. Breech kept them there as guards. When he disappeared, I took over the operation to secure the station. Mr. Blue worked for me."

"You gave him the orders to destroy the place?" Kane asked.

"I did. We were hoping to break the circuit between the transmitter and the virals and thus cut off their energy source." She paused for a thoughtful second, and then said, "Obviously it didn't work."

Lakesh tugged at his nose again. "I think I understand now. In many plasma states, electrical currents need no voltage to drive the circuit. Any electric current is the transport of electric charge, but in many cases, such transport is already implied by the structure of the individual magnetic field and the plasma form itself."

Grant's face arranged itself in a foreboding scowl. "What are you talking about?"

Erica said, "Electrons and positive ions trapped in a dipole field tend to circulate around the magnetic axis, without gaining or losing energy. Ions circulate clockwise, electrons counterclockwise, producing a net circulating clockwise current, known as the ring circuit. No voltage is needed—the current arises naturally from the motion of the ions and electrons in the magnetic field."

"So are you telling us that these ghost-walkers can never run out of energy?" Brigid demanded dubiously.

Erica shook her head. "As plasma forms, they will always be drawn to electromagnetic fields to sustain themselves… 'magnetic mirroring' is the term."

"That implies a degree of self-awareness," Kane said.

"Perhaps," she admitted. "I don't know enough about it to hazard a guess."

"If Breech left the ghost-walkers there as guards," Lakesh commented, "where did he get himself off to?"

"He watched the same final report from Spiros Marcuse as we did," answered Erica diffidently. "Breech went to Area 51 for the containment unit. If he finds it and everything else pertaining to the theta transmitter, he will have access to technology that will make him unstoppable."

"What makes you think he's turned against you?" Grant wanted to know.

Erica manipulated keys on the board. "*This* does. Mr. Blue brought this message back from the station two days ago. It was left in the control room, in an envelope addressed to the consortium."

The image on the screen wavered, shifted and

filled with an extreme close-up of Quintus Breech's genially smiling face. "Hello," he said in a vibrant yet mellow voice. "I want you to watch closely."

The perspective changed, pulling back as the cameraman withdrew, revealing the crater at the base of the mesa. Judging by the brightness of the sunlight, the time of day was high noon. Breech gestured to a fair-haired man garbed in the drab consortium coverall standing twenty or so yards away. His arms hung limply at his sides and he listed slightly. He seemed unaware of his surroundings, his mouth partially open.

"You recognize Mr. Brown," Breech stated matter-of-factly. "One of the minor cogs in the consortium's mighty wheels. I've had to sedate him to keep him from running away."

Breech paused, then his smile broadened to a grin. "Running away from what, you may ask? I invite you to observe and take notes."

Closing his eyes, Breech breathed deeply through his nostrils. His face locked tight in a mask of concentration. Flickering greens of different hues and intensities suddenly appeared above Breech's head. The orbs swirled around him, almost like a miniature emerald-hued blizzard.

"What in the name of God—?" Lakesh blurted.

Eyes still shut, Breech lifted his right hand, the palm on a direct line with Brown's chest across the crater. A small circle of fierce smoking green appeared on the center of Brown's coverall, as if a magnifying glass of unimaginable heat had suddenly been focused there. A flare of green flame fanned out from between his shoulder blades.

Brown jerked and staggered backward. He cried out. The flash of jade fire vanished, leaving a charred area in the material of his garment. Uttering a choking sound as if his throat had closed, he toppled backward to the crater and lay there, outflung limbs twitching violently. The flesh of his face blistered and bubbled, and his hair smouldered. His eye sockets filled with a semiliquid gel that oozed down his cheeks.

Quintus Breech lowered his right hand and opened his eyes. He flexed his fingers. Face sheened with perspiration, he turn back toward the camera. His tone was grave. "I am embarking on a new course, one that will put me at odds with my mentors at the Millennial Consortium. But my course is a matter of conscience, not profit or philosophy. It is one of reality. Our world is one that breeds violence, madness and greed.

"Although your technocratic ideals might one day restore sanity to this country, to this planet, it will take many years before any long-term benefits can be measured. What is required now is immediate, unalterable discipline. The madness must end, and only overwhelming force can prevail against all the anarchies running loose. What you witnessed is just a small sample of the kind of power I will be able to command."

Breech paused to offer a cold, menacing smile. Softly, he said, "Do not seek to stop me. And that means *you*, Erica."

The image flickered and dissolved into pixels.

Brigid glanced at Erica. "So you know him."

"I do. We were close at one time."

"I can't say I'm surprised," Brigid replied. "So... he can control the ghost-walkers and summon them to siphon off and channel their plasma energy?"

"Apparently," Erica stated. "Don't ask me how. I'm as much in the dark about it as you are."

"Well, I can't say I disagree with the man's attitude," Kane said conversationally.

Grant and Brigid kept their own counsel, but Kane knew they shared his thoughts. Years before, the Cerberus warriors had declared war on the dark forces devoted to maintaining the yoke of slavery around the collective neck of humankind. It was a struggle not just for the physical survival of humanity but for the human spirit, the soul of an entire race.

Over the past five-plus years, they had scored many victories, defeated many enemies and solved mysteries of the past that molded the present and affected the future. More importantly, they began to rekindle of the spark of hope within the breasts of the disenfranchised fighting for survival in the Outlands.

Apparently that spark of hope wasn't sufficient to satisfy Quintus Breech.

No one spoke for a long moment. Then Lakesh

intoned, "I presume the power Mr. Breech refers to is the theta-pinch fusion generator."

Erica nodded. "I'm afraid so."

"And it's in Area 51," Kane declared. He did not ask a question.

"Again," Erica replied, "I'm afraid so. And since you are the only person I know who has ever been inside the place, that's why I came to you."

Kane cast a slit-eyed glare in her direction. "Then you should know I don't have any great interest in returning."

"I do. But you should know there is more than likely a great deal of technology still in the place." A lazy smile played over Erica van Sloan's lips, and she dropped her voice to barely above a conspiratorial whisper.

"Not to mention hybrids and perhaps even…hybrid spawn that you may have fathered."

Chapter 16

Kane barely restrained himself from backhanding the woman's smile off her face. Between clenched teeth, he rasped, "Shut up, Erica. You don't know what you're talking about."

Her laugh had a taunting lilt. "I know you wish that were the case. I've seen tapes of your time there, Kane. You can maybe delude yourself that what you experienced there never happened, but don't expect me to go along with it."

Kane knotted his fists but did not respond. He glared at her, and she smiled with feigned innocence.

Pushing his chair away from the computer station, Lakesh stood up. "Erica, you have never improved your people skills. You won't gain Kane's assistance by insulting him."

Erica's one visible eyebrow rose. "Did I insult you, Kane? If I did, I apologize. I was under the assumption you appreciated straight talk."

As Kane met the woman's unblinking gaze, he grudgingly realized she was right. For many months following his ordeal at Area 51, he had never shared the details about his captivity. Over the past few years, especially after the death of Quavell, the vivid memories had softened at the edges, receding into the blur of the distant past.

He took a deep, calming breath. "I didn't impregnate any of the hybrids. Quavell told me the experiments were failures."

"Quavell could only guess," Erica pointed out.

"As you can you," Brigid interjected sharply. She speared Lakesh with a challenging stare. "Do you believe Erica's story?"

Lakesh sighed regretfully. "We have no reason not to. After all, we know that the plasma bugs—the virals—killed our man Higson."

Grant planted his fists on his hips. "How do we know the rest of it is true? It's only supposition that Breech went to Area 51."

All of them remembered Lakesh's briefing about the place, prior to the first mission there. He told them that Area 51 was, in the latter years of the twentieth century, a place as fabulous to Americans as Avalon had been to Britons a thousand years earlier.

Financed by the American government and also known as Dreamland and Groom Lake, Area 51 was a secret military facility about ninety miles north of Las Vegas. At the center of the six-by-ten mile block of land was a large air base the predark government only reluctantly admitted even existed.

Lakesh claimed the site was selected in the mid-1950s for testing of the U-2 spy plane and later, due to its remoteness, Groom Lake became America's traditional testing ground for experimental "black budget" aircraft. The sprawling facility and surrounding areas were also associated with UFO and conspiracy stories featuring alien technology that was back-engineered and retrofitted.

None of the Cerberus warriors had a reason to doubt Lakesh's history, since one of the experimental aircraft that rolled from the hidden hangars of the Area 51 complex was the Aurora. In New Mexico, Grant had downed a small, prototypical version of the stealth plane, and later Kane, Brigid and Lakesh had seen to the destruction of a far larger and more deadly Aurora aircraft that had been kept in deep storage beneath Mount Rushmore.

The majority of the Dreamland complex lay underground to prevent unauthorized observation from satellites or overflights. And more importantly, Area 51 was first code-named Mission Snowbird. All of them at Cerberus had learned that Mission Snowbird and Project Sigma, two subdivisions of the Totality Concept's Overproject Majestic, were the only ones that dealt directly with the so-called Archon alien technology.

"Time may not be of the essence," Erica declared grimly, "but it *is* a factor. I know you have the mat-trans destination code for the unit there."

Lakesh made an exaggerated show of lifting his right wrist, shooting the cuff and eyeing his watch. "It's too late in the day to mount a mission anyplace. Even if we agree to do this, we'll require several hours of prep time."

"Besides," Brigid said, "you need Kane to be your guide, and he's not a hundred percent yet. He was stung by one of the virals."

Erica swung her head toward him, her expression both surprised yet skeptical. "Really? And you recovered?"

"It was just the one," Kane said blandly.

"But he was unconscious for nearly twenty-four hours," Brigid continued. "He's still a little weak."

Kane opened his mouth to protest, then he caught Brigid's eye and repressed a smile. The sunset-haired former archivist was stalling for time. He could only guess at the reason, but he assumed it was a sound one.

"We'll assign you quarters," Lakesh said to Erica. "And we'll let you know our decision in a few hours."

Erica stood up, smoothing her bodysuit over her hips. "I hope you don't plan to hold me hostage."

Grant snorted derisively. "We don't have the resources to pay the consortium to take you back. Nobody has that much jack."

Everyone chuckled, but Erica ignored the gibe. Lakesh waved over Carson, one of the Moonbase émigrés. "Please escort Dr. van Sloan to a guest suite."

As the young man and led the tall, black-haired woman out of the ops center, Brigid dropped into her chair at the computer station. Her fingers clattered over the keyboard. "I want to see the DVD again…maybe I can get a better idea of how the theta-pinch process actually works."

Lakesh nodded approvingly. "Good idea. I'll consult the database for any existing records on the research."

He glanced questioningly at Kane. "In the interim, might I suggest you rest…and perhaps clean up?"

Kane ran a hand over his stubbled jaw. "Yeah, I think I will."

Grant turned toward the exit. "I'll stop by the armory and put some ordnance together for a dark-territory probe."

The two men strode down the main corridor until they reached the T junction. Grant turned left toward the armory.

"Hey, just one question," Kane called after him.

Grant paused. "What?"

"We're really going to go through with this mission, aren't we?"

Grant presented the image of pondering the question, then he shrugged. "Well, since it's crazy and dangerous, yeah—I imagine we will. Try to get some rest."

Kane turned down the corridor to the wing holding the apartments and dormitories. His four-room suite was substantially larger and better appointed than his old flat in the residential enclaves of Cobaltville.

In the bathroom, he stripped out of his clothes and stepped into the shower, adjusting the water so it was as hot as he could stand it. The entire bathroom quickly filled with billowing clouds of steam.

Kane soaped himself up, working a lather all over his bruised and scarred body. He methodically shaved by feel. He stayed beneath the shower longer than was necessary, wanting to scrub every microscopic grain of sand from his pores. His muscles felt sore.

Kane had no trouble admitting to himself that the prospect of returning to Area 51 disturbed him greatly. Although his conscious memories of his experiences there had faded somewhat, they occasionally surfaced in his dreams.

After the destruction of the Archuleta Mesa medical facilities, the barons were left without access to the techniques of fetal development outside the womb, so both the baronial oligarchy and the entire hybrid race were in danger of extinction.

Baron Cobalt reactivated the Area 51 installation, turning it into a processing and treatment center and transferred the human and hybrid personnel from the Dulce facility—those who had survived the destruction there, at any rate.

But the medical treatments that addressed the congenital autoimmune system deficiencies of the hybrids were not enough to insure the continued survival of the race. The necessary equipment and raw material to implement procreation had yet to be installed. Baron Cobalt had unilaterally decided that the conventional means of conception was the only option to keep the hybrid race alive.

Because of their metabolic deficiencies, the barons lived insulated, isolated lives. The theatrical trappings many of them adopted not only added to their semidivine mystique, but also protected them from contamination both psychological and physical.

Although all of the barons were extremely long-lived, cellular and metabolic deterioration was part and parcel of what they were—hybrids of human and Archon DNA. Just like the caste system in place in the villes, the hybrids observed a similar one, although it had little do with parentage. If the first phase of human evolution produced a package of adaptations for a particular and distinct way of life, the second phase was an effort to control that way of life by controlling the environment. The focus switched to an evolution that was cultural rather than physical.

The hybrids, at least by their way of thinking, represented the final phase of human evolution. They created wholesale, planned alterations in living organisms and were empowered to control not only their environment but also the evolution of other species. And the pinnacles of that evolutionary achievement were the barons, as high above ordinary hybrids bred as servants as the hybrids were above mere humans.

When Cerberus learned of Baron Cobalt's plan, Kane and Domi penetrated Area 51 but were captured. Domi was found by a little group of insurgents led by the hybrid female Quavell, while Kane was sentenced by Baron Cobalt to what amounted to stud service.

During his two weeks of captivity, he was fed a steady diet of protein laced with a stimulant of the catecholamine group. It affected the renal blood supply, increasing cardiac output without increasing the need for cardiac oxygen consumption.

Combined with the food loaded with protein to speed sperm production, the stimulant provided Kane with hours of high energy. Since he was forced to achieve erection and ejaculation six times a day every two days, his energy and sperm count had to be preternaturally high, even higher than was normal for him.

Although Kane was supposed to be biologically superior, he knew the main reason he was chosen to impregnate the female hybrids was simply due to the fact male hybrids were incapable of engaging in conventional acts of procreation, at least physically. Their organs of reproduction were so undeveloped as to be vestigial.

Kane wasn't the first human male to be pressed into service. But the other men before him had performed unsatisfactorily due to their terror of the hybrids. At first the females selected for the process donned wigs and wore cosmetics in order to appear more human to the trapped sperm donors. The men had to be strapped down and even after the application of an aphrodisiac gel, had difficulty maintaining an erection.

Such a problem wasn't something a hybrid, baron or no, was likely to ever experience. What made the barons so superior had nothing to do with the physical. The brains of the barons could absorb and process information with exceptional speed, and their cognitive abilities were little short of supernatural.

Almost from the moment the barons emerged from the incubation chambers, they possessed IQs so far beyond the range of standard tests as to render them meaningless. They mastered language in a matter of weeks, speaking in whole sentences. All of Nature's design faults in the human brain were corrected, modified and improved, specifically the hypothalamus, which regulated the complex biochemical systems of the body.

They could control all autonomous functions of their brains and bodies, even to the manufacture and release of chemicals and hormones. They could speed or slow their heartbeats, increase and decrease the amount of adrenaline in their bloodstreams.

They possessed complete control over that mysterious portion of the brain known as the limbic system, a portion that predark scientists had always known possessed great reserves of electromagnetic power and strength.

Physically, the barons were a beautiful people, almost too perfect to be real. Even their expressions were markedly similar to one another—a vast pride, a diffident superiority, authority and even ruthlessness. They were the barons, and as such, they believed themselves to be the avatars of the new humans who would inherit the Earth.

But since they were bred for brilliance, all barons had emotional limitations placed upon their enormous intellects. They were captives of their shared Archon hive-mind heritage, which did not carry with it the simple comprehension of the importance of individual liberty to humans.

Smug in their hybrid arrogance, the baronial oligarchy did not understand the primal beast buried inside the human psyche, the beast that always gave humans a fair chance of winning in the deadly game of survival of the fittest.

Returning his thoughts to the present, Kane noted that his fingertips were wrinkled and had turned pink. He decided he was as clean as he was likely to be. He started to turn off the faucet when a soft hand touched his back. He jumped, stumbling, biting back a surprised curse.

Erica van Sloan materialized out of the steam. Her naked limbs glistened with droplets of water vapor. Kane stared at her full, gem-crested breasts, flaring hips and the black triangle at the juncture of her rounded thighs. Her tumbles of black hair clung to her damp shoulders.

Her single good eye gleamed with violet light. Erica said softly, "I knocked, but when you didn't answer, I let myself in. I hope you don't mind."

Get FREE BOOKS and a FREE GIFT when you play the...

LAS VEGAS

GAME

*Just scratch off
the gold box with a coin.
Then check below to see
the gifts you get!* →

YES! I have scratched off the gold box. Please send
me my **2 FREE BOOKS** and **gift for which I qualify.** I understand
that I am under no obligation to purchase any books as
explained on the back of this card.

▶ DETACH AND MAIL CARD TODAY! ▶

© 2007 WORLDWIDE LIBRARY
® and TM are trademarks owned and used by the trademark owner and/or its licensee.

366 ADL ENWS

166 ADL ENX4
(GE-LV-08)

FIRST NAME

LAST NAME

ADDRESS

APT.#

CITY

STATE/PROV.

ZIP/POSTAL CODE

7	7	7	Worth TWO FREE BOOKS plus a BONUS Mystery Gift!
🍒	🍒	🍒	Worth TWO FREE BOOKS!
🔔	🔔	♣	TRY AGAIN!

Offer limited to one per household and not
valid to current subscribers of Gold Eagle®
books. All orders subject to approval.
Please allow 4 to 6 weeks for delivery.

Your Privacy - Worldwide Library is committed to protecting your privacy. Our privacy policy is available online at
www.eHarlequin.com or upon request from the Gold Eagle Reader Service. From time to time we make our lists
of customers available to reputable third parties who may have a product or service of interest to you. If you
would prefer for us not to share your name and address, please check here.☐

Chapter 17

"As a point of fact, Erica," Kane snapped, "I do mind. This is a pretty cheap tactic, even for you."

Kane didn't bother snatching a towel to cover his nudity. Modesty had not been instilled as a virtue—among the ville bred. As for Erica, she had always been proud, even vain, about her body. Nor did she make an effort to disguise her appreciation of Kane's.

Ignoring her visual inventory, Kane stepped out of the shower stall and took a towel from the rack. "Are you playing for time or just playing?"

"Neither," Erica answered. "The shower in my quarters doesn't have working hot water."

"So you just strolled naked over here?"

Erica shrugged and stepped past him into the stall. "I put on a robe. It's on your bed."

She turned the faucet handle and exhaled a deep sigh when the stream of hot water sprayed over her breasts. Kane watched her for a few seconds, and then realized her nude proximity was affecting him. He felt his penis engorging, thickening and hardening.

She glanced at him and said wryly, "Ah, there it is. In the flesh, this time."

"What are you talking about?"

"I told you I'd seen tapes of you in Area 51…in particular during your seeding session with Quavell."

Kane's jaw muscles knotted. "I could just throw you out of here."

Erica laughed. "With that thing pointing at me? You should just order me to throw up my hands— or my legs."

Spinning on his heel, Kane stalked out of the bathroom and saw a yellow terry-cloth robe lying at the foot of his bed. From his clothes closet, he quickly took a black T-shirt and jeans. By the time he finished dressing, his body responded more or less to his conscious control again.

He glanced at Erica, still in the shower stall, and he couldn't help but feel a twinge of lust mixed with frustration. His feelings about the woman weren't easy to sort out. Over the past few years, Erica had been an enemy, an ally, a neutral player and then an ally again. He had no idea what role she played now.

"Hey," Erica called. "Would you mind washing my back?"

Kane stopped short of responding that he wouldn't mind stabbing her there, but instead retorted, "You're about as clean as it's possible for you to get."

She turned off the water and stepped out of the stall, wrapping up her hair in a towel turban. As she strolled into the bedroom, wet, naked flesh glistening, Kane tossed her the robe and said gruffly, "Get out."

"Always the charmer," Erica said with an exaggeratedly sweet smile, sliding her arms into the sleeves. She took a tantalizing long time tugging the robe closed.

"I don't have to charm you."

"Good thing, because you're really terrible at it. But that doesn't mean you can't be cordial. We've worked together before."

Kane stalked into the living room and entered the small kitchenette. "You wildly overestimate your standing with us."

Erica leaned against the doorway, inspecting her fingernails. "Has no woman ever gotten into your life and softened you up?"

Kane felt the back of his neck flush hot with anger. He knew she made a mocking reference to Brigid Baptiste. "If one hadn't, you and I wouldn't be having this conversation."

Erica widened her one eye in disingenuous surprise. "Why? Because we'd be too busy fucking?"

"More likely it would be because I'd have killed you a long time ago."

In a tone brittle with barely suppressed anger, she shot back, "You're not one for this forgive-and-forget business, are you?"

"You noticed."

From a cabinet he took a bottle of Scotch that had been discovered in the bowels of the Cerberus redoubt. The seal hadn't been broken in two centuries until he, Grant and Baptiste shared a few sips a couple of years before. Neither one of his friends developed a taste for the stinging intoxicant, but with practice he came to appreciate it.

He poured a dash of the liquor into a cup and took a careful sip. Erica stirred from her place in doorway. "Is that Scotch?"

He nodded, struggling to keep his face immobile as the liquor scorched a path down his esophagus.

She moved closer. "Do you think you can share?"

Wordlessly, he handed her the bottle by the neck. She took it, smelled the rim, then tilted her head back and took a long swallow. He watched, hoping for an explosion with fountainlike effects or the very least a convulsion much like Brigid had done. Instead she swallowed three times, her one eye gleaming with cunning.

Kane reached for the bottle, but Erica stepped sideways, avoiding his hand, then lowered the bottle and gasped out, "Hah! That was good! It's been a long time."

She pushed the bottle back into Kane's hands. He could only stare at her in shocked silence. She smiled, pirouetted on her toes and nodded to him graciously. "Thank you. That was lovely. A very good blend."

Kane raised the bottle to his nose and sniffed it suspiciously.

Erica laughed. "When I was in college, I used to drink a fifth of bourbon every weekend. I'd always win drinking contests. You people born in this age don't have the constitution for real liquor. Home-brewed popskull is what you're used to and you can only drink a little of that before you get sick or go blind."

Defiantly, he took a sip from the bottle. "It's not surprising that a shark can drink anything."

Erica didn't appear to be offended. "A wolf insulting a shark? That's a new one."

Kane didn't question her on her use of the word *wolf*. Among Sky Dog's band of Cheyenne and Lakota, he was known as Unktomi Shunkaha, the Trickster Wolf.

Wistfully, Erica said, "I wish you had a cigarette, though. I always smoked when I drank. Preferably a mentholated one."

"Pretty filthy habit for someone as fastidious as you."

She cocked her head at him. "You smoke cigars, right?"

"Sometimes," he admitted. "My supply is limited and I'm not too inclined to share."

Kane spoke the truth. The nuclear holocaust had pretty much completed what twentieth-century government legislation had begun in regards to tobacco, since it was no longer cultivated as a crop.

Hardly anyone but Outlanders used tobacco in any form any longer. There were mild drugs available that were much safer and less offensive to others. Smoking had certainly been forbidden in the all the Administrative Monoliths and the residential Enclaves of the baronies.

Fortunately, upon arriving at Cerberus, Kane and Grant learned that the redoubt had a well-stocked and functioning hermetically-sealed humidor.

Kane returned the bottle to the cabinet. "I'm tired of sparring with you. Why are you really here?"

"I told you…there was no hot water—"

"I mean Cerberus," he broke in impatiently. "You could've found layouts of Area 51 in other places. The resources of the Millennial Consortium are pretty broad."

"Broad, but not deep. The consortium's main focus is on commerce, establishing trade routes to build a new economy."

"Right," he drawled sarcastically. "That's why they never go anywhere without an army in tow."

Erica's lips curved in a knowing smile. "Most new societies are built by armies, and the Millennial Consortium is no different. One of their founders discovered a cache of predark weapons and vehicles, all of it in pristine condition, most of it prototypical. None of it had never been used in the field."

"Found where?"

."I'm not sure of that," she said frankly. "But in the vaults, they found Calico firearms, several wars worth of ammunition and a number of vehicles— what we call the Scorpinauts."

Kane vividly recalled the low-slung, boxlike vehicles. Propelled by eight massively treaded wheels, four to each side, the machines were sheathed in armor plate and studded with rocket pods and sealed weapons ports. At the end, jointed armatures sprouted two swivel-mounted .50-caliber machine guns, looking like a pair of foreclaws.

Kane, Brigid and Grant and had first encountered the Scorpinauts a couple of years before in China. Lakesh had described them as omnipurpose Future Combat System vehicles designed to replace tanks in a variety of ground-war situations. He opined that the consortium had found the vehicles in a COG vault.

From rectangular turrets protruded the tapered, ten-foot-long snouts of 40 mm cannons. The barrels were locked in a backward position, giving the FCS vehicles the aspects of mechanical scorpions, with the fore-mounted machine guns representing claws and the cannon barrels the stinger-tipped tails.

The Millennial Consortium had supplied the Scorpinauts to the warlord Wei Qiang to bolster his bid to conquer China. A few months later, the Cerberus warriors saw them in use in Europe.

While she spoke, Erica sank down on the one

armchair, oblivious to Kane's grimace of aggravation. Smoothly, she crossed one leg over the other.

"The consortium is tech rich in many ways, but intel poor. At this juncture, serviceable intelligence is more important than material goods. You have firsthand experience with both the interior and exterior of Area 51."

Kane's mouth quirked in a smirk. "I didn't see a whole hell of a lot of it."

Erica nodded in understanding. "But you've seen more than any agent of the consortium has, certainly more than anyone I ever met. It's estimated there are over a hundred miles worth of tunnels and passageways spread out over three or four subterranean levels."

"In which case, why are you so worried that Breech can find his way around well enough to stumble on the theta-pinch transmitter equipment?"

Taking a deep breath, the shelf of her breasts pushing at the bodice of her robe, Erica said flatly, "There's no point in dancing around the subject anymore. You've probably guessed that I had inside information about the transmitter experiments and the location of the station at the mesa."

"We guessed that some time ago."

"I also had inside information about the approximate location of the transmitter experiments in Area 51."

Kane gazed at her for a silent second, gauging the implications of her words. Then he snorted out a laugh. "Now I get it. You and Breech had hooked up—you intended to use the consortium's resources to gain your own power foothold within the organization. You two planned to take them over, but Breech went maverick on you."

Erica chuckled but there was no humor in it. "That was my plan, yes, but Quintus Breech wasn't privy to it. He's a man out of his time. He should've been born three hundred years ago."

"What do you mean?"

"He's a scientist of the old school, always seeking to better the lot of mankind by giving them more knowledge about the universe. But once Quintus found out what the transmitter was actually capable of accomplishing—"

The shiver that passed through Erica van Sloan's body held elements of a horrified shudder. "I think he became an obsessive-compulsive monster. He never was very emotional, even though I tried to awaken that in him. Quintus thinks he's found the way to free the souls and minds of humanity. He calls himself a visionary."

"He sounds more like another in a long line of goddamn megalomaniacs," Kane said bitterly.

Erica pulled away the towel turban, shook out her hair and nervously began finger combing it. "All across history, humans dreamed of building a better world. In my time, when I was a child, I thought the better world would be a couple of hundred years in the future, in the twenty-third century. I imagined it as a utopia where humanity was united and giant starships flew across the galaxy, exploring strange new worlds and seeking out new worlds and civilizations."

"That hasn't happened," Kane growled, "thanks to people like you."

"I know," Erica replied sadly. "Now the possibility of achieving such a utopia has receded so far away I can no longer believe it will ever happen. But Quintus Breech does—and he's going to lay the groundwork for that brave new world of the future, no matter how many people he has to kill in the process."

Chapter 18

Kane squeezed his eyes shut against the harsh light. He placed his hands against the sides of his head, fearing for a moment the sudden surge of pain within his skull would blow his head apart. Within seconds, the worst of the agony receded.

He blinked repeatedly, trying to bring the world back into focus. He flexed his fingers, brushing the tips against the interlocking hexagonal floor plates of the mat-trans unit. He felt the pins-and-needles static discharge prickling from the polished plates even through the gloves of his shadow suit.

The floor plates had already lost their silvery shimmer and the last wisps of spark-shot mist disappeared even as tendrils of it crawled over his field of vision. He knew the vapor was not really a mist at all but a plasma waveform. Beneath the platform, he heard the emitter's characteristic hurricane howl cycling down to a high-pitched drone.

Kane continued to lie on his back, his stomach churning, his head swimming. He took slow, deep breaths, wondering again at the enduring mystery of why a jumper could begin a gateway transition standing erect, but almost always ended it lying down.

Hearing a soft moan beside him, Kane slowly turned his head, not wanting to exacerbate the throbbing pain in his head. He knew from experience the throbbing would recede soon as long as he didn't move too quickly. Although the nausea seeped away, he knew better than to sit up until the dizziness faded.

Erica van Sloan stirred from her prone position on the platform, kneading her temples with her fingers. "I feel sick."

He hiked himself up on an elbow and said unsympathetically, "I told you not to have that big supper."

All things considered, temporary queasiness and light-headedness were trivial compared to traveling hundreds, sometimes thousands of miles in a handful of seconds. Occasionally, the toll exacted was terrible, as when he, Brigid and Grant jumped to a malfunctioning unit in Russia. The matter-stream modulations could not be synchronized with the destination lock, and all of them suffered a severe case of debilitating jump sickness that included hallucinations, lassitude and projectile vomiting.

Erica raised her head and squinted around at the armaglass walls enclosing the chamber. "Are we where we're supposed to be?" she whispered.

Kane eyed the walls, noting their pale green hue. He remembered the color from the first time he had

made a mat-trans jump from Cerberus to Area 51.
"I believe so."

"Goddamn well better be," Grant grunted, pushing himself to a sitting position. "I hate these
things."

"So we've heard," Brigid said dryly, carefully
rising to one knee. She squeezed her eyes shut
against the spasm of vertigo.

"Are you all right?" Kane asked.

Her lips creased in a wan smile. "Even though
it's been a while since we've traveled by the mat-
trans, you'd think we'd have gotten used to all the
side effects by now."

Like Kane and Grant, Brigid was clad from
throat to fingertip to heel in a one-piece black garment that resembled doeskin. The Cerberus warriors had opted not to wear BDUs over the shadow
suit for the mission, inasmuch they figured they
would be inside the base and not in the surrounding desert-like terrain.

Raking her hair out of her eyes, Erica lifted her
wrist chron to eye level. In a puzzled tone, she said,
"According to my watch, barely ten seconds have
passed since we activated the inducer of the Cerberus unit. How can that be?"

"There are occasional time-dilation events when
you use the mat-trans," Brigid answered. "I thought
you knew that."

Erica regarded her superciliously. "And why
would I know that, Baptiste?"

"Because of who you were sleeping with toward the end of the world as you knew it," Brigid countered. "Silas Torrance Burr, the head of Operation Chronos."

Erica didn't respond. She knew exactly to what Brigid referred. A major subdivision of the Totality Concept had been devoted to exploring the nature of time. Operation Chronos was built on the breakthroughs of Project Cerberus, but it had not been as successful.

During development of the mat-trans gateways, the Cerberus researchers observed a number of side effects. On occasion, traversing the quantum pathways resulted in minor temporal anomalies, such as arriving at a destination three seconds before the jump initiator was actually engaged.

Lakesh proposed that constant jumpers might find themselves physically rejuvenated if they accumulated enough "backwards time." Conversely, jumpers might find themselves prematurely aged if the quantum stream pushed them further into the future with each journey. Operation Chronos exploited these temporal anomalies, using the gateway technology, to develop time travel.

Silas Torrance Burr and his colleagues employed a practice they termed "trawling," focusing on subjects in the past and pulling them forward to the twentieth century. Lakesh had heard rumors of their many attempts and failures. Without access to the specs and data of Operation Chronos, Lakesh could not duplicate their work, so he determined to circumvent it. He saw to the creation of the Omega Path Program and linked it with the mat-trans gateway.

The concept was sound—to dispatch Kane and Brigid back through time to a point only a month before the nukecaust so they could hopefully trigger an alternate event horizon and thus avert the apocalypse.

The Omega Path successfully translated them into a past temporal plane, but they came to learn it was not their world's past, but another, almost identical to it. Thus their actions had no bearing on their world's present and future.

Lakesh could only speculate on the underlying system of physics at work. Operation Chronos hypothesized that time was not continuous but made up of subatomic particles jammed together like beads on a string. According to this chronon theory, between each bead, each individual unit of time might exist in an infinite series of parallel universes, fitted into the probability gaps between the chronons.

"The temporal issues are another reason we prefer to use the interphaser," Brigid continued, rising to her feet. "You don't lose consciousness, you don't get dizzy and you don't throw up. More importantly, you aren't disassembled at the subatomic level, squirted along a carrier wave and reassembled in a booth like this one."

Erica's supercilious stare became one of annoyance. "Don't lecture me. I know how the interphaser works. It opens a localized wormhole between two naturally occurring vortex points and forms a quantum conduit between the vortices. I'm a physicist myself, remember?"

Grant slowly pushed himself to his feet. "It's kind of hard to tell since you switch sides so often."

Kane smiled thinly as he stood up. "That's not quite fair. Erica has ever only been on one side. Her own."

He extended a hand to the woman, who affected not to notice. She rose swiftly, then staggered, leaning against the wall. "I think I'm suffering from inner-ear problems."

"You'll be all right in another couple of minutes," Brigid said, making sure her TP-9 autopistol was still snugged its cross-draw slide holster.

The three Cerberus warriors quickly checked their ordnance. Flat, square ammo pouches were attached to their lower backs by Velcro tabs. Long combat knives, the razor-keen blades forged of dark blued steel, hung from scabbards at their hips. The abbreviated Copperhead subguns dangled from combat webbing.

Kane and Grant checked the Sin Eaters in their rather bulky power holsters strapped to their forearms. They carried war bags full of odds and ends taken from the Cerberus armory, some selected for their maximum destructive capabilities and others for altogether different functions. The former Mags were experienced enough to know they could not plan for all contingencies and were always prepared to improvise.

Erica carried a case containing emergency medical supplies, including hypodermics of pain suppressants, ampoules of stimulants and antibiotics. A Heckler & Koch VP-70 autopistol was holstered in a shoulder rig she wore over her dun-colored coverall.

All of the ordnance was supplied by the Cerberus armory, quite likely the best stocked arsenal in post-nuke America. Glass-fronted cases held racks of automatic assault rifles. There were many makes and models of subguns, as well as dozens of semiautomatic pistols and revolvers, complete with holsters and belts.

The armory also housed heavy assault weaponry like bazookas, tripod-mounted 20 mm cannons, mortars and rocket launchers. All the ordnance had been laid down in hermetically sealed Continuity of Government installations before the nukecaust. Protected from the ravages of the outside environment, nearly every piece of munitions and hardware was as pristine as the day it was first manufactured.

Lakesh himself had put the arsenal together over several decades, envisioning it as the major supply depot for a rebel army. The army never materialized—at least not in the fashion Lakesh hoped it would. Therefore, Cerberus was blessed with a surplus of death-dealing equipment that would have turned the most militaristic overlord green with envy.

Kane moved to the door, straining to hear any sound through the slab of greenish armaglass. The color was appropriate, he told himself grimly, considering the hue of the ghost-walkers. All of the jump chambers in the Cerberus mat-trans network were color coded so authorized travelers could tell at a glance into which redoubt they had materialized.

The system seemed like an inefficient method of differentiating one installation from another, but Lakesh had once explained that before the nuke-caust, only personnel holding color-coded security clearances were allowed to make use of the network. Inasmuch as their use was restricted to a select few of the units, it was fairly easy for them to memorize which color designated what redoubt.

"I don't hear anything," Kane said.

Brigid moved up beside him, lifting her left wrist. A small motion detector was strapped around it. Made of molded black plastic and stamped metal, the device's window exuded a faint glow. The motion detector indicated no movement within the radius of its invisible sensor beams.

"No welcoming committee," she said. "Or if there is, they're not moving."

Kane nodded in acknowledgment and gripped the wedge-shaped handle placed in the center of the door. He heaved up on it. With a click of solenoids, the panel of dense, semiopaque material swung outward on counterbalanced hinges.

Cautiously, Kane shouldered open the door. Sin Eater unleathered, he stepped off the platform into a bare-walled anteroom. He looked around, seeing nothing and hearing only a distant electronic hum.

With hand gestures, he indicated that it was safe for everyone to leave the mat-trans unit. They joined him at the doorway. Both Brigid and Grant uttered wordless murmurs of surprise and dismay. Even Kane, who had been there before, was impressed.

The control room was immense, nearly twice the size of any they had seen in other redoubts. Kane estimated it measured eighty by a hundred feet, which made it even larger than the ops center in Cerberus.

Brigid sniffed the air and winced. "Do you smell that?"

Kane inhaled gingerly through his nostrils and caught a faint odor of decay. "Yeah, I do. Something is dying its little heart out."

He moved into the control complex, automatically walking heel-to-toe as he always did in a potential killzone. Three aisles of computer stations lined the walls, and almost every chair was occupied—by a corpse.

Their heads were tilted back, exposing the decomposition of their noses and the flesh peeling back around their lips. The skin on their faces was discolored, mottled and so thin that the cheekbones protruded.

Although his stomach roiled, Kane cast a glance over his shoulder at his companions and said quietly, "There was a welcoming committee after all. Now we know why they weren't moving."

Chapter 19

"It looks like they've been scalded from the inside out," Brigid said, tentatively probing a man's face with a forefinger. The flesh peeled away, but her expression didn't alter. Her mind operated efficiently in a matrix balanced between clinical curiosity and horror.

Grant swept his dark gaze around the ops center. "Who—or what—did this to them? The viral or Breech with his death touch?"

"A combination most likely," Erica murmured. She gestured toward several of the bodies. "Look—some of them have scorch marks on their clothes, but some don't."

Kane frowned, eyeing the positions of the bodies. "What the hell were they doing? Just sitting here waiting to be parboiled when Breech and his men gated through?"

Brigid glanced at the consoles, and then moved to a row of monitor stations. All the screens were blank, showing only snow. "Maybe there's a vid record of what happened here."

Her fingers clattered over a keyboard, and pale

black-and-white images flashed onto the screens. Two of screens lit up with exterior views, showing the rolling plains of

desert terrain, most of the details washed out by brilliant noonday sunlight. Sheer rock walls rose on every side, exposing layers of sediment. The lifeless and sere lake basin spread out like a vast bowl of desolation.

There was nothing left of the lake, not even a few puddles. It looked as though an impossibly huge animal had stomped a hoof print into the center of the basin, sinking it well below the foothills of the Timpahute Mountain Range.

Kane touched a switch beneath a screen and what appeared to be a mile's worth of ruins came into focus, looking like a line of compacted rubble. Nearby, the sunlight winked from a litter of metal scrap, fire blackened and slagged.

"Nobody cleaned up after the battle," Grant commented somberly.

Kane shrugged. "No need." He murmured as an afterthought, "That was a hell of a fight, though."

Grant grunted. "Tell me about it."

Kane assumed Grant's remark to be rhetorical and he didn't respond. He had witnessed only the aftermath of the bloody battle between two forces out in the dry lake bed. Grant had led the assault in an armored vehicle.

More screens flickered with images, but they

showed essentially the same dimly lit and bare corridors.

"There have to be more personnel here than the dead ones. Even a hybrid or two," Brigid said flatly.

"There was nothing to keep anybody here once the baronies fell," Kane said.

"And no place for them to go," Grant interposed, "except to the Outlands, where the hybrids would have been killed on sight."

"I thought all the hybrids changed," Erica said, "when *Tiamat* activated their genetic switch. They turned into the Nephilim."

"No, not all of them," Kane replied.

Erica nodded. "Right. Only the Quad-Vees."

The hybrids had been divided into classes. The Quad-Vees were bred as the highest-ranking order, one step beneath the barons but still servants, what once were referred to as majordomos. The Quad-Vees possessed a higher percentage of human DNA than the baronial breed of hybrid, but they were still superior to humanity. But only the baronial oligarchy possessed the dormant Annunaki gene.

According to information gathered by the Cerberus personnel over the past few years, most myths regarding gods and aliens derived from a race known in ancient

Sumerian texts as the Annunaki but also known in legend as the Dragon Kings and the Serpent Lords.

A species of bipedal reptile that appeared on

Earth at the dawn of humanity's development, the Annunaki used their advanced technology and great organizational skills to conquer the Mideast, most of Europe and the African continent.

They reared great cities, built cities and spaceports and influenced the evolution of Homo sapiens. They were also consumed by abounding pride, arrogance, and more than a few displayed an insatiable appetite for conquest and control. The Annunaki faction led by Enlil had developed and imposed complex, oppressive caste and gender systems on early human cultures to maintain that control.

The original Annunaki had arrived on Earth nearly half a million years before from an extrasolar planet known as Nibiru, traveling in a mile-long spaceship named *Tiamat*.

For aeons, the sentient *Tiamat* floated in a region of dead space called by Kurnugi by the Annunaki. She awaited the time when she would be summoned to fulfill her role as a Magan, a repository where the souls of the dead slumbered between incarnations, preparing for rebirth. A blending of inorganic and organic, composed of an incredibly ancient and complex genetic code, *Tiamat*'s countless subsystems that constituted her programming made her self-aware.

When the physical bodies of the Annunaki Supreme Council ceased to function, the electromagnetic pattern of their individuality broke free of the organic receptacle and was downloaded into a vast data storage bank aboard the ship. *Tiamat* maintained them until they could be uploaded into new organic receptacles—the bodies of the hybrid barons.

When the barons reached their final stage of evolution as the overlords, so too did the Quad-Vees. They became the Nephilim, serving as the foot soldiers of the overlords. According to ancient legend, the hybrid offspring of the cursed fornications between fallen angels and human women were called the Nephilim. They were believed to be soldiers in the armies of darkness.

"The ops center spy-eye system is off-line in here," Brigid announced irritably, nodding to a screen shot through with a pattern of pixels. "There's no vid at all."

"Quite the coincidence," Erica commented, walking over to a body slumped over in a chair.

"It would be if it was," Brigid stated, "but it's not. The only other option is to find a record of the last mat-trans activity. Since this unit is part of the official Cerberus network, I ought to be able to access the playback."

She strode across the ops center to the master mat-trans console and began manipulating the keyboard and the mouse. As she did so, Erica van Sloan called, "Kane, come over here, would you?"

Kane obliged, watching Erica gently pushing the corpse's head to one side. "This is one of the hybrids," she said.

Despite the near fleshless state of the skull, Kane instantly recognized the domed configuration of the cranium, the gracile build of the body and the pronounced supraorbital ridges arching over the large eye sockets.

"Not a Quad-Vee," Kane commented, "but at least we know there are still some hybrids here. Or there were."

He patted down the corpse and from a zippered breast pocket removed a magnetically striped key card. One corner of the plastic rectangle was melted.

"At least now we can open the damn doors around here," he declared.

Erica glanced at it disinterestedly and turned away.

Brigid, her attention focused on an indicator screen, said, "There was definitely mat-trans activity here three days ago. But I'd have to remove the memory matrix of the imaging scanner to find out the particulars—who gated in and the jump point of origin."

Grant blew out a weary sigh. "So we're just strolling blind into dark territory again."

"We ought to be used to it by now," Kane said wryly.

"I am," Grant shot back. "That's why I don't like it."

Kane turned toward the exit on the opposite side of the huge room. "Let's get to strolling."

The four people marched up the long aisle between the computer terminals and through a square doorway that opened up on an expanse of featureless corridor. The overhead neon light strips shed a pale illumination on the dusty linoleum floor. The hall ended against the sealed doors of an elevator shaft.

"The lift is the only way into and out of the control room," Kane stated. "When Domi and I gated in, we had to force the doors and climb the access ladder."

Grant eyed the sealed doors dubiously. "We don't have to do that now?"

Kane swiped the key card through a scanner inset into the metal plate beside the frame. "We'll find out."

The two panels rolled smoothly aside. The lift car was large with polished-chrome handrails. The four people tentatively stepped inside. Only one button glowed on the interior wall, imprinted with an arrow pointing upward.

"Let's give it a try," Erica said, depressing the button with her thumb.

The doors closed and within seconds, the car began to ascend. Eyes narrowed, Grant demanded, "Where will it stop?"

"Where it's programmed to, most likely," Brigid replied nonchalantly.

"That's not an answer."

"Let's try not to worry too much about it until we get there," Erica said soothingly.

Grant glared at her. "I'm not worried."

Kane repressed the urge to tell him, You should be.

The elevator stopped with a gentle bump. The doors opened onto a featureless corridor. Brigid scanned for motion with the detector on her wrist and shook her head. "Nothing. I can't say I'm impressed with what I've seen of the legendary Area 51 so far."

Kane smiled crookedly and stepped out. During his two weeks' captivity in the base, he had seen very little that was more dramatic than one hallway and office after another. He walked point, with Grant hugging the wall to his right and Brigid to his left. Erica brought up the rear. Their shoe soles occasionally squeaked on the floor tiles, but they heard nothing else.

The corridor ended at a T junction. Beyond it a round tunnel stretched in either direction as far as the eye could see. A small, burnished-metal shifter engine and two passenger cars rested in perfect balance atop a narrow-gauge monorail track. The rail disappeared into the darkness to the left and to the right.

"These little trains were the fastest way to get around the place," Kane said.

Grant and Brigid eyed the train suspiciously. "How does it run?" she asked. "Doesn't the rail have to be powered up?"

Before Kane could reply, the engine suddenly

emitted a soft electric hum. He took a quick step back, muttering, "Okay, that's kind of creepy."

"I don't know why you'd say that," Erica declared. "It's a sign the place is still inhabited."

"And that we're being watched," Grant said grimly, glancing around.

"I figured we've been observed since the moment we arrived," Erica replied matter-of-factly. "Just because we can't see them doesn't mean there aren't spy-eyes everywhere."

"This is a bit too blatant of an invitation," Kane said uneasily.

"We don't know that Breech is the one who issued it," Brigid pointed out. "You claimed Area 51 was factionalized, right?"

"Yeah, back when the barons were fighting among themselves. But that fight is done."

"Some of the people here may not know that," Erica ventured. "Or if they do, they might have been your allies. Getting in the train is a risk, but it's one I vote we take."

"We'll keep that in mind," Grant growled, "when this becomes a democracy."

Kane glanced down the tunnel, from the left to the right. He gusted out an exasperated breath, then stepped down into the passenger car. He looked up expectantly at his friends. "Aren't you coming?"

Brigid and Grant hesitated only a second, and then they seated themselves in the passenger car. Erica squeezed in between them.

They waited in uncomfortable silence for a moment, then the electronic hum from the engine rose in pitch. With a slight lurch, the train began sliding along the rail, swiftly building up speed. Overhead light fixtures flicked by so rapidly that they combined with the intervals of darkness between them to acquire a strobing pattern. Neither man spoke as the train sped down the shaft.

The rail curved lazily to the right, plunging almost noiselessly into a side chute. Lights shone intermittently on the smooth walls, small drops of illumination that did little to alleviate the deep shadows.

"How fast do you think we're going?" Grant asked.

Kane grinned. "Since when did a little speed make you nervous?"

Grant only glowered at him resentfully.

The train hissed along the rail, speeding down the shaft, passing several well-lit platforms. Each one was emblazoned with a two-digit number.

"Twenty-five," Brigid said as they shot past a station. "How many are there?"

Kane shook his head. "A whole hell of a lot. This place is the size of a city…a couple of cities, maybe. So the monorail is the major transportation system."

They whizzed past two more stations. "If the power is cut, we'll be trapped like rats in the tunnel," Grant said tensely.

Kane considered his friend's words and said, "We should take the initiative, then."

When he saw the distant glimmer of another station, Kane began pulling back on the emergency-brake lever. The metal shoes caught the track with prolonged screeches.

"What are you doing?" Erica demanded.

"If we're really being watched, then we should cause a little confusion. Assuming the watchers are allies, they won't be too upset. And if they're not inclined to be friends, then anything we do that's unexpected can only be to our benefit."

Kane continued to increase the pressure until the car slid to a halt in front of the platform marked 28. As they disembarked, Grant glanced down the tunnel, paused, then thrust his head forward, eyes slitted. "Uh-oh."

Kane followed the big man's gaze. "Uh-oh what?"

In the darkness of the tunnel, twinkling like the stirred embers of a distant fire, glittered a pattern of green lights.

Chapter 20

The four people sprinted down the corridor, running flat-out. Kane didn't risk a misstep by looking over his shoulder. He had no idea of how fast the viral swarm could move, but he had a feeling the green orbs could attain greater speeds than humans.

As they rounded a corner, Grant panted, "See, this is exactly the kind of shit I was worried about!"

"Why didn't you say something before we left?" Kane snapped.

"Would you have paid any attention?"

Kane didn't respond to Grant's wheezed question. He focused his attention on a door at the end of the corridor. It was partially ajar, allowing feeble light to spill out. He noted it was a heavy hatch-cover type of door, made of dull metal.

"That's convenient," Brigid said.

"Probably a trap," Erica rasped.

Kane agreed, but he had no breath to reply.

"We can't afford to be choosy," Brigid said.

As they ran toward the door, Kane slowed his pace, casting a glance over his shoulder. He saw nothing but the featureless expanse of corridor, but before he could begin to feel relieved, around the corner flew the cluster of green sparks. The swarm paused as if getting its bearings, flickering and shifting. Then the orbs darted forward. His flesh crawled as if an army of ants crept along between his skin and the shadow suit.

"Go!" he half shouted, putting a hand between Brigid's shoulder blades and propelling her along.

The four people sprinted down the corridor as the green orbs drew closer. Their thudding footfalls echoed, drowning out all other sounds. Kane ran as he had run few times in his life. Memories of Higson and of the corpses in the control room wheeled through his mind like a tape on a continual-replay loop. The breath seared his lungs and his heart pounded against his ribs. His laboring legs seemed weighted with half-frozen mud.

Erica and Grant stumbled over the raised lip of the hatchway. Kane shoved Brigid ahead of him and grabbed the wheel lock of the door with his left hand. With his right, he fired his Copperhead, spraying a steady stream of rounds down the corridor with a sound like the prolonged ripping of stiff canvas.

The muzzle-flash smeared the murk with strobing tongues of flame. Little flares sparked in the dimness as the rounds struck and ricocheted from walls and the floor. Kane knew that a sustained full-auto burst only wasted ammunition, but he focused on driving the virals back long enough so he could close the hatch. The darting orbs were completely unaffected by the brief barrage, the bullets passing through them.

Grant reached around Kane and grabbed a cross brace on the inner side of the door. Kane threw himself backward and Grant pulled the hatch closed with a muffled clang. Putting both hands on the wheel, he spun it until solenoids caught with snapping of latches. Kane swiftly dogged the lock.

Grant drew in a lungful of air. "How do we know those things can't pass right through metal?"

Erica shook her head, backing away. "We don't. At best we're only buying some time."

"Time to do what?" Grant snarled. "Run from one room to another, chased by those fucking things? Breech can probably set them loose on us anytime he wants."

"No," a soft voice whispered. "He can't."

Kane, Grant and Brigid skipped quickly around, guns questing for targets.

"Walk straight ahead," the voice continued, so finely projected that they had trouble believing the words weren't being spoken next to them. "The viral won't be able to penetrate the hatch cover. It is shielded against EMPs."

"EMPs?" Kane echoed.

"Electromagnetic pulses," Brigid murmured, eyes flicking back and forth. She raised her voice and demanded, "Who are you?"

"Just do as I say if you want to live."

The four people glanced at each other. There was a familiar timbre and cadence about the voice, but no one spared it much thought. Kane reached out and touched the metal of the hatch. Faintly he felt a vibration, then a distant series of staccato raps, as of knuckles knocking against the other side at an inhumanly fast tempo.

"They're trying to get to us." Turning away, Kane said, "We can't stay here, so we might as well go forward."

Taking point, Kane led them through a narrow passageway that after a few steps became a labyrinth of crisscrossing pipes and wheel valves. Pieces of dismantled machinery lay scattered on the floor.

"This must be a maintenance accessway," Erica said.

They maneuvered around fuse boxes and cooling systems, all the machinery that kept the installation alive. Grant bumped his head on low-hanging pipes more than once. He swore furiously and Erica shushed him into silence. She kept twisting her head to listen for sounds of pursuit and stared with burning, fearful intensity at every wedge of shadow they passed.

When the passageway terminated at a closed door, Kane didn't hesitate. Lifting the handle, he took a deep breath and threw the door open wide. The laser autotargeter of the Copperhead cut a bright red thread through the gloom. Looking around, he experienced a sense of déjà vu.

"I've been here before," he said.

"Yes," a lilting voice said. "You have indeed."

Kane whirled and saw a small, graceful figure shifting in the shadows. When he caught a glimpse of an overlarge cranium, he understood why the room was so poorly lit. The optic nerves of hybrid eyes possessed a natural sensitivity to high light levels, and so their vision functioned more efficiently in a semigloom.

"Please," the hybrid said. "All of you may enter."

Kane stepped farther into the room, allowing his companions to move in on either side of him.

"Let's have a look at you," Brigid said.

The figure edged closer to them, but he maintained a discreet distance. His inhumanly large eyes were shadowed by the sweeping supraorbital ridges characteristic of hybrids. His cheekbones and chin were very prominent, his pursed mouth little more than a slit.

His hairless skull rose high and smooth, and his small ears were set very low on the hinge of his jaw. Despite the shapeless gray coverall he wore, the hybrid's body was excessively slender. He didn't look to be more than five feet tall. He rested a long-fingered hand on a black plastic tube holder strapped to his right thigh.

"What's your name?" Kane asked.

"Varnley."

Kane squinted, examining his face. "You're not a Quad-Vee."

"Obviously."

"We've met before."

The hybrid nodded. "Yes." His eyes slid from Kane to Erica van Sloan. "Nor is this the first we have met. I attended to your needs the last time you were here—Imperial Mother."

GRANT WHIRLED ON ERICA, his teeth bared. "What does he mean? You've been here before?"

Erica tried to keep her expression composed but she took an involuntarily step away from Grant's sudden flare of anger. "Yes. Shortly after Kane made his escape and Baron Cobalt's forces were dispossessed. I served as the liaison between the barons and Sam. Ancient history."

"But you've lied to us—again," Brigid Baptiste intoned. "Nothing ancient about that."

"I didn't really lie to you," Erica said defensively. "I said I didn't know my way around."

"You were here long enough to memorize the mat-trans lock code," Kane stated grimly. "And you, of course, passed it on to Breech."

"That fits my criteria of a lie by omission," Brigid snapped.

Erica shrugged but didn't reply.

Varnley cleared his throat. "Excuse me—"

The Cerberus warriors turned their attention to the hybrid.

"The imperial mother was not here but for a day. She was escorted to and from the gateway unit." His eyes fixed on Kane. "You saw far more of this installation than she did."

"It's not how much she saw," Kane retorted, "but the fact she withheld that information from us."

"I submit that is immaterial now," Varnley said. "The arrival of Breech and the unleashing of destructive energy throughout this installation should be your immediate concern."

Kane grudgingly accepted the hybrid's words. He glanced around the room. "The last time I was here, this place was the headquarters of Area 51's fifth column—the nest of insurrectionists."

Varnley nodded. "Yes, that is true. We were led by Quavell."

Both Grant and Brigid knew Quavell acted as the de facto leader of a group of resisters within Area 51.

"Where are the rest of your people?"

"If you arrived via the mat-trans gateway, then you know where they are."

Brigid's eyebrows rose. "All we found were corpses."

"I know. I was there when they were killed. I barely escaped."

"How did you manage that?" Grant rumbled suspiciously.

For the first time, Varnley's face showed an emotion—confusion mixed with fear. "I am not sure. I surmise my survival had something to do with this."

From the tube holster at his thigh he drew out a

slender silver wand that tapered down to a very narrow tip. Kane's belly turned cold when he recognized it as an infrasound wand. Grant's reaction wasn't so restrained—he snapped up his Copperhead.

The Cerberus warriors experienced a brief, shuddery flashback to the hybrid horde they had fought off over five years earlier inside the Archuleta Mesa installation. That had been their first encounter with both hybrids and the deadly infrasound wands.

Miniaturized masers converted electric current to directional ultrasonic waves and turned innocuous silver rods into weapons that could kill or cripple. The vicious Baroness Beausoleil had tortured Grant with a rod, and he still retained exceptionally vivid memories of that incident.

Varnley appeared unaware of Grant's extreme reaction. Quietly, he said, "When I turned this on to full power, the viral seemed disturbed by it and did not attack me like they did my colleagues. I was able to make my escape."

"What were all of you doing in the control room?" Erica demanded.

Before Varnley replied, Grant said, "Put that damn thing away."

Varnley blinked at him in mild surprise, but he obeyed without question. Turning to Erica he said, "The man you call Breech asked us to meet him there and run diagnostics on all of the systems."

Brigid's eyes narrowed. "Let me get this

straight—you people here were cooperating with the Millennial Consortium?"

Varnley shook his head. "I know very little of this consortium you speak of…but we were indeed cooperating with Quintus Breech. We saw no reason not to do so."

Skeptically, Kane asked, "Since when do you cooperate with strangers who gate into Area 51 unannounced?"

Varnley's high forehead acquired a crease of surprise. "He did not come here unannounced. We knew of his arrival. That's why all of us were in the control room when he arrived."

Grant grimaced in angry frustration. "Maybe you'd better start at the beginning."

Varnley nodded and turned toward a long table pushed against the far wall. "Perhaps I should. And perhaps the imperial mother should reconsider keeping all of her secrets, as well."

Chapter 21

"I have to say I'm surprised to find you here, Varnley," Kane said.

"Anyone or just me in particular?" the hybrid inquired.

The five people stood around a long table pushed against a rear wall. Grant studied several cross-section blueprints of the Area 51 installation sandwiched between layers of transparent Lucite.

"This place is the size of some states," he complained.

"Very true," Varnley agreed. "That is why there isn't one comprehensive map of the layout. It is divided by sections and if you don't know your starting point, you have no frame of reference. Once the baronies pulled their security forces from base, many of the personnel left behind went off to explore. Most never returned. They either became hopelessly lost and perished or they found their way to the surface and struck out on their own."

"You do know what happened to the barons, don't you?" Brigid asked.

Varnley nodded curtly. "Bits of it. I was told the barons assumed their true forms."

Erica's mouth twisted as if she tasted something exceptionally foul. "Yes...they became hybrids of hybrids. Their Annunaki genetic material that had lain dormant in their DNA was stimulated and it became predominant."

Varnley's delicate nostrils flared as he inhaled deeply. "Yes. And the Quad-Vees here made an evolutionary jump, as well. They became drones."

"Something like that," Brigid said. "We're still not sure of the process. But that doesn't explain why any hybrids or humans stayed here."

Varnley stared at her, confused, as if he didn't understand the meaning of her observation. "We new humans had responsibilities."

"Responsibilities?" Grant echoed, glancing up from the maps. He didn't respond to Varnley's euphemism of *new humans* to describe hybrids. "Like what?"

Varnley made a vague gesture with one long-fingered hand. "Kane never told you?"

Kane frowned. "Told them what?"

Varnley waved a hand toward the opposite wall. "Of the infants here in the nursery. We could not leave them."

Kane's belly lurched sideways and Brigid's eyes widened. As she spun around in the direction Varnley gestured, he said flatly, "There is no reason to rush."

Kane felt guilt settle over him like a heavy cloak. "The babies died?"

Varnley nodded. "The Quad-Vees had the specialized medical training to treat their conditions. They often served as nurses and even doctors to the barons."

The Cerberus warriors knew he spoke the truth. None of them could argue that the hybrids, the so-called new human race, were as intellectually superior to humankind as the Cro-Magnon was to the Neanderthal, but they paid a heavy price for their superior abilities. Physically they were fragile, their autoimmune systems at the mercy of infections and diseases that had little effect on the primitive humans they ruled. Nor could they reproduce by intercourse. The nine barons were the products of in vitro fertilization, as were all their offspring.

Once a year, the oligarchy had traveled to an installation beneath the Archuleta Mesa in Dulce, New Mexico, for medical treatments. They received fresh transfusions of blood and submitted to a regimen of biochemical genetic therapy designed to strengthen their autoimmune systems, which granted them another year of life and power.

"So when the Quad-Vees stationed here became the Nephilim, they abandoned the babies," Brigid stated grimly.

"Our personnel was severely depleted," Varnley said defensively. "By eighty percent, I estimate."

Brigid walked toward the door. After a moment,

Kane followed her down a dimly lit corridor. The passage ended, at a square room nearly twenty yards across. Because the overhead lighting was as dim as in the hallway they had difficult seeing the rows of little plastic boxes, transparent cubes with no tops to them.

Reluctantly, Brigid and Kane stepped into the room, peering into the boxes. What they saw caused their breath to seize in their lungs. Within every box, covered by thin sheets of cloth, lay the skeletal remains of infants.

Brigid Baptiste shook her head in sad, angry frustration. "This was our fault, you know...the aftermath of destroying the Archuleta Mesa facility."

Kane did not speak, remembering what Quavell had told him when she first gave him a tour of the nursery. She'd said the mesa was more than just a medical treatment center for the barons. It served as the centerpiece of their community. She'd called it the hybrid heart."

Hugging herself, Brigid husked out in a voice barely above a whisper, "How many?"

"According to what Quavell told me," Kane answered in the same hushed tone, "only twenty-three out of the two thousand in the incubation chambers of the Archuleta Mesa installation survived."

He didn't tell her the rest. He saw little need. Without access to the medical technology and treatments, the survivors sickened and died in the months following the installation's destruction. The infants Quavell cared for suffered from a variety of infections and malnutrition.

Kane remembered how he stood there and looked down to see a hybrid infant who seemed all ribs and swollen belly, blindly groping for him with its tiny, spindly fingers. Its hand found and closed around his thumb. The touch was no more substantial than gossamer, than a cobweb.

Even now, years later, as he remembered gazing down at the infant's bald, scabrous head, a pressure built in Kane's chest, then spread to this throat. He had witnessed and occasionally been forced to participate in many acts of cruelty as a Mag and after, but he had never felt so stricken with guilt. Quavell's whispery words ghosted through his memory.

"What you see here is the last generation of your loathsome new human…here lie your despised enemies, Kane. Will it make you feel better if I concede defeat on the part of the hybrids? You have beaten us. We surrender. You won that victory not in battle, not with cleverness and not with the old-fashioned human ingenuity you value so much. You won by the simple dint of striking at our most vulnerable resources…our babies."

Varnley's voice floated down the passageway. "Perhaps it is all for the best. The purpose to which they were bred no longer exists. There no barons to serve, no Program of Unification to carry forward."

Both Kane and Brigid knew to what he referred.

A century before, Unity Through Action was the rallying cry of the early Program of Unification. It awakened the long forgotten trust in a central government by offering a solution to the constant states of hardship and fear—join the unification program and never know want or fear again. Of course, any concept of liberty had to be forgotten in the exchange.

One the basic tenets of the unification program was taking responsibility. Since humanity was responsible for the arrival of Judgment Day, it had to accept the blame before a truly utopian age could be ushered in. All humankind had to do to earn this utopia was follow the rules, and be obedient to be fed and clothed—and accept the new order without question.

For most of the men and women who lived in the villes and the surrounding territories, this was more than enough. Long-sought-after dreams of peace and safety had at last been transformed into reality. Of course, fleeting dreams of personal freedom were completely crushed, but such abstract aspirations were nothing but childish illusions.

In fact, almost every tradition of the predark world that survived the nukecaust, the skydark and the anarchy that followed, was spit upon as an illusion. Even the ancient social patterns that connected mother, father and child were broken. That break was a crucial one in order for the Program of Unification to succeed. The existence of the family as a unit of procreation and therefore as a social unit had to be eliminated.

Kane shook his head, trying to drive away the memories. "Let's go, Baptiste."

When she didn't move, he reached out to touch her shoulder, but she evaded him. Leaning away, she stared at him with a penetrating emerald gaze. Her voice strained, she demanded, "How can we ever make this right?"

"We've already made it right," he retorted flatly. "We beat the barons, we beat the overlords. We freed humanity from their bondage. That makes this if not right, at least justified."

Brigid stared into his face without speaking and then stepped around him, striding back down the hallway. Kane waited a few seconds before following her. His response hadn't even convinced himself, so he knew he hadn't persuaded Brigid.

When they reentered the big room and rejoined everyone at the table, Grant asked, "What about the regular 'old' humans who were stationed here? What happened to them?"

Varnley lifted his narrow shoulders in a shrug. "The majority simply absconded with the vehicles remaining in the depot and departed. To where, I have no idea."

Kane said, "There were a number of female hybrids here. They weren't all Quad-Vees."

"No…very few were, in fact. Those females had already attached themselves to human males. They accompanied the men when they left. Apparently, the females had become accustomed to the physical pleasures you showed them that were possible when they participated in Baron Cobalt's breeding program. They were loath to give that up."

Erica smiled smugly, and Brigid cast Kane a sharp, sidewise glance but he affected not to notice. He wasn't very surprised by Varnley's explanation.

Visceral emotions did not play a large part in the psychologies of the new humans. Even their bursts of passion were of the most rudimentary kind. Although the tissue of their hybridized brains was of the same organic matter as the human brain, the millions of neurons operated a bit differently in the processing of information.

Therefore, their thought processes were very structured, extremely linear. When they experienced emotions, they only did so under in moments of stress, and then so intensely they were almost consumed by them, whether that emotion was anger or lust.

"How many people are here now?" Erica asked. "Excluding Breech and his people?"

Varnley's tightly composed face suddenly twisted in a naked display of grief and despair. "Excluding Breech and his party and you four...I am the sole survivor of the garrison of Area 51."

Chapter 22

"How did Breech get the run of this place?" Erica asked.

Varnley's one-word response was flat. "Trickery."

"Yeah, we guessed that," Grant grunted. "What was the trick?"

"A simple stratagem, really," Varnley admitted. "Breech gated through into the installation, bearing gifts."

Brigid arched an eyebrow. "Gifts?"

"Provisions…food, drink and medicine. We were running dangerously low on supplies here. He also brought data pertaining to the theta-pinch experiments that had been conducted at the Phantom Mesa facility and transferred here. We were intrigued."

"Why?" Kane demanded.

"Breech communicated with us openly, scientist to scientist. Although he claimed to be a representative of the Millennial Consortium, he did not expend much time or effort proselytizing us as to their cause. Rather, he focused on the benefits of the unrealized benefits of the theta-pinch transmitter. He claimed it would revolutionize our world…restore order, science and sanity to it."

"That's the sales pitch of the Millennial Consortium," Grant rumbled. "Sounds like Breech just adapted it for a new audience."

"And you bought into his bullshit," Kane stated darkly.

Varnley turned a wide-eyed, disingenuous stare on him. "Why would we not cross-check the database? When we did, we found evidence that the researches Breech referenced had indeed been conducted here. We were understandably interested."

"Especially with full bellies," Grant commented. "Who is 'we' exactly?"

"The people who stayed behind. There were eighteen of us. We were too disinclined to make new lives in a baronless world, one controlled by anarchy. I will not deny our existence here was cheerless and pointless. But we believed it would be better than the alternative. When Breech arrived, we hoped for a new beginning."

Kane nodded, sympathizing with the hybrid. The past two hundred years of history had been filled with endings, beginnings and false starts.

The new beginning for humankind began on January 20, 2001. The detonation of a nuclear warhead in the basement of the Russian embassy in Washington, D.C., triggered a chain reaction, like the toppling of a row of dominoes. By the end of that day, the world in general and America in particular had been transformed into a shockscape of ruined nature, a hell on Earth. In North America, all major cities, all commercial, political and industrial centers were swallowed up by blazing columns of hellfire.

Earthquakes split the geography of the West Coast, volcanoes dormant for centuries burst into explosive life, coastlines disappeared and islands took their place. Tidal waves, tsunamis hundreds of feet high, battered the Pacific seaboard.

Sometime late that Saturday afternoon, the nuclear winter, or skydark, began. Massive quantities of pulverized rubble were propelled into the atmosphere, clogging the sky for a generation, enveloping the planet in a thick cloud of radioactive dust, ash, debris, smoke and fallout. After nearly twenty years of endless nights, of freezing temperatures even in subtropical climates, of fallout storms, well over another million people had perished. The entire atmosphere of the planet had been hideously polluted by the nukecaust, producing all manners of deadly side effects in the ecosphere.

In the century following the atomic megacull, what was left of the world filled with savage beasts and even more savage men. They lived beyond any concept of law or morality and made pacts to achieve power, regardless of how pointless an exercise it seemed.

Survivors and descendants of survivors tried to build enclaves of civilization around which a new human society could rally, but there were only so many people in the world, and few of these made either good pioneers or settlers.

It was far easier to wander, to lead the live of nomads and scavengers, digging out Stockpiles and building a power base on what was salvaged.

Some of the scavengers used what they had found in the Stockpiles and elsewhere to carve out fiefdoms, tiny islands of law and order amid a sea of anarchy. These people formed ruling hierarchies, and they spread out across the ruined face of America. They profited from the near annihilation of the human race, enjoying benefits and personal power that otherwise would have been denied them if the nukecaust had not happened.

The hierarchies spread out and divided the country into little territories, much like old Europe, which had been ruled over by princes and barons. The different hierarchies conquered territories and claimed them as baronies. Although these territories offered a certain amount of sanctuary from the crazed anarchy of outlying regions, most of them offered as little freedom.

At first, people retreated into baronies for protection, and then as the decades went by, they remained because they had no choice. Generations of Americans were born into serfdom, slavery in everything but name. Whatever their parents or grand-

parents had been before skydark, they were now
only commodities and they cursed the suicidal fool-
ishness of their forebears who had brought on the
nightmare.

The alternatives were few; one could live the
life of a nomad or join the marauding wolf packs
or set up robber baronies. Whichever option was
chosen, lives tended to be brutal and short. The
blood that had splattered the pages of America's
frontier history was a mere sprinkling compared to
the crimson tide that flooded postnuke America.

In the century following skydark, baronial territories were redefined, treaties struck among the
barons. The city-states became interconnected
points in a continent-spanning network. Control of
the continent was divided among the nine baronies
that survived the long wars over territorial expan-
sion and resources. The pretenders, those who ar-
rogantly carved out their own little pieces of
empire, were overrun, exterminated and their territories absorbed.

The Program of Unification was ratified and
ruthlessly employed. The reconstructed form of
government was still basically despotic, but now it
was institutionalized and shared by all the formerly
independent baronies.

Unity Through Action spread across the Outlands by word of mouth and proof of deed. It offered a solution to the constant states of worry and
fear—join the unification program and never worry

or fear, or think again. Humanity was responsible for the arrival

of Judgment Day, and it must accept that responsibility before a truly utopian age could be ushered in.

Synchronized with this forward step in social engineering came technical advances. Technology, most of it based on predark designs, appeared mysteriously and simultaneously with the beginning of the unification program. There was much speculation at the time that many previously unknown Continuity of Government Stockpiles were opened up and their contents distributed evenly among the barons.

Although the technologies were restricted for the use of those who held the reins of power, life overall improved for the citizens in and around the villes. To enjoy the bounty offered by the barons, people only had to surrender their will.

The barons' legions of black-armored Magistrates were charged with the task of encouraging people to surrender their wills. Formed as a complex police machine, the Magistrate Divisions demanded instant obedience to baronial edicts. In a little under a century, both the oligarchy of barons and the Mages who served them had taken on a fearful, almost legendary aspect. The unification program established a social order by which generations of Americans were born into serfdom, slavery in everything but name.

The doctrines expressed in ville teachings encouraged humanity to endure a continuous hardship before a utopian age could be ushered in. Because humanity had ruined the world, the punishment was deserved. The doctrines ultimately amounted to extortion—obey and suffer, or disobey and die.

The dogma was elegant in its simplicity, and for most of her life, Brigid Baptiste had believed it. Then she stumbled over a few troubling questions, and when she attempted to find the answers, all she discovered were many more troubling questions. The attempt to find answers to those questions had turned her, Kane and Grant into exiles on the planet of their birth.

His thoughts returning to the present, Kane asked, "How did all eighteen of you manage to be in one place so Breech could conveniently knock you off?"

"By another simple stratagem," Varnley answered. "He asked us."

"Very nicely, I guess," Grant drawled sarcastically. "I wish you people were in charge of Area 51 the last time we visited. It would have saved everybody a lot of trouble...not to mention bullets."

Varnley ignored the jibe. "Breech asked all of us to convene in the control room so we could meet with his scientific staff and compare notes. The request made sense to us, inasmuch as the main database was there."

The hybrid paused for a long moment, his heavy-lidded eyes closing. He opened them again, and he seemed to stare into the past. "We assembled as he asked us to. When Breech and his people stepped out of the gateway unit, he asked me, 'Is everyone here?'

"I answered in the affirmative. Then the viral came out of the gateway, moving with such speed none of us were able to react until it was too late. The orbs attacked everyone. As I said, I activated my infrasound wand and drove the viral back long enough for me to escape. But before I did, I saw Breech killing some of my comrades with a type of energy discharge from his weapons."

Varnley broke off, swallowed hard and said, "That was three days ago."

"And you've been in hiding ever since?" Erica asked.

"I would not characterize my actions in such a fashion. Breech and his people were not looking for me. I simply stayed out of their way as they journeyed to Section Y-95."

"What's there?" Brigid inquired.

"According to the database, that was the section of the installation dedicated to alternative-energy researches—atomic fusion, zero point and pinch plasma physics."

Erica combed a frustrated hand through her hair. "Three days ago? Breech has possession of the theta-pinch transmitter by now."

"Perhaps," Varnley said contemplatively. "But I

examined the research. Years of training would be required to properly operate the device. Even the project's chief scientist, Spiros Marcuse, abandoned the experiments."

"Breech is a brilliant man," Erica said curtly. "Far more intelligent and resourceful than Spiros Marcuse could ever hope to be."

"I cannot debate you on that point," Varnley replied. "But the technology employed for the pinch-plasma transmitter is not simply that manufactured by twentieth-century engineers."

Grant frowned. "What do you mean?"

"The transmitter is based on a science so advanced that the technology of the Totality Concept is very small in comparison."

Kane stared at the hybrid, waiting for him to elaborate. When he didn't, Kane said, "I think I can guess the rest—it's Annunaki science, isn't it?"

Varnley's prim mouth pursed in a smile. "And perhaps some Danaan scattered among it, as well."

Chapter 23

"The best solution is to get out of here," Varnley said, "but we cannot reach the gateway unit because of the viral."

The hybrid led them on a circuitous route down a maintenance shaft originally built as an accessway for repair crews. Pipes, conduits and ventilation ductwork ran up and down all around them.

"The entire lake bed is honeycombed with chambers and tunnels that twist and turn and lead everywhere. No one that I have met has ever explored all the passages."

"That's good for us and the viral," Grant commented dourly. "They can go places we can't. I'd like to know how they can track us."

"As would I," Varnley said, "but Breech cannot see us and I assume he cannot send his viral after us."

"Why do you assume that?" Brigid asked grimly. "He may have complete power over it by now."

"If that's the case," Erica commented, "then that is all the more reason we can't let the power rest only in his hands."

Kane, following closely behind Varnley, glared over his shoulder at the dark-haired woman. "When did this become a 'we' operation, Erica?"

She threw him a frosty smile, her one eye glinting like an amethyst in the dim light. "We always end up on the same side eventually, don't we?"

Repressing a shudder, Kane turned away. He retained exceptionally vivid memories of glimpse of their future, afforded to him by his future self, conveyed from thirty years hence. Erica van Sloan ruled in a preeminent position of global power following a long conflict called the Consolidation War.

However, the actions undertaken by Kane, Grant and Brigid to make sure such a future never came to pass shifted probabilities sufficiently to set in a motion an entirely new series of events, which in turn created a branching timeline. Unfortunately, the shifting of probabilities more than likely set into motion the rebirth of the Annunaki pantheon.

"This place reminds me of the tunnel running beneath the Tartarus Pits in Cobaltville," Brigid murmured.

"Yeah," Kane agreed, grasping a rung. "But it doesn't smell as bad."

Ville society was strictly class and caste based, so the higher a citizen's standing, the higher he or she might live in one of the residential towers. At the bottom level of the villes was the servant class, who lived in abject squalor in consciously designed ghettos known as the Tartarus Pits, named after the abyss below Hell where Zeus confined the Titans. They swarmed with a heterogeneous population of serfs, cheap labor and black marketeers.

Varnley clambered up a network of pipes that stretched across the wall. "Follow me. It's not hard."

The Cerberus warriors exchanged glances, and then did as Varnley instructed. They pulled themselves to the top of the wall and saw it was an outer barrier with another wall a few yards beyond it. The inner and outer walls were joined at regular intervals by load-bearing metal trusses. Although spaced several feet apart, they formed a latticework that could be climbed like a ladder. They proceeded to climb between the walls, their amber-colored Nighthawk microlights illuminating the way.

They balanced themselves precariously between the walls, edging their way carefully. The passage narrowed and the fit became tight but they squeezed through. It curved slightly then ended at a series of staple-shaped metal rungs embedded into the wall.

Without pausing, Varnley began scaling the rungs nimbly, hand over hand. Craning his neck and tilting his head back, Kane saw that the ladder stretched up to a round metal hatch. The hybrid climbed with surprising agility, clutching at and kicking himself off the rungs.

Kane followed Varnley, not trying to imitate his method of climbing. His war bag dragged at him, throwing his balance off. The hand-over-hand process caused his bruised shoulder to throb. He heard a distant hum of machinery, then a clanking sound above him. He glanced up as Varnley pushed open the hatch cover, then averted his eyes as a bright beam of light cut blazed down.

Shielding his eyes, Varnley said softly, "We're here."

"Where is here?" Grant rumbled impatiently.

With his stick-thin arms, Varnley heaved himself up and over the lip of the hatch. He said only, "Hurry."

The Cerberus warriors and Erica climbed out of the shaft and stood in a wide corridor. Neon strips glowed from the ceiling. The light they exuded wasn't all that bright, but it seemed brilliant in comparison to the gloom of the passageway.

Glancing around, Kane said, "I've been here before."

Varnley nodded and began walking swiftly. "Yes. It is a secondary security checkpoint."

They all fell into step behind the hybrid. They reached a large observation window inset into the right-hand wall and carefully edged around the frame for a look at what lay on the other side.

They saw a large room lined with two aisles of computer stations. A huge flat-screen vid monitor covered the facing wall. The screen was divided into small square sections, each one showing a different black-and-white view of the interior and the exterior.

"There is no one about," Varnley whispered, going through the door.

"Then why are you whispering?" Brigid asked.

Varnley did not respond. He strode to the screen and began stroking keys on the board. Two squares flashed with a flat, sandy expanse of unbroken desolation.

"I thought all the spy-eyes were inactive," Grant said.

"There are many electronic eyes and ears throughout this installation," Varnley declared. "Even if Breech knew the location of all of them, it would take him several years to deactivate them all. And that would be by working at the task full-time."

Brigid put on her spectacles and peered at the screens. The glasses weren't for appearance only. After years of sifting through nearly illegible pre-dark documents, books and computer files, her vision had weakened. Eyestrain often led to nagging headaches that spread from her eye sockets up into her skull.

A few years before Brigid had suffered from a serious head injury, and it seemed her vision had been further impaired by the wound that had laid her scalp open to the bone and put her in a coma for several days. Now the only sign of it was a faintly pink, horizontal line on her right temple that disappeared into the roots of her hair. Although her recovery time had been little short of phenomenal, she had noticed she needed her glasses more and more in the months following her release from the infirmary.

Slowly Brigid scanned the bowl-shaped dead lake bottom. Groom Lake was surrounded on all sides by looming mountain chains, making it the ideal location for the predark military to conduct its experiments in secrecy. About five miles away, a scattered collection of structures, control and guard towers rose from the ground, reminding her of the broken-off stumps of teeth.

The line of structures was completely dwarfed by a building so tremendous in size that it was easily seen without the aid of the binoculars. Lakesh had said the largest aircraft hangar of predark days was built in Area 51, but *large* didn't even begin to cover it. Brigid estimated it was over three-quarters of a mile long, a quarter-mile wide and at the very least a hundred feet tall. The cavernous hangar could comfortably house the entire Cerberus redoubt, with room left over for Cobaltville's Tartarus Pits.

The other structures were nearly obliterated by wind-blown sand. It was difficult to tell where the lines of the buildings had fallen. Everything was half-buried. The region exuded an atmosphere of abandonment, of not having seen a living soul in many, many years.

"Nothing out there," Erica said with a touch of asperity.

"I did not expect to see anything, but it is best to check," Varnley replied calmly.

He touched another key and several others screens flickered. One was almost black, and for a moment they didn't see anything. Then they caught a hint of movement that resolved itself an image of men passing through the shadows of a vault-walled chamber. Four men in coveralls walked across a huge room, through a set of double doors with wire shields in front of them.

Varnley leaned forward, eyes intent. After a few seconds of silent studying, he said, "That is the section known as the Prometheus wing. It is located several levels below this one."

"Prometheus?" Erica echoed. "Why is it called that?"

"In the ancient Greek myth Prometheus had challenged the lightning of Zeus and brought fire down to Earth to warm the hearts of men," Brigid said.

Erica regarded her superciliously. "I know that. Don't confuse me with the dullards you have to associate with. I asked *why* the wing was called that, not for a lesson in mythology."

"From what I recall," Varnley said, "it was the facility where the final phase of testing took place."

"All things being equal," Grant said, "the Prometheus wing is where we'll find Breech."

Eric suddenly drew in a sharp breath. "And other things, too."

On the screen, the viral spun before the shielded double doors. The orbs danced, they twisted, they flashed in pinwheels of light.

Chapter 24

"I don't get this at all," Grant complained as he marched down the corridor. "Where are those goddamn plasma bees coming from? Is it the same swarm that chased us in New Mexico?"

Brigid's lips pursed in thought. "I don't see how. They must reproduce in some way. I have to agree with Spiros Marcuse's theory that they're combination of radiations and plasma waveforms held together by a magnetic field."

The five people reached a big elevator, which they all entered. Reaching out for a polished brass handrail, Erica said, "That wouldn't account for their apparent intelligence."

Kane pressed a button on the wall. A pair of heavy doors rumbled shut, and an overhead light came on. "And why they're green."

The elevator shot upward at breathtaking speed, making Kane's stomach feel as if it were sinking into the soles of his boots.

Varnley cocked his head at a puzzled angle. "I don't understand."

"What's to understand?" Kane countered. "The viral is green."

"They are all different colors," the hybrid stated matter-of-factly.

"They only look green to us," Grant said.

"My eyes see in a far broader range of the spectrum than yours."

Brigid nodded musingly. "That may mean something."

"Like what?" Erica inquired.

"If the viral is composed of radiation, then Breech might have a method of controlling it using high-frequency radiation in the radio-wave spectrum."

Grant grunted. "So he may be using them as a pack of hunting dogs."

"Or," Varnley ventured, "they may be intelligent but their intelligence might be a different order than what we human beings understand."

Kane repressed the urge to smile at Varnley's inclusion of himself as a human. Eyeing the hybrid surreptitiously, he again wondered just how many truly human people populated Earth, but there was no way to hazard an accurate guess. Even the intelligence-gathering apparatus of the Magistrate Divisions in the villes could not learn with any certainty about what was transpiring beyond the continental boundaries of the country. Radio waves would not reach across the sea because lingering radiation and atmospheric disturbances disrupted shortwave carrier bands.

After two centuries, the aftereffects of the nuke-caust and the skydark were more subtle, an underlying texture to a world struggling to heal itself, but the side effects of the war still let themselves be known from time to time, like a grim remainder to humanity to never take the permanence of the planet for granted again.

One of the worst and most frequent side effects had been chem storms, showers of acid-tainted rain that could scorch the flesh off any mammal caught in the open. They were lingering examples of the freakish weather effects common after the nuke-caust. Chem storms were dangerous partly because of their intensity, but mainly because of the acids, heavy metals and other chemical compounds that fell, with the rain possessing the corrosive potency to strip flesh from bone in less than a minute.

Fortunately, chem storms were no longer as frequent as they had been even a century before, but there were still a number of places where the geological or meteorological effects of the nukecaust prevented a full recovery. These regions were called hellzones, areas that not even the passage of time could cleanse of hideous, invisible plagues.

The cargo elevator jolted to a stop and the doors opened up on a huge, dark space. Varnley led them into a multileveled man-made cavern so vast its true dimensions could not really be gauged. The far end ran away into the murk, and the ceiling was lost in the shadows. Large rectangular containers were arranged in orderly fifty-foot-tall aisles, stretching as far as they could see. The containers were made of lightweight, corrugated metal with hinged lids.

Smooth ramps sloped between levels, and were wide enough to permit forklifts and motorized dollies to carry their loads. At regularly space intervals were wide square apertures leading out of the huge chamber. Gleaming monorail tracks laced out in every direction, plunging into the apertures. On one track stood a small shifter engine with a chrome nose coupled to a flatcar holding three metal crates.

Kane walked over to it and glanced up and down the narrow track. "Which way?" he asked.

Varnley nodded in the direction the nose of the engine was pointed. "There."

"There's no passenger car," Erica pointed out.

"You're not too special that you can't ride on the flatcar," Brigid retorted. "You haven't been the imperial mother or Tui Chui Jian in a long time."

"Yeah," Kane remarked snidely. "You'll make good ballast."

Erica's eye widened and her mouth opened to voice a profane rejoinder when Varnley waved her to silence. "I hear something."

Kane tilted his head first to one side, then the other. "I don't."

"Nevertheless."

As Kane stepped to the rear of the flatcar, he put a foot on the metal rail. A steady vibration shivered through it. Then, from an opening in the wall two hundred yards away plunged a blunt-nosed shifter engine. He glimpsed three men wearing dun-colored coveralls seated within it. He didn't need to see the Calico subguns in their hands to know they wielded them.

A series of whipping cracks reverberated in the cavernous chamber, and bullets ricocheted from metal. The echoes of the shots were swallowed up by the high ceiling.

"Move, move!" Grant bellowed, jumping onto the flatcar, his Sin Eater slapping into his palm.

Erica and Varnley climbed into the compartment of the engine while Brigid and Kane joined Grant on the flatcar, squeezing between the crates. As they did so, the bullet-shaped engine emitted a high-pitched whine. The whine quickly rose in pitch, and with a slight lurch the train slid almost silently along the rail.

More autofire rattled and bullets hit the floor around the rail, gouging scars. Another bullet punched a dimple in the side of a metal-walled crate.

"Hang on," Varnley called.

All of them felt a shock of acceleration as the train plunged into the tunnels. Overhead light fixtures flicked by so rapidly that they combined with the intervals of darkness between them to acquire a strobing pattern.

The monorail car carrying the millennialists came rocketing after them a few seconds later. The bores of the weapons in their hands spit tongues of flame. Little spouts of concrete sprang up the right of the flatcar. Brigid positioned herself to return the fire, squeezing off three rounds from her TP-9 in such rapid succession they sounded like one extended report.

The Calicos of the millennialists continued to hammer, and bullets smacked into the flatcar with flat clangs. Kane cursed and ducked instinctively. He squeezed off a short triburst from his Sin Eater. The rounds struck sparks from the nose of the pursuing train.

The track curved to the left, and Grant, Kane and Brigid grabbed the edges of the flatcar as the boxes went sliding. Bullets rattled loudly all around them, sparks flaring from the points of impact. Gritting his teeth, Kane felt as if he were trapped in a recurrent nightmare where the same things happened over and over again, no matter what actions he took.

"They're obviously willing to kill us," Brigid commented. "Not just slow us down."

Pushing himself to one knee, Kane called to Varnley, "How far is the Prometheus wing?"

"Not much farther," Varnley shouted back. "Perhaps only five miles."

The pursuing engine screamed along the track like an out-of-control express train.

"Only?" Grant echoed incredulously. "We can't keep this shit up for five miles."

"What do you suggest?" Brigid asked.

Reaching into his warbag. Grant pulled out a canister-shaped RG-34 high-explosive grenade. "This will stop the chase pretty conclusively."

"Yeah," Kane agreed, "providing you time the throw just right."

A bullet struck the crate beside him and he ducked. "I think the time is right."

Grant slipped the spoon, pulled the pin, then dropped the grenade. It bounced along the rail for several yards, then exploded. The pursuing engine drove straight into the bloom of flame and concussion.

The car leaped from the rail, flipped, rolling end over end. The men inside were catapulted out, their limbs flailing the air like those of rag dolls. Metal fragments clattered and clanged loudly all along the tunnel.

"That," Brigid said flatly, "as they say, is that."

Kane rose up and turned around looking over the heads of Erica and Varnley. As their train went around a curve, he stiffened. "Ah, hell."

Brigid and Grant looked in the direction he stared. The plasma swarm glowed in the center of the tunnel, exploding like silent sky rockets.

"They're multiplying," Erica cried out, her voice hitting a high note of fear. "To trap us!"

"Maybe another grenade would work," Grant said, although he sounded skeptical.

"I don't think so," Brigid replied. "The explosion would get us, too."

"Do we take the chance of smashing through them?" Kane demanded. "Or stopping and surrendering?"

Grant snorted. "I don't think viruses take prisoners."

"Me, neither," Brigid put in. "Let's keep going."

Erica pushed herself up from the passenger compartment. "Let me out! I'll take my chances!"

Reaching over, Kane slammed her back into her seat. "We do this together. You wanted to come along and now you're in it as deep as we are."

He clenched his teeth as the engine arrowed straight for the cloud of green-glowing orbs.

Chapter 25

The bullet-shaped engine plunged on like a missile. The swarm of orbs did not shift position.

"I don't think we can bluff them," Grant said tensely. "And slowing down won't do any good."

Varnley half rose, light glinting from the slender infrasound wand grasped in his right fist. The humming, shivering tip inscribed a blurry semicircle. The viral cloud suddenly quivered, then the orbs in the center of the swarm spun away, leaving a large gap.

The monorail car plunged through the hole in the green-glimmering cloud. Glancing behind him, Kane watched the swarm spiral first to the right, then to the left, but not re-form into a cloud shape.

"They don't appear to be coming after us," he announced.

"The jolt of infrasound probably damaged them," Brigid said. "Maybe even destroyed a few."

"Wouldn't that be nice," Grant put in wistfully.

The monorail carriage swerved around a curve in the tunnel, and the viral cloud was lost to view. The shifter engine and the flatcar glided smoothly along the rail. Up ahead glowed the light of a train platform. Varnley adjusted the controls and their speed slackened. When they came abreast of the platform they saw the letters and numbers Y-95 stenciled on the wall above it.

With a scrape of brake shoes, the train gradually slowed to a halt. Everyone disembarked, assembling on the platform. Erica shook her head half in exasperation, half in relief. "That was very fast thinking, Varnley. I underestimated you."

Varnley's blank expression did not alter, but Kane received the distinct impression he was pleased with the praise. Grant gazed uneasily at the corridor stretching away from the station, not liking how it plunged into darkness.

"We'd better get going before the bees regroup and come buzzing after us again," he said.

The Cerberus warriors paused long enough to put on dark-lensed glasses. The electrochemical polymer of the lenses gathered all available light and made the most of it to give them a limited form of night vision. They strode swiftly along the corridor, alert for any unusual sound. The floor sloped upward at a gradual angle. Handrails lined both walls.

The group moved swiftly and fairly silently, their boots making only faint rasping sounds. They walked steadily forward toward odd, distant noises that emanated from the darkness ahead of them.

The incline terminated at a flat landing. A few

yards away stood the wire-shielded double doors they had seen earlier on the monitor screen. The skin on the back of Kane's neck tightened and prickled as he became conscious of a distant, almost inaudible reverberation on the other side of the barrier.

"The Prometheus wing, I presume," Brigid said softly.

Everyone stood and stared, not moving. Finally Grant said, "I don't see any millennialists or virals."

"Me, either," Kane muttered. "But that doesn't mean they're not around."

"So far this has a convenient feel to it," Brigid commented.

"Yes," Erica agreed. "So we might as well take advantage of it before everything becomes very inconvenient."

The black-haired woman took a tentative step forward, then another. Gusting out a sigh, Kane stepped in front of her, his Sin Eater held in a double-handed grip, barrel pointing upward. Brigid and Grant automatically took up positions on either side him, weapons at the ready.

Kane paused at the pair of doors, listening. The throbbing drone grew louder, like the murmur of a far-off crowd. The sound was not unfamiliar. He nodded to Grant and Brigid, then pushed open the right-hand door with the toe of his boot. It swung aside easily. Slowly, he eased over the threshold, pausing for his eyes to become adjusted to the deep gloom. It was much darker than in the corridor. He saw a chamber hung with large-scale maps of the United States and Europe. They were dimly illuminated from beneath. He quickly picked out red concentric circles emblazoned over various countries.

Brigid entered and came to his side. She glanced at the maps and said quietly, "First-strike targets."

"I figured."

One by one the group of five slipped through the door. They walked across the chamber, toward another set of doors on the far side. As their vision accustomed to the murk, they could see rising all around them a complex array of machine relays, connectives and many pieces of electronic equipment that didn't seem to belong.

The other door opened just as easily as the first, but the light was much stronger. Kane pushed it open with a shoulder. He and his companions emerged on a broad shelf that thrust out over a cavernous gallery nearly twenty feet below. They stood at a metal handrail, staring down at the fusion generator. Twelve feet tall, it resembled two solid black cubes, a slightly smaller one placed atop the larger. The top cube rotated slowly, producing the drone. The odor of ozone was very pronounced.

"Is anybody surprised to see that?" Kane asked quietly.

No one answered. The Cerberus warriors had seen identical machines in several places across the world over the past five-plus years. The two-tiered generators derived from the same source as the light panels—the Annunaki.

Long ago Lakesh had put forth the initial speculation they were fusion reactors, the energy output held in a delicately balanced magnetic matrix within the cubes. When the matrix was breached, an explosion of apocalyptic proportions resulted, which was what caused the destruction of the Archuleta Mesa installation.

"Now we know there's Annunaki tech being used," Erica said. "Partly, anyway."

Brigid frowned. She looked at the complexity and extent of the circuitry surrounding the generator. Lines ran across the floor and into the walls. "I've never seen a generator hooked up like that before. It seems to be only a component instead of a power source."

Suddenly the droning throb died. The uppermost cube of the generator stopped rotating. The entire gallery fell silent, as still as the crypts where the bones of the ancient dead were interred.

Brigid's throat tightened. "Something's happening," she husked out.

Then directly above the top cube of the generator a spiral of green lights appeared, seeming to bleed into existence from thin air. The huge viral formation floated lazily in the gallery.

While everyone watched, too paralyzed with shock to move, the shape changed from a spiral to a cloud, still floating lazily around the generator. Terror tightened a fist around Brigid's heart. While she watched, the cloud became a tight ball of dancing red light.

Under other circumstances, Brigid Baptiste would have thought the prismatic changeover in color was beautiful, but the sight of it made her throat constrict.

"Maybe we should back away," Kane said flatly.

As soon as he spoke, crooked threads of red lightning erupted out of the viral cloud. They whiplashed around the people standing on the ledge, and for only an instant Brigid glimpsed a skein of blood-hued electricity crawling over her face.

THE RED ORBS WANTED answers. They asked Brigid questions only her subconscious mind could answer, and she saw no reason not to tell them truth as she remembered it. She was, after all, trained to preserve the truth.

For ten of her first twenty-one years, Brigid had trained to be an archivist in Cobaltville's Historical Division, and then for six years had worked as one. Despite the common misconception, archivists were not bookish, bespectacled scholars. They were primarily data-entry techs, albeit ones with high security clearances. Midgrade senior archivists like herself were primarily editors.

A vast amount of predark historical information had survived the nukecaust, particularly documents stored in underground vaults. Tons of it, in fact, from novels to encyclopedias, to magazines printed on coated stock, which survived just about anything. Much more data—usually government documents—was digitized and stored on computer diskettes.

Although she was a fairly high ranking archivist, Brigid wasn't among the highest. Those in the upper echelons were responsible for viewing and editing—or suppressing—the most-sensitive material. Still, she had glimpsed enough to know there were bits and bytes of information that were still classified, even two centuries after the nuking.

Her primary duty was not to record predark history, but to revise, rewrite and often times completely disguise it. The political causes leading to the nukecaust were well-known. They were major parts of the dogma, the articles of faith, and they had to be accurately recorded for posterity.

Scheming, wicked Russkies had detonated a nuclear warhead in the basement of their embassy in Washington, D.C., even while they negotiated for peace. American retaliation had been swift and all-encompassing. The world had come very close to transforming into a smoldering, lifeless cinder spinning darkly in space.

People were responsible. Russian people, American people, Asian people. People had put irresponsible people into positions of responsibility, so ergo, the responsibility for the nukecaust was the responsibility of people. Humanity as a whole.

Brigid had believed that, of course. For many years, she had never questioned it. Humankind had been judged guilty and the sentence carried out forthwith. As she rose up the ranks, promoted mainly through attrition, she was allowed even greater access to secret records. Though these were heavily edited, she came across references to something called the Totality Concept, to devices called gateways, to a place called the Anthill Complex, and to projects bearing the code names of Chronos and Whisper, which hinted at phenomena termed "probability wave dysfunctions" and "alternate event horizons."

Then, toward the end of her sixth year as an archivist, Brigid read the *Wyeth Codex,* which contained recollections, observations, speculations and theories about the environmental conditions of postnukecaust America. The author, Mildred Winona Wyeth, also delved deeply into the Totality Concept and its many different yet interconnected subdivisions. In her journal, she maintained that the technology simply did not exist to have created all of the Totality Concept's many wonders—unless it had originated from somewhere, or someone else.

Despite her exceptional intelligence and education, Wyeth had no inkling of the true nature of the Totality Concept's experiments, but a number of her extrapolations that they were linked to the nukecaust came very close to the truth.

In the decades following its discovery, the *Wyeth Codex* had been downloaded, copied and disseminated like a virus through the Historical Divisions of the entire ville network.

That particular virus had infected Brigid years ago, when she found a disk containing the *Codex* at her workstation in the archives. After reading and committing it to memory, she had never been the same woman again.

Now a different kind of virus infected Brigid Baptiste—only this time, she understood on some level that it didn't want to infect her, but to turn her into a replica of itself.

Chapter 26

The hum of electronics and a steady, castanet click-ing insinuated itself into Brigid's mind. She came awake slowly. First the black void turned to gray, then to a pale, shimmering red.

Pain consumed her body. Her head pounded rhythmically, in cadence with her heartbeat. She tried to open her eyes, but she couldn't see anything but a dull reddish blob and she wondered if she had lost her sight. She tried to put her hands under her, but they seemed to be somewhere else, beyond her control. Her stumbling thoughts probed for the reason why.

Grinding her teeth, Brigid mentally explored her body, noting its position and posture. She realized she lay on her back and when she tried to move, cramping needles of agony shot up her shoulders and arms. A persistent pressure compressed her wrists, squeezed them so tightly together her hands were no more than numb, half-remembered presences at the ends of her arms. By a tentative exploration with her fingertips, she felt hard straps pinning her wrists.

She turned her body, aware of the tremors that went through her. Nausea became a clawed animal trying to tear its way out of her stomach. It was all she could do to swallow the column of burning bile working its way up her throat.

Brigid shifted her legs, and they trembled violently. She struggled frantically, managing to angle her elbows to lever herself up, but her body went into convulsions. She fell back, panting. She realized her body was dissociated from the messages of her mind. Every order from her brain seemed to confuse her nerves and muscles. She tasted fear, a sharp, bitter tang as of freshly sheared copper wire.

Somewhere in the distance she heard a hoarse male voice. She couldn't distinguish the words, but she wasn't sure if was because the voice spoke a foreign language or because her neurons were misfiring so badly her mind could no longer recognize words.

She opened her mouth to call for help, but shut it again. Although her thoughts moved like half-frozen mud, she knew it was best to keep as silent and as motionless as possible. She opened her eyes wide, blinking repeatedly. The wavering red glow slowly resolved itself into a distorted low-angle view of the two-tiered generator. A hazy crimson aura surrounded it.

When Brigid realized she lay at its base, memory and awareness returned in a simultaneous rush. She strained at the binding around her wrists but she felt no slack. She kicked her legs, thrashing wildly. She guessed that the exposure to the energy of the viral had scrambled her nervous system. Pain thudded at the back of her head, and she stopped struggling. She sucked in a long lungful of air, trying to calm down.

A man's voice, somewhere behind her said, "That's right…fighting it only makes the effects worse. You'll recover in a moment. Relax."

A hand inserted itself between the back of her neck and floor and lifted her to a sitting position. Brigid blinked repeatedly and a man's dark face swam into focus. He wore a beige coverall, begrimed with oil, grease and bloodstains.

"You took an EMP jolt," he said soothingly. "Pretty mild, considering the size of the viral. That's why your eyes aren't working right…the eyes are particularly vulnerable to EM radiation."

With effort, Brigid said, "You're Quintus Breech." She was dismayed by how weak her voice sounded.

The man nodded. "One and the same. I've seen pictures of you in the consortium files. You're Brigid Baptiste. You look just like your pix."

"I can't say the same for you." Brigid studied him. He did not resemble the dapper Quintus Breech she had seen on the DVD. His face showed raw abrasions and two of his teeth were missing.

He shrugged. "You can't tinker around with the power of the quantum field and not get kicked around a little."

"Or die," Brigid said, her voice growing stronger.

Breech smiled crookedly. "Yeah, there's that. But I'm prepared."

"You are?"

"Sure. When it my time comes, I'll accept it without complaint. There won't be any monuments erected over my grave, but I'll have made my contribution."

"To what?"

"To the next step in humanity's evolution. That alone is a worthwhile epitaph."

Brigid eyed the man, looking for any signs of dementia. He seemed sane enough, and his stoic attitude toward death was one she understood.

She had learned to accept risk as a part of her way of life, taking chances so that others might find the ground beneath their feet a little more secure. She didn't consider her attitude idealism, but simple pragmatism. If she had learned anything from her friends, it was to regard death as a part of the challenge of existence, a fact that every man and woman must face eventually.

She could accept it without humiliating herself, if it came as a result of her efforts to remove the yokes of the barons from the collective neck of humanity. Although she never spoke of it, certainly not to the cynical Kane, she had privately vowed to make the future a better, cleaner place than either the past or the present.

"Where are my friends?" Brigid asked.

"Safe." Breech smiled wryly. "That is, about as safe as they could be under the circumstances."

"I don't like the sound of that."

Breech's smile disappeared. "There's no reason why you should."

"I suppose you and Erica had a lot to talk about."

Breech's face brightened. "She's here?"

"You didn't see her?"

"No—the viral incapacitated all of you, but when we came to collect you, I couldn't find her. At first I thought she might have stayed behind."

"You seem happy that she's here."

A line of consternation appeared on Breech's brow. "Why wouldn't I be? I love her."

Brigid stared at him, surprised into speechlessness for a long moment. "Your men tried to kill all of us, Erica included," she stated.

Breech sighed. "I know."

Putting his hands under her arms, he heaved her to her feet, steadying her as her legs wobbled. Brigid attempted to take a forward step, but lost her balance and nearly fell. Breech caught her. She breathed harshly, listing from side to side.

"Can't you cut my hands loose?" she demanded angrily. "So I can at least catch myself if I fall?"

"If you were anyone else, I would," he replied regretfully. "But you're no ordinary woman. Just aim yourself for that door."

Breech pointed to a bevel-framed doorway a few yards away.

Carefully, as though she walked on a heaving deck, Brigid went toward the opening, with Breech's hand at her elbow. Her face was locked in a mask of concentration as she blocked out everything but the necessity to take the next step, and the next, and the next.

"I'm sorry that a couple of my men got trigger-happy," Breech said. "My staff is fused out and some are worse off than others. I've been forced to discipline them."

Brigid glanced at the abrasions on his face. "Looks like it's been a two-way street."

Breech forced a smile. "It's been something of a study in behavioral neurology."

"What's been?"

"How different people react to exposure to the EM field. I'm probably a little mad myself."

"I don't doubt it," Brigid said grimly.

As they walked toward the door, Breech said, "You might still feel a little queasy, so if you need to throw up, just let me know."

"I am feeling a little sick to my stomach. Why is that?"

"Radiation."

Brigid felt her heartbeat speed up. "What kind of radiation?"

"I'm not sure," he replied uncertainly. "The wavelength is in the ultrahigh frequency. Only very sensitive equipment can detect it, much less measure it."

"You're talking theta-band emissions, aren't you?"

Breech glanced at her in surprise. "I'm afraid so. You know about the transmitter?"

"As much as it's possible to know about Annunaki technology."

Quintus Breech nodded contemplatively. "I figured we were dealing with retroengineered alien tech. I think there might be some Danaan in it, too."

They stepped over the threshold into the adjoining room, and Brigid's gait faltered. It was filled, from wall to ceiling, with an intricate mass of circuitry. Indicator lights glowed, switches clicked steadily, which she recognized as the castanet clatter she had heard earlier, and a multitude of little chevron-shaped panels pulsated.

Brigid swept her gaze over it and said, "As a general rule the Tuatha de Danaan didn't use such extensive machinery."

"Yeah, that's what Erica said, too."

"So, what is all this gear?"

Breech turned earnest eyes upon her. "I was hoping you could tell me."

"I've never seen anything like this," she stated. "Especially the red glow around the generators. You must have a theory about it."

Breech nodded. "At first, I assumed the generator was a power source, a self-perpetuating feed shunt from the quantum stream. Now I'm not sure. If you know about the Annunaki—"

He broke off, his jaw muscles bunching.

"What?" Brigid asked.

Quintus Breech inhaled a deep breath. "If you know about the Annunaki and the Archons, maybe you can tell me if any of them are still alive in this machine."

Brigid's eyes narrowed. "I don't understand."

"I don't, either. Erica told me about the Archons and their genetic relationship with the Danaan and the Annunaki, but this device doesn't seem to be of their creation. But I've been told about the First Folk and how they used some kind of energy that almost destroyed the world. Protoplanic? Does that ring a bell?"

A chill finger ran up and down the buttons of her spine. The First Folk, the so-called Archons, had used the technology from both the Annunaki and the Tuatha de Danaan, redesigning it and blending both into a single form with several functions. However, the Danaan and Annunaki forbade the sharing of advanced scientific knowledge with humanity.

Lakesh had speculated the solution to both the riddle of the so-called Archons and humanity's mysterious origins lay in ancient religious codices. He had finally come to accept that he could not penetrate the convoluted conspiracy of secrecy that had been maintained for twenty thousand years or more.

The few surviving sacred texts contained only hints, inferences passed down from generation to

generation, not actual answers. Ancient documents
that might have held the truth had crumbled into
dust or were deliberately destroyed. Regardless,
historical records of nonhuman influence on Terran
development ran uninterrupted from the very dawn
of humankind to the present day.

Always it was the same—human beings as
possessions, with a never-ending conflict bred
between them, promoting spiritual decay and per-
petuating conditions of unremitting physical
hardship. And always, secret societies were created by human pawns to conceal and to protect
the true nature of humanity's custodians—or
masters.

Such societies traced their roots back to ancient
Egypt, Babylon, Mesopotamia, Greece and Sume-
ria. Throughout humankind's history, secret coven-
ants with mysterious nonhuman entities known by
a variety of names in variety of places—the Nagas,
the Oannes, the Titans and lastly the Archons—
were struck by kings, princes and even presidents.

The secret societies acted more or less as the
plenipotentiaries of the entities, and their oaths re-
volved around a single theme—the presence of the
beings must never be revealed to humanity at large.

The First Folk, the hybrid race propagated by the
Annunaki and the Tuatha de Danaan, functioned
much like a secret society. It was their duty to keep
the ancient secrets of their ancestors alive, yet not
perpetuate the same errors as their forebears, espe-

cially in their dealings with humans, with whom they shared a genetic link.

Humankind was still struggling to overcome a global cataclysm, striving again for civilization, and the graceful First Folk did what they could to assist. They insinuated themselves into schools, into political circles, prompting and ensuring men made the right decisions.

Due to the First Folk's influence, humankind enjoyed a thousand years of relative peace and harmony, during which the Atlantean civilization arose. Lam, a leader of the First Folk and Balam's father, sought to convince the Annunaki and Danaan representatives to allow humanity to grow and evolve without strictures. Instead, the two races threatened to visit another cataclysm upon Earth and hurl humankind back into savagery.

The First Folk knew their forebears had too many weapons in their arsenals, stolen and adapted from other worlds they visited and exploited, for them to be able to defend Earth. Nor did they possess the resources to fight an all-out war, but once they had aroused their forebears' suspicions, they had no choice but to take quick, preemptive action.

They employed an energy they called proto-planic. According to what Brigid had been told, the force demolished an Annunaki settlement on the Moon and killed the royal family.

A blow-back effect, a reverse reaction that the First Folk had not foreseen, very nearly destroyed the Earth. It decimated human and the First Folk civilizations. In their attempts to defend human-kind, they had inadvertently brought about the destruction their forebears had threatened.

After the global catastrophe, the First Folk transformed themselves to adapt to the new environment. Their muscle tissue became less dense, motor reflexes sharpened, optic capacities broadened. A new range of psychic abilities were developed that allowed them to survive on a planet whose magnetic fields had changed, whose weather was drastically unpredictable.

In the process, the physical appearance of the First Folk changed from tall, slender, graceful creatures to small, furtive shadow dwellers. Although the survivors of the custodial race were viewed by humans as demons and monsters, they still tried to protect humanity over the long track of time, as they clawed their way back up from barbarism. At the dawn of Earth's industrial revolution, the First Folk's descendants, the entities later known as Grays and Archons, feared more reprisals from their forebears. As protective coloration, they fabricated a convoluted false history designed to confound any enterprising human who got too close to the truth.

"Well?" Breech prodded urgently. "I need to know. Is this protoplanic energy?"

Brigid shook her head. "I wish I could tell you."

Brigid could not answer Breech's question, but

she knew that the circuitry in the room represented a science of an ordered, systematic knowledge that led to the control of the forces of nature, if not the universe itself.

The extent of the forces, how vast their effects, she had no way of even guessing, but she had the unsettling sensation that the machines channeled the same energies that had destroyed the world aeons before.

Chapter 27

Breech led the way down a spiral flight of metal stairs and entered a vault-walled chamber. The room was circular and much larger than had looked possible.

A gleaming spire rose from the center of the floor, reaching like a spear through an aperture in the high ceiling. Four huge metal rings surrounded its base, but as they ascended upward, they decreased in diameter. There were perhaps fifty of the rings visible. A dim glow came from the hole in the roof, illuminating the rings. A pale nimbus, a kind of wavering halo, shimmered from each ring.

"It looks like a supercollider," Brigid commented.

"Close," Breech replied. "It's a large ion collider expeditor. Known in the old vernacular as ALICE."

"You put this together?" Brigid demanded. "You built this?"

"No," said Breech. "ALICE was already here."

He gestured to the base of the spire, and she saw hair-thin filaments stretching out from it, disappearing into sockets on the floor. "We just hooked up the power feeds."

"Why?"

Breech regarded her with hollow, haunted eyes. "I thought—I hoped—we could engineer a new beginning. A fresh start for humanity."

Brigid gritted her teeth against a pain stabbing through her skull. "By cobbling together old Archon tech that predark scientists realized was too dangerous to use?"

"I didn't know it was Archon tech...not exactly, anyway."

"But you put it together nevertheless." Her tone held a sharp, accusatory edge.

"We had to. That was the plan. The transmitter itself was already assembled. It just needed to be connected to the generator. We did that."

"And now?"

He swallowed hard. "And now we can't turn it off. It's drawing power from somewhere, and I have the feeling it's building to critical mass, which can have a terrible effect on space-time itself."

As Brigid stared at the spire, she became aware that shifting patterns of light and changing colors on the rings brought pain to her eyes and a corresponding throb in her head.

"You have a feeling," she snapped, "that it's generating the so-called protoplanic force used by the Archons?"

Taking her by the elbow, he guided her around

the spire. "It's a little more than that. In general relativity and related theories, the distribution of the mass, momentum and stress due to matter interacting with a nongravitational field is called an energy-momentum tensor. Are you familiar with the term?"

"Only insofar as the Einstein field equation is applied to it. I do know that his equation isn't very specific about what types of matter or energy fields are admissible in a space-time model."

Breech gave her a fleeting, appreciative smile. "Erica was right. You are far more intelligent than most people in this day and age. All right, I believe the energy conditions within the generator and the transmitter are channeling properties that represent all states of matter and all energy states. Eigenvalues and eigenvectors are unrestricted and they are imposed at the level of tangent space."

Brigid frowned. "And that means what exactly?"

Breech laughed, but it sounded forced, with a screechy undertone of hysteria. "If I knew what it meant exactly, you and I wouldn't be having this conversation. But my theory is that enough power is already concentrated in the transmitter to warp the fabric of space-time all over the planet."

"The power has to be drawn from somewhere other than the generator."

"I agree. I think it's drawn from subspace and its nature is being modified and focused by the theta-pinch transmitter."

"Focused into what?" Brigid asked.

Breech turned his stricken face toward her. "That's why we're talking, Brigid. You're the one with experience with this kind of technology."

Brigid smiled crookedly, without humor. "No one really has experience with it. But I'll do what I can to help you if my hands are freed and you take me to my friends."

Breech nodded agreeably. "All right. You're a hands-on type of scientist. So you need your hands."

Reaching into a pocket of his coverall, he pulled out a small knife and slashed through the nylon straps around Brigid's wrists. She brought her arms around in front of her, flexing her fingers and massaging circulation back into her hands.

Gazing at Breech challengingly, she asked, "And my friends?"

He jerked his head toward the left. "This way."

Brigid followed him around the spire, then rocked to a clumsy halt, her stomach lurching. Grant and Kane were bound hand and ankle to a pair of metal frameworks in the shape of Xs. Both men were conscious, but they did not look well—their eyes bore glassy sheens and their faces glistened with perspiration.

Two men wearing the consortium coveralls stood on either side of the frameworks. They looked distinctly unhealthy, their complexions waxy, their eyes surrounded by dark rings.

Brigid made a move to lunge toward Kane and Grant, but Breech latched on to her right arm and pulled her back. "They're all right. They haven't been harmed."

"Then why are they bound?" she demanded, wresting out of his grip.

"Mainly so they won't cause trouble until—" Breech broke off and averted his gaze.

"Until what?" she snapped.

"Until," said a musical voice from behind her, "they can serve as vessels for the vent discharge."

Brigid whirled around and watched Varnley approach, tapping the tip of his infrasound wand against the palm of one hand. Although his high-planed face revealed no emotion, she suddenly knew the hybrid had betrayed them.

Struggling to tamp down the surge of fear so it was not evident in her voice, Brigid asked, "What's going on here, Varnley?"

Varnley's eyes flicked toward Breech. "Should you tell her, Quintus, or shall I?"

"So you're the real brains of this operation," Brigid declared.

Varnley's thin lips creased in an imitation of a smug smile. "Rather more colloquial than I might phrase it, but yes—I've been working with Quintus Breech and his disaffected consortium agents."

"Why?" Brigid blurted. "You helped him to murder your own people here?"

"Of course." Varnley shook his head in mock pity. "It was my idea to get rid of the competition."

"Competition for what?"

"What do you think?" Kane called out. "He's the latest entrant in the ongoing 'tomorrow the world' sweepstakes, with absolute power as the prize."

"And it's corrupted absolutely again," Brigid said grimly, glaring first at Varnley then at Breech.

Varnley waved the infrasound wand diffidently. "Don't be so melodramatic. I learned about the theta-pinch transmitter many years ago. It was always my ambition to use it to further the baronial agenda."

"The barons are gone," Grant barked.

Varnley didn't glance in his direction. "But their agenda remains."

"Which is what?" Brigid asked, not trying to soften the hard edge of contempt in her tone.

"To unify humanity and the world."

Kane uttered a sound between a snarl and a laugh. "We've heard that one before. Just about everybody who said it to us is dead…including your barons."

"Of that I have no doubt. But with this machine—" he nodded toward the transmitter "—I can force that unity myself. All it takes is a bit of transformation."

Brigid suddenly understood—and she felt sick. "By turning humanity into a viral form of life? Into ghost-walkers?"

"That phenomenon is a side effect of the theta radiation," Breech said. "It's not what it was designed to do."

"Even so," Varnley stated, "humanity is already primitive, driven by a kind of herd instinct, living and reproducing in groups. Why not reduce all of that to its most base components?"

"The barons are no more," Brigid said evenly. "You've become the puppet of a lost and dead conspiracy."

Varnley regarded her with a mocking smile. "Think you so? Isn't it axiomatic of conspiracies that someone or something else always pulls the strings?"

"Of ignorant puppets," Brigid shot back, "yes."

"I am not that, I can assure you. The puppet masters of this world have always been the Archons."

"You're over your head, Varnley," Kane stated. "It's the Annunaki."

The hybrid finally deigned to glance at him. "Do you think you've been able to rip away the cloak of secrecy that has been maintained for over twenty thousand years? Hardly. You were tricked by another diversion, one concocted by the barons."

Although the Cerberus warriors had encountered mentally unstable hybrids in the past such as Baron Sharpe, it hadn't occurred to Brigid that they also might fall prey to simple denial.

"We've had this discussion before," Breech said coldly. "You're deluding yourself. The baronies have fallen, the villes overwhelmed by chaos. The baronial agenda failed. Get used to it."

Without altering his expression of detachment, Varnley slashed Breech viciously across the right cheek with the point of the infrasound wand. The man staggered back, clutching at his face and crying out. Fortunately the device wasn't powered up. If it had, Breech's facial bones would have shattered like spun crystal.

"I suggest *you* get used to it," Varnley countered. "You helped me reach this point in the plan, but that doesn't mean I'll tolerate disrespect from humans."

Brigid intoned, "And the next stage of human development is what—reducing us to single-celled organisms? No, not even that…just a collection of electrical impulses and ionized gas?"

Varnley nodded. "Yes. Not everyone obviously. We new humans will still need servants."

"Slaves," Grant said.

Appearing not to have heard, Varnley continued, "The energy contained in the transmitter's capacitors needs to be bled off at regular intervals. When exposed to undiluted discharge of the energy, it transforms organic matter into the viral."

Holding a hand to the cut on his face, Breech said, "That's what happened to most of my staff. The men who chased you in the tunnel had refused to cooperate. They weren't so much trying to kill you as kill Varnley." He paused, his eyes seething with hatred. "I wish they'd succeeded."

"If they had," Varnley retorted dismissively, "then Erica van Sloan would have no doubt died, as well."

He turned toward Brigid. "However, the sacrifice of your friends may not be necessary."

"Why not?"

"With your help, we may be able to turn off the transmitter or at least reduce its power needs."

"I thought you wanted to turn everyone into ghost-walkers," Brigid said.

"That was not the original plan," Breech put in. "Believe me."

"What is the plan, then?" Grant demanded hoarsely, lifting his head. The man standing on his right slammed him back against the framework with a hand pressed against his forehead.

Breech's shoulders slumped. "Erica told me about the theta-pinch experiments in New Mexico. I went to Phantom Mesa station to claim the technology that still existed. When I activated it, the transmitter…"

He trailed off, coughed and asked, "You saw the video record, right?"

Brigid eyed him keenly. "Your people were turned into ghost-walkers…and you were changed, too."

He nodded and raised his hands, palm outwards. The skin was black, crusted and flaking away. "Yes, but because I didn't get a direct jolt, the changeover has been progressive with me. I'm turning into a ghost-walker, but by degrees. I've been able to delay the process by venting the radiation that is transforming my cellular structure."

Lowering his hands, Breech stated, "When I found out stage two of the experiments had been moved here to Area 51, Erica secretly provided me with the gateway coordinates."

"What does she plan to do with the transmitter?" Brigid asked.

"Erica described it as a self-sustaining source of free, transmittable energy. Photovoltaic technology, she called. She said a man named Tesla invented it. She said that if we controlled the energy, then we would control the world."

Kane uttered a scoffing sound. "Why am I not surprised?"

Breech squared his shoulders. "We're as qualified to lay down a foundation for a new society as the goddamn Millennial Consortium. If they have their way, we'll all be a bunch of laborers."

Brigid cast a glance toward Varnley. "That's the underpinnings of the baronial philosophy, so I can see why you two got along…at first."

Desperately, Breech said, "None of that matters now. We don't control the power here. The generator and the pieces of equipment to channel the protoplanic force are building up to a critical mass…we're taking global decimation!"

A rush of sympathy rose in Brigid. "Let Kane and Grant go free, and I'll stay here to help you figure out how to power down the generator."

"No," Varnley snapped. "Bleeding off the energy keeps the reactor within the generator at a manageable level."

"We're only buying time that way," Breech said. "The intervals between the venting have become shorter and shorter. The color of the viral has changed from green to red...that means something. We're all dying here, anyway. We don't have to take the planet with us."

Uncertainty flickered in Varnley's eyes. "I have a counterproposal. Baptiste stays here and her friends become part of the viral collective."

Before Brigid could answer, footsteps rang on the risers of the metal staircase. They turned to see a man in the consortium coverall slowly trudging down the steps.

Varnley called to him, "Lennox, did you find any trace of the van Sloan woman?"

The man addressed as Lennox shook his head, his face a doleful mask of exhaustion.

From above his head floated Erica van Sloan's voice. "No, but I found a trace of Lennox."

Chapter 28

Everyone watched in surprised silence as Erica strode down the stairs with the barrel of the Calico subgun trained on Lennox's back.

Uttering a cry of relief, Breech rushed toward the woman, arms outspread. "Erica! Thank God!"

She snapped up the Calico. "That's far enough, Quintus. Don't make me shoot you."

He stumbled to a clumsy halt, lowering his arms. Face twisting in confusion, he stammered, "What are you—? I don't understand! Tell me—"

"You're probably radioactive," Erica broke in harshly. "And you look and smell like shit."

"Ain't love grand," Brigid murmured.

"Shut up, Baptiste," Erica said curtly, pushing Lennox away from her. "I'm the only chance you, Kane and Grant have of getting out of here alive."

Varnley sidled around Brigid, lifting the infra-sound wand but not activating it. "How were you able to escape the viral?"

Erica's lips quirked in a superior smile. "The EMP emitted by the virals affect the brain. Mine isn't quite like everyone else's…or yours for that matter."

Varnley frowned. "What do you mean?"

"The SQUIDs implants," Brigid announced. "Right?"

Erica tapped her forehead. "On the money. I maintained consciousness long enough to get out of the viral's effect radius and lay low."

"Until now," Breech said accusingly. "You were eavesdropping."

"Just long enough to form an idea of what's going on here." Erica took a deep breath, as if she were steeling herself for an unpleasant task. "Quintus, baby…I'm afraid you're screwed."

The air in the room suddenly became hot. The switches stopped their steady clicking. The silence that took their place was of the void, of the grave.

"The final countdown has begun," Erica continued. "Venting won't stop the reactor from reaching critical mass now, so you might as well release Kane and Grant and say your goodbyes."

Brigid saw Breech's face go from fear to complete horror. He clutched at himself. "Something is happening, inside of me—"

"It's the protoplanic force, baby." Erica's voice held a note of sympathy. "It works by mass-to-energy conversion…the ultimate expression of fusion power."

Breech doubled up. Brigid reached out for him, touching him. Heat blazed through her hands, even through the fabric of her gloves. Crying out, she recoiled.

"The viral and the ghost-walkers are intermediate stages of the protoplanic event," Erica went on. "Depending on the length and intensity of exposure, the victims can be converted immediately to the viral or it takes a while…like with you. The life span of both forms is only a few days."

Foam flecked Breech's writhing lips. "You knew this?"

"I guessed…I'd hoped I was wrong…what the Archons called protoplanic force is really fusion nucleosynthesis ramped up to the ultimate degree."

Softly, she added, "I'm sorry, Quintus, I really am. But you were dead when you were first exposed in Phantom Mesa station."

Breech started to speak again, then cried out in pain. He lifted his hands before his face. Pale light pulsed from the palms. He croaked, "Kill me."

Varnley stepped forward, thumbing the power switch of his infrasound wand. He pointed the tip at Breech's head. "This will be painful, but only for a second."

"Don't!" Erica cried out in alarm. "It won't make a difference."

Varnley whipped the wand toward her. "Will it make a difference if I kill you?"

The silver rod emitted a high-pitched hum. Brigid heard the sharp clang of impact, and then Erica staggered backward, the Calico flying from her hands.

Brigid drove a elbow into Varnley's midsection,

and he folded over with a gasp. Grasping his arm with both hands, she snapped his elbow against the point of her knee. The joint cracked loudly. The hybrid shrieked in pain, and Brigid snatched the wand from his fingers.

She whirled around toward Kane and Grant. The millennialists moved away from the framework to intercept her. The staccato hammering of two subguns echoed.

Brigid fanned the air with the gleaming wand, thumbing the power output to full. The hum became a high-pitched buzz. Several pops concussed the air, and the deflected bullets screamed in all directions, ricocheting off metal. One of the millennialists cried out and slapped at himself. Both men turned and ran around the base of the spire.

Reaching Kane and Grant, Brigid touched the vibration-blurred tip of the wand to the slender chains hooked to their manacles. The links split and fragmented with chiming sounds. The two men jumped off the frameworks and glanced around. They saw their weapons resting on a small table behind them.

As they retrieved them, Varnley, cradling his broken elbow, stumbled against Breech. The man instinctively touched him, laying his hands flat against Varnley. A torrent of incandescence engulfed the hybrid's body. He burst into flame, transformed into fire-wreathed scarecrow. His body exploded from within.

"Oh, my God," Brigid husked out.

In a raspy whisper, Breech said, "I can't control the reaction going on within me...but I might be able to absorb more of the energy and balance it all out."

Whirling, he staggered toward the base of the transmitter. He slapped both hands onto one of the ALICE rings of metal encircling it. Throwing back his head, he screamed. The light shimmering from his hands blended with the colors wavering from the rings. An incandescent cocoon settled around him. White flame exploded from the spire, but there was no sound of a detonation. Bursts of light blazed up and down the shaft. Thick, spark-shot smoke plumed out, billows of roiling vapor all but blinding them.

"Let's get the hell out of here," Kane said, kicking himself into a sprint.

"I don't know if running will do any good," Brigid stated flatly. "If the transmitter starts discharging, no place will be far enough away."

"Let's take our chances," Grant panted.

As they came around the transmitter, the millennialists ran from the opposite direction, Calicos stuttering. Kane triggered his Sin Eater and bullets pounded through a dun-colored torso. The man went down, blood spurting from three holes neatly grouped over his heart.

The cloud of smoke dimmed the lights, but Grant dropped his pistol sights over the other millennialist and depressed the trigger stud. The bullet slammed through the man's forehead, punching him backward with such force his head struck the floor first.

Great whorls of color danced around the metal rings, growing in size and brilliance. The Cerberus warriors joined Erica at the base of the staircase. She stared, transfixed, her one eye reflecting the shifting colors like a kaleidoscope. A halo surrounded Quintus Breech's body. As they watched, the halo inexorably expanded like ripples in a pond.

The edges of the ripples curled in upon themselves and then seemed to break apart, turning into millions of glittering orbs. They were all of different colors, ranging across the visible spectrum.

"He's become a viral," Erica said between gritted teeth.

"Great," Kane muttered. "Time for us to go before he expects us to join the club."

They turned toward the staircase but froze when they saw multicolored specks of light flickering over the steps. A swift glance told Brigid there were thousands, perhaps hundreds of thousands of the orbs. They darted toward the transmitter like a monstrous swarm of bees drawn to a hive.

"It's all the surviving virals," Erica said, her voice hushed with a combination of fright and awe. "Quintus is calling them, summoning them."

"Why?" Grant demanded.

Erica didn't answer. All of them stared unblinkingly as the viral swarm blended together into one giant cloud. One group overlapped with another, changing form, twisting into a helix pattern, then a monstrous ball and finally into a crisscross of streaks, shooting back and forth.

"Quintus is absorbing them into his matrix," Erica whispered. "He's smothering the chain reaction."

By degrees the viral swarm oozed into the rings surrounding the transmitter shaft. The entire structure became shot through with tiny lightning strokes of dazzling light.

"They're entering the ALICE," Brigid exclaimed. "Becoming inert particles."

"Is that good?" Kane asked doubtfully.

Grant snorted. "It's better than the alternative."

The entire viral cloud faded, becoming a faint, feathery mist. Brigid, Kane, Grant and Erica van Sloan stood rooted to the spot at the foot of the spiral staircase. They looked for some sign of movement, a fleeting, flitting glimpse of an orb, but they saw nothing around the base of the transmitter.

"Is that it?" Kane demanded.

"Things don't always have to end with an explosion," Brigid said with a wan smile. "Even though that's sometimes more satisfying."

Erica said quietly, "This was all an accident, really. The same kind of accident that destroyed my world two centuries ago. Humans playing with the power universe and getting their fingers burned. Another lost dream."

Grant regarded her scornfully. "Now you get judgmental. If it had all worked out, you'd claim it was your destiny or some crap like that."

"I'm tired of arguing," said Brigid, turning toward the staircase. "Let's get out of here."

Erica van Sloan and Grant followed Brigid Baptiste up the stairs. For once, Kane brought up the rear. He paused long enough to look at the spire of the transmitter, thinking that it marked a graveyard of ambitions and lost dreams.

* * * * *

Power Struggles

While the Cerberus warriors and the overlords are locked in a cold and bitter truce, other forces seek to tear apart the fragile postapocalyptic Earth. In their time as barons, the overlords tried to take over the world, but now, evolved into their godly forms, many of their human minions are leaderless, and some resent their abandonment. Marduk wants Greece on his own terms, and even his old human slaves' established efforts are considered doubtful.

Gods of Technology

New Olympus is involved in a brutal war against Marduk's forces. Though they are outnumbered by Nephilim and vat-grown mutants, the Olympians make up for it with sheer power in the form of towering mechanical demigods. Battered and overwhelmed human survivors lose to whichever tyrant wins out. Only by trusting a robotic monster can the Cerberus warriors hope to bring peace and freedom to a war-torn region.

Chapter 1

Artem15's flat-treaded, semiclawed metal foot sank into the hillside with all the ponderous weight of her three-thousand-pound clockwork-geared frame. The robot's pace seemed leisurely as she topped the small swell in the terrain, but it was just an illusion cast by her towering fifteen-foot height. Each swing of her long, mechanized legs was accompanied by the soft, melodic whistle of polished joints grinding against each other.

Artem15 was a decidedly female construct. There was no disguising her feminine breastplate, contrasting with the masculine-sculpted copper torsos of her fellow mechanically suited warriors. Her head, a camera-laden module with ruby-red optics placed where the eyes would be in a bronze-forged representation of a woman's face, was hunched between shoulder-mounted guns. A mane of glimmering golden ribbons of polished and colored steel wool hung like real hair, not obscuring her red camera lenses, but cascading down her back.

Diana Pantolpoulos, who piloted the one-and-a-half ton mobile war suit was one of the elite. Thus she had been rewarded with the identity Artemis. A mere combat drone bore a red ID number painted onto a coppery simulation of a pectoral muscle. The rank-and-file drone pilots strode into battle with ID stencils, not names drawn from the gods of ancient Greece.

The mane of Diana Pantopoulos's suit glimmered like fire in the sunset, two fat, braided ropes of gold-polished cable falling forward to provide her metallic breasts a modicum of modesty, keeping the Artem15 armor from flashing naked breasts on the battlefield. Though the war suit pilot called the metals that made up the armor copper and bronze, they weren't. They were far older materials, crafted by beings whom Hera Olympiad had identified as the gods themselves. The specifics really didn't matter to Diana, because inside the robot walker, she was not just another subject of the New Olympian nation state; she was Artem15, the Artemis of the third millennium.

She swiveled her camera head to the left, spying Are5, with his green copper Mohawk jutting from forehead to the back of his neck, sharp and aggressive as a circular-saw blade. A glance to the right showed Apo110, his burnished yellow locks a more masculine rendition of her own red-gold wig.

The three of them were Hera's representatives of the pantheon known as Strike Force Olympus. The trio towered twice as tall as a man, and they bristled with cannons and wielded massive manipulator claws that could fold into fists easily capable of crushing a boulder. The god-themed robot warriors had their own weapons, based on their larger-than-life inspirations, while the robot drones that they led were styled after helmeted Spartan warriors; one forearm was concealed under a buckler five feet in diameter, while the other arm ended in a spike-knuckled claw that could fold into a two-foot-wide monster fist.

Artem15 looked down into the valley. The commander units and their squadron of Spartan troopers were standing as a copper-colored wall overseeing a writhing mass that she knew could be nothing but the opposition. The dark one, Thanatos, did not possess the industrial means to match the mechanized might that shielded New Olympus, but the Hydrae hordes below, the warriors of Tartarus, had been produced in clone farms. Despite their primitive technology, they still posed a deadly threat to the Greeks who had striven to rise from postapocalyptic barbarism in the shattered island nation. Thanatos's legion of black scale-skinned Hydrae snarled, glaring up as one, creating the image of a thousand-handed, thousand-eyed organism of astonishing size. Artem15 knew that the clone horde did indeed act as if it were under the command of a hive mind. Though armed only with muskets and bayonets, the simplest weapons that Thanatos could produce, they were a fearsome force that threatened to overwhelm the town Strike Force Olympus had sworn to protect.

Artem15's pilot clicked on the loudspeaker built into her head unit. "You have only one chance. Turn back, and you all shall live."

As one, the Hydrae horde surged up the hill, their bare, claw-toed feet digging into the grassy slope. The front line opened up with their muskets, and Artem15's copper-colored breastplate shuddered under a sheet of lead balls. The smooth, polished surface sported dozens of pockmarks, creating a terrain of dimples, dents and craters on the lovingly sculpted torso plate.

Artem15 triggered her shoulder-mounted guns. The built-in weapons were belt-fed blasters that fired cartridge ammunition, faster and more powerful rounds than the musket balls, but required more craftsmanship to make.

The other mechanized units matched her actions except for Are5, who deployed his twin thermal axes. The Mohawked war machine leaped across the gulf of fifty yards between the formation of robots and the churning throng of clones, clawed feet crashing into the writhing enemy force. Are5 would engage in conflict his way, which had carried battles to success on a hundred occasions.

Three thousand pounds of machinery easily crushed a dozen Hydrae under the huge, four-taloned feet. The force of Are5's impact jarred the hillside loose. A small landslide rushed down the slope, tripping up scores more Hydrae as the wave of freed soil cascaded into shins and thighs. While the other war suits relied on their shoulder-mounted machine guns, Are5 preferred a more hands-on approach. His twin double-headed ax blades, heated to five hundred degrees Fahrenheit by internal thermal elements, carved through flesh in wide, sweeping strokes that separated torsos and severed limbs all around him. The axes had been folded and stored in customized forearm housings, and Are5 used the axes to clear a fifteen-foot-wide swath in two body-shredding swings of the robot's long arms. The clone horde had taken the war god avatar's bait and swarmed toward him, rising to the challenge of bayonet versus red-hot ax blade.

Artem15 let her shoulder guns fall silent, drawing one of her javelins. Like the goddess of the hunt she emulated, the war armor she piloted favored the slender, accurate, explosive spears. A powerful throw launched the warhead-tipped javelin at over a thousand feet per second, and though Artem15 could easily and accurately toss the spear two miles, at the spitting-range distance between her and the savage Hydrae, it was like shooting a bullet into an anthill. The custom-tipped spear burst through relatively fragile humanoid forms, tearing them to pieces before the internal fuse was finally armed with the right amount of kinetic energy and impacted on the mass of one reptilian. The deceleration-based fuse enabled the gore-spattered missile to explode and scythe out a deadly storm of shrapnel, clearing out a crowd of mutants who rushed to overtake Are5.

To her left, Apo110 unleashed the heat of the sun itself. Greek fire consumed a flank of irate clones who had swept around in an attempt to outmaneuver the guardian war machines. Powdered, aerosolbased orichalcum reacted on contact with sunlight and flashed brilliantly, long tongues licking through the scale-skinned Hydrae and leaving behind only blackened bones. Robot drone troopers lashed out with spike-adorned, two-foot-wide metal fists even as their shoulder guns blazed incessantly. The Spartan suits featured massive arms able to deliver nearly seventy tons of kinetic force with each punch. Even without the lethal spikes, the massive paws of the clockwork warrior robots would have turned any smaller humanoid into a pulped mass of gore. The spikes were there to keep a glancing punch from merely tossing a stunned opponent to the ground.

"Dammit! Get off!" a Spartan pilot yelled.

Artem15 turned her head and spotted a swarm of scaled flesh piled into a mound twenty feet high. She watched as a clockwork fist burst through the surface before being swallowed again by the writhing melee. She triggered the shoulder weaponry, but for every two she knocked aside, four more rose. The Hydrae were indeed like their namesake Hydra as they swarmed over the cleared body.

"Artie! There's more heading to the town!" another Spartan called. "A second formation is in motion!"

Artem15 whirled away from her beleaguered ally. "Airy, Pollie! Hold the line here! You two, with me!"

Hydraulic leg pistons hurled Diana into the air with enough force to shove her deep into her pilot's couch. The twenty-yard bound took her to the top of the hill. Those same hydraulics compressed on landing, cushioning the impact. The two drone infantry she'd directed to follow her were close on her heels, and together they shoved off down the far slope of the hill, riding their front and hind toes like skis as they utilized gravity and forward momentum to rocket down the hillside. Moving at over one hundred miles per hour, they closed the distance to intercept the maddened clones charging to the town.

The town's militia, armed with pikes and crude muzzle-loaders, were braced for the enemy assault. Artem15 admired the courage of those she was sworn to protect, but she knew that the Hydrae were bred for ruthlessness, great strength and endurance. The picket line of human defenders was outnumbered by the savage attackers whose aplomb for killing made them more than a match for simple citizens defending their homes.

Artem15 opened fire with her shoulder guns, perforating the flank of Hydrae as they bypassed the mechanized hilltop force. Three pairs of machine guns, however, were not enough to counter the Tartarus hordes. Artem15 drew another of her javelins and hurled it into the heart of the group. The detonation of the 70 mm warhead devastated the back half of the column of Hydrae mutants. Bodies stumbled and tripped over downed brethren.

The town's militia opened fire with their own primitive muskets and bolt-action rifles, joining the fight. As the Hydrae at the head of the charging remnants fell with bullets puncturing their organs, the remaining attackers renewed their charge, leaping over black-scaled corpses twisted in the dirt.

The New Olympian pilot reached for another javelin, but the horde was suddenly too close to the skirmish line defending the town. They would be caught in the spear's blast radius. Artem15 leaped, soaring over the space between herself and the Hydrae as the first bayonet sank into a citizen's chest. Anger stirred inside the metal-wrapped warrior's heart. With a feral rage that Are5 would have been proud of, she landed on the necks of a half-dozen clones, her four-toed hydraulic leg squashing them into the soil with the force that only a ton and a half of metal propelled at 150 miles per hour could produce. As she landed, Diana bellowed through her suit's loudspeakers, an inarticulate, amplified war cry that froze a score more of the deadly clones.

Her backup opened fire, slicing through the stunned and distracted Hydrae, ending their vatborn lives in a hail of bullets. Artem15's throat filled with bile, however, as she saw Greek men and women twist and fall alongside the Hydrae.

"Fall back!" Artem15 ordered. "I'll hold the line!"

The horde of attackers twisted, eyeing Artem15 as she drew her javelin from its hip quiver. They lunged forward, snarling, swinging, stabbing their bayonet-tipped muskets, determined to down an elite clockwork warrior. Pike-sharp points penetrated her armor, razor-sharp steel coming far too close to Diana's all too vulnerable human body in the pilot's compartment. She didn't dare sweep the enemy away, not if she wanted to protect the New Olympians who raced back to shelter. Diana had vowed to defend the citizens with her blood.

A clawing bayonet opened a gash on her cheek. Another needled into her thigh. The strength and fury of the Hydrae horde were more than the metal skin of her war suit could fend off.

Artem15 stabbed the earth with her javelin, and the warhead belched out a sheet of flaming death and flying metal. The concussive shock wave and heat were dampened by the cushioned tub of armor that cradled her pilot's seat, and the mobile suit's armor deflected the notched razor wire that had wrapped the explosive core of the javelin's point. Hydrae corpses were hurled off the armored battle suit's massive frame.

Dazed by the nearby detonation, Artem15 looked down to her hydraulic right arm. The metal sleeve that protected the skeleton's carpal manipulators and ulna framework had peeled back like the petals of a steel flower. The clockwork gears and pistons, composed of secondary orichalcum, had withstood the powerful detonation as if it were nothing more than a stiff breeze.

The attacking Hydrae, however, were retreating, fearing another lethal javelin strike.

"Artie!" Are5 called out. "Artie, report!"

She took a tentative step, noting that the right leg's mechanisms had been knocked out of alignment. The metal components of her legs were vulnerable to explosive displacement. She'd need realignment back at the base.

"I'm still standing, Airy. So is the town," she stated. "But it'll take some extra time to walk home."

"Thank Hera," Are5 answered.

Artem15 glared silently at the two backup units as they stood between the fleeing Hydrae and the besieged townspeople. Diana pulled aside her microphone and opened the window on her cockpit. "You two!"

The pair took a step closer and their own cockpit windows opened. They both knew what was coming.

"You fired on your fellow citizens," she hissed.

"They were overwhelmed," one offered. "We couldn't rescue them. They were dead anyway."

"That is *not* your call to make," Diana said. She looked at the tangle of human and mutant bodies. Six Greek men and women lay among the scores of Hydrae mutants. Bite marks and bayonet wounds marred faces and chests, but she also saw the ugly puckers of gunshot wounds on the humans. "They trusted us to die for them. Instead, they died because I was too slow and you were hasty."

The warrior drone heads lowered.

"Remember this in the future," she snarled. She turned away from the drones. "Airy, Pollie, how goes it?"

"The Hydrae are pulling back," Apo110 answered. "They no longer have any stomach for battle."

"Airy?" Diana called.

"Broke one of my axes again," Are5 complained. "But I found something in the mix. You have to come see this."

"Bring it back to base," Artem15 replied. "I'm too slow as it is to make the walk worth it. If it's that important, then we have to show Zoo and Her Highness, as well."

Are5 transmitted his camera image to her screen. "Just look, Artie."

It appeared to be another reptilian variant, similar to the basic Hydrae clone. However, where the scaled hordes of Thanatos were naked, bony-limbed and distorted abominations, this reptilian was tall, strong and of perfect build. He also wore a second skin that conformed to his muscular frame, glinting in the sunlight like metal.

"What the hell is that?" Artem15 asked.

"Beats me, but we're bringing the remains back," Are5 confirmed.

Artem15 turned to glare at her Spartan units. "Go back with the rest of the main force. I've got some thinking to do."

As the war robot limped back to Strike Force Olympus headquarters alone, Diana looked at the stored image of the lifeless, metal-skinned newcomer, trying to cope with the mystery.

IT TOOK AN EXTRA HALF HOUR for Artem15 to return to base. When she arrived, she backed the war suit into its storage berth. Mechanics swarmed around, looking at punctured and blood-caked steel skin.

"Lord, Artie, you fucked this suit up again," Ted "Fast" Euphastus noted. He was the head of maintenance for the magnificent clockwork machines that had been discovered by the goddess-queen of New Olympus.

"Just shut up and fix it," Diana grumbled. "Where's my chair?"

"We're bringing it," Carmine, another repairman, said. He looked at the dented, distorted chest plate. "Damn shame those mutants had to mess up a nice pair of boobs. We'll get right to work on—"

Diana crawled out of her couch, glaring at the metal-breast-obsessed mechanic. Carmine froze as angry blue eyes gleamed from the half-fused mask of a burned, ruined face. "Do whatever the hell you want. Do I really look like I give a damn about a pair of robot tits?"

Carmine shook his head as Diana unplugged the

cybernetic trunk cable from its port at the base of her spine. She swung the metal-capped stumps of her half thighs out and into the seat of her wheelchair. Slender, ropy arms braced themselves on the wheelchair's armrests, and she lowered herself down. Her gymnast-tight arm muscles stood out as they flexed under the weight of her torso and half legs.

"You're bleeding," Fast noted.

Diana looked down at the blood that soaked through the bandage she'd placed on a bayonet injury. "I took care of it while Artie was walking on autopilot."

She peeled off her leather flight helmet and thin, strawlike hair fell in a wet tangle over her eyes. "It's just a scratch, Fast."

Fast's lips quivered with concern, but something drew his attention from the red splotch on her thigh. A silence had fallen over the hangar, and Diana spun her chair to see what was going on.

Hera Olympiad would have been impressive just with her six-foot-tall, voluptuous body and piercing green eyes. However, clad in a shimmering silver skin that conformed to her athletic body, making her appear like a naked silver statue, she truly was unmistakable as the goddess-queen of New Olympus. Only her finely featured face was visible through a window in the otherwise seamless gleaming metal skin. She strode with focus toward Diana in her chair.

"My apologies, Queen," Diana began, dipping her head in a bow to the woman who had come to Greece in search of mythic technology.

Hera had come from a place called Cobaltville, but had chosen to remain in Greece, utilizing the wonders she'd unearthed to become the defender of the inhabitants of the shattered islands. Before Hera's arrival, their problems with barbarian pirate raiders had grown worse with the rise of the Hydrae under the command of a madman named Thanatos. With the discovery of the Hephaestian mobile suits, Hera had single-handedly ensured peace and tranquility under the protection of the New Olympians.

"No, my child," Hera said. She gestured toward the battered frame of Artem15. "Metal can be reforged, but our villages cannot be so readily repopulated. Once more, your heroism honors me, Diana."

Smooth metallic fingertips grazed tenderly down the scar tissue that made up the left side of Diana's young face. The goddess-queen's touch was cool and soothing to her numbed skin.

"Then what, milady?" Diana asked.

"Airy has shown me what he showed you," Hera said. Her emerald eyes shimmered, as if pebbles had been tossed into green ponds. "We are facing a demon from my past. I will brief you all, but the creature you discovered was not born in the vats of Tartarus."

"From where, then, my queen?" Diana asked.

Hera looked out of the slowly closing hangar doors, her silvery skin burning bright in the reflected sunset bleeding over the distant line of hills. "The creature was sent from my old home, Cobaltville. My baron had sent me, seeking an advantage over his fellow barons. Now he no longer needs that advantage."

The hangar doors clamped shut, and Hera's chrome flesh no longer shone bright. The shadows of the hangar were reflected in black hollows and voids on her mirrored skin. It seemed as if a light had been doused.

"The New Olympians must now face a real god, my child," Hera sighed.

Diana followed her queen, forcefully propelling her wheelchair to match the goddess's long strides.

Chapter 2

"Anything…for…you, dear Domi," Mohandas La-kesh Singh mocked himself in a pitched, nasal tone. He would have said it softer, smoother had he not been forced to grunt from the effort it took his 250-year-old body to crawl over the boulder-strewed hillside in the Bitterroot Mountains. Born before the nukecaust in 2001, Lakesh had maintained his life-span initially through cryogenic stasis. The gifts of new, blue eyes and the more important vital organs were due to his involvement in the Totality Concept, a super secret program of scientific research that en-abled the revival of nine godlike beings to dominate the more manageable, surviving human populace.

Lakesh's brilliance made him irreplaceable in constructing the technology behind the matter-transfer system that linked the many redoubts span-ning the apocalypse-ravaged globe. He had been so important that the old barons kept him as young and healthy as their science could allow. Those medi-cal efforts paled in comparison, though, to Sam's nanotechnology. San's mere touch had transferred an armada of microscopic nanites to Lakesh, and the miniature rebuilders had repaired the ravages of age on a molecular level. He currently appeared to be in his mid-to-late-forties.

Lakesh was pushing his physical limits on this odd little hike led by Domi, who moved with pantherlike surefootedness ahead of him. Originally a child of the Outlands, Domi had survived the sexual servitude of Guana Teague in the hellish underworld of Cobaltville known as the Tartarus Pits. Though she was often described as an albino, with porcelain-white skin, hair the color of bone and pink eyes, she was scarcely as frail and as delicate as the albinos that Lakesh had known of in the twentieth century.

Feral, not fragile, was the term most often associated with Domi, from her lapses into simple, broken English when under stress to her fury in battle when defending those she cared for.

When Domi became his devoted lover, Lakesh was at first concerned that he was merely the man she had chosen because the original object of her affection, Grant, had developed a relationship with Shizuka, the leader of the Tigers of Heaven. Lakesh had feared that he was either her rebound from rejection, or just a means to make Grant jealous.

That wasn't the case. Their mutual affection was real and strong. Domi remained fiercely loyal friends with Grant, the man who had stood up for her to the cruel Guana Teague, but Lakesh could see that the love the two felt for each other was not sexual at all. Grant had become the surrogate big brother that Domi had always wanted, and the little albino had filled the same surrogate sibling role for the former Magistrate.

Domi looked back to the exhausted Lakesh. Her face broke into an impish grin. "Need a rest?"

At just a hair over five feet, Domi looked as if she had been carved out of ivory. Her muscles were tight and firm, and if she were older than twenty-five years, her smooth, unlined face and near perfect physical conditioning didn't betray it. She wore cutoff jean shorts and one of Lakesh's khaki safari shirts, which billowed down from her shoulders like a tent. She tied off the tails under her breasts, leaving her washboard stomach exposed. Aside from her scant clothing, she also had a small gun belt with her equally small Detonics Combat Master and a waist-level quiver for the lightweight crossbow slung across her slender shoulders.

"Not at all," Lakesh lied, restraining his desire to gulp down air like a landed fish. "Though, Domi dearest, it would have just been easier to tell me where you like to go hunting."

Domi raised a white-blond eyebrow. She then looked at the small sheath of quarrels bouncing against her upper thigh. "Oh. This."

"I understand the feral needs—" Lakesh began, but before he could finish, she bounded down off the boulder she stood on and planted a kiss on his lips.

"You are smart about a lot of things," she replied. "But my trips aren't just about getting fresh squirrel meat."

Lakesh felt his cheeks redden. "Then what is this about?"

"Some really neat things," Domi answered cryptically. "It's not far now."

Lakesh mopped his brow, then took a swig of water from his canteen. "Mystery soon to be solved."

"Making fun of the way I used to talk?" Domi asked, but her smile and tone belied any challenge in her words.

"No, just out of breath," Lakesh sighed.

She gave him a soft pat on the cheek, then tapped his stomach with the back of her hand. "This is the other reason. You need some exercise."

Lakesh blew out a breath that fluttered through his lips in a rude response to Domi's implication. That only made the albino girl grin even more widely, and she gave his abdomen a playful pinch.

"Come on," Domi said, taking his hand in hers. They moved a little more slowly now, letting Lakesh regain his wind as they followed a narrow trail that wound to the mouth of a cave.

"Welcome to my version of an archive," Domi announced.

Lakesh's eyes tried to adapt to the dimmer illumination inside the cavern when a growl filled the air. The Cerberus scientist whirled at the sound, wishing he'd brought a firearm for himself when a small gray bolt of fur lunged at him.

"Moe! No!" Domi shouted. She intercepted the flying little fur ball inches from Lakesh's face. "Bad Moe! That's the man you're named after. Be nice."

She held up a small creature with the familiar bandit mask of a raccoon in front of Lakesh's face. A pointed, little brown nose wrinkled. "Sniff him. He's friendly. He's *our* friend."

Lakesh's eyes finally adjusted and he could see the little gray-and-black creature, far less menacing in appearance than in growl. Blue eyes met blue eyes as Moe touched noses with Lakesh. A moment later, a tiny pink tongue began lapping at Lakesh's cheeks.

"Hold him for a moment," Domi said, handing the animal off to Lakesh. The raccoon continued to sniff and nuzzle Lakesh as the albino girl walked to where she'd stored a small battery-operated lantern. She clicked it on, and Lakesh looked around the cave, seeing plastic storage shelves and containers, each laden with all forms of odd knickknacks and faded though once garish periodicals and paperbacks. Moe crawled up onto Lakesh's shoulders, but aside from the odd feeling of tiny hands in his graying hair and the softness of fur on the nape of his neck, the little beast hadn't so much as scratched him.

Lakesh's eyes danced across cracked old figurines, time-worn stuffed animals and bald plastic dolls sitting at eye level on several shelves. "This looks like a teenage girl's room."

Domi nodded, as if doing mental math. "Maybe. That's the first stuff I collected. I might have been a teenager back then."

"You come here all the time?" Lakesh asked. His fingertips ran over a plastic crate filled with a mix of ancient comic books and ratty old magazines.

"Sometimes," Domi said. She pulled a black cartoon mouse off one shelf, inspecting it. She pushed the stuffed animal's eye back into its face, kissed its furred forehead and put it back on the shelf.

"A lot of old toys," Lakesh noted. "The things that would be at a garage sale. Old puzzles, picture books, even old LPs and tapes."

Lakesh wiped dust off an album cover, then his eyes widened. "The Blue Oyster Cult? Oh, that takes me way back."

Domi grinned broadly.

"We have a lot of this in the computer archives. You don't need to hunt all this down. Why?" Lakesh asked.

"At first, before I met Grant, I'd always wanted a room of my own. Full of stuff that I owned," Domi explained. She picked up a doll that Lakesh had thought was bald, but it was just white skinned and white haired, dressed in what appeared to be a hand-sewn version of a shadow suit. Lakesh could see where Domi had trimmed its hair, arms and legs in proportion to foot-tall doll representations of Kane, Grant, Brigid Baptiste and even himself. "In the Outlands I didn't own nothing more than the clothes I wore."

"Own anything," Lakesh unconsciously corrected. He walked to the familiar-looking dolls set on a rocky shelf. "What…what are these?"

"My family portrait," Domi said. "The people I love."

Lakesh felt his throat tighten for a moment. Domi was a fiery young woman, quick to anger and voracious as a lover, and Lakesh realized the depth of caring she possessed was evident in the loving detail applied to each of the tiny totems standing together. Each had been carefully sculpted and repainted and painstakingly dressed to be a perfect miniature doppelgänger.

Taking a step back, he felt the corner of a container scratch his calf. Lakesh looked down at the box. In large letters on top of the crate, Read was scrawled in marker. More boxes were beside it, but unmarked, save one with a strip of tape marked To Brigid.

"Those are ones I know she hasn't read yet," Domi said. "She gave me a list. When the box gets full, I bring 'em down for her."

Domi put her miniature self back with the rest of its family. Lakesh saw two versions of himself, the old, withered self before Enlil-as-Sam had bestowed the gift of rejuvenation upon him, and one that more closely matched his appearance now. Lakesh admitted, though, that the hook-nosed little doll seemed to be considerably more handsome than he currently felt.

"Quite a library," Lakesh said, fighting his narcissism over the miniature doppelgänger. "But why not use the archives?"

Domi shrugged. "Those aren't *my* books. This is where I am. This is me and mine here. My people. The things I've learned. The shit I think is cute. And Moe."

Lakesh scratched the butt of the fur ball on his shoulder. "Called Moe because he's so smart?"

Domi's eyes widened, lips parting for a moment as she was caught off guard. "Uh, yeah. Smart. Right."

Lakesh mentally flashed back to all of the times that Domi had sat in his lap, his fingers giving her shoulder a squeeze, or scratching her back. He could easily imagine the situation reversed for Domi and the raccoon, the young albino sitting on the floor of the cavern, Moe curled in her lap as her fingertips absently scratched its back, mirroring her pose whenever Lakesh read to her, teaching her how to read. Domi winced as she noted the mental gears turning in her lover's eyes as he figured out the equation.

Lakesh leaned in close to Domi and kissed her tenderly. He never had felt more in love with the feral creature who had grown so much since he'd first met her. "You are truly the sweetest, best thing ever to come into my life, precious Domi."

Her cheeks turned almost cartoonishly bright red at the statement.

With an inevitability that both Lakesh and Domi had grown used to, their Commtacts—subdermal transmitters that had been surgically embedded into their mastoid bones—buzzed to life.

The familiar twang of Bry sounded in their ears. "Lakesh, Domi, where are you?"

With a resigned sigh, Lakesh answered, the vibrations of his speech carrying along his jawbone to be transformed into an outgoing signal by the cybernetic implant. "We're about two hours' hike from the redoubt."

"Two hours at your speed? Or Domi's?" the sarcastic technical wizard asked.

Lakesh rolled his eyes, eliciting a smirk from his companion and a chittering chuckle from Moe the raccoon. "What's wrong, Bry?"

"I picked up something on satellite imagery from over the Mediterranean. The remains of Greece to be exact," Bry responded. "Atmospheric disturbance indicative of—"

"Annunaki dropships," Lakesh finished, worry tingeing his words. His mood soured instantly, and even resting his arm across Domi's suddenly taut shoulders did little to help him. He looked down to the girl who was listening in on her own Commtact.

"Send out a Sandcat to meet us at Road 6," Domi

interjected. "Marker 12. We'll be down there in fifteen minutes."

Seemingly recognizing the urgency in his mistress's voice, Moe bounded off of Lakesh's shoulder. Domi gave the raccoon a loving hug and a kiss on the end of its pointed nose. "Be good, Moe."

The raccoon chittered a response, then darted out of the cave.

Regretting the hike's abrupt end, Lakesh followed Domi out of her personal archive and down the rocky slope of the hill.

KANE STOOD, a silent sentinel at the Cerberus Redoubt's entrance as the Sandcat rolled up. His cold blue eyes regarded the modified armored personnel carrier as it slowed to a halt, its side door swinging open to allow Lakesh and Domi out. The six-foot-tall former Magistrate was always an imposing figure, but the dour expression darkening his features gave Lakesh a momentary pause.

"They're still alive," he pronounced grimly.

"Perhaps," Lakesh replied. "Just because Bry saw evidence of a dropship means nothing. Someone else might have come into possession of one of their craft. It could have been uncovered by the Millennial Consortium, or Erica could have traded for one before *Tiamat's* destruction."

Kane's eye flickered momentarily at the scientist's suggestions, but he didn't relax. "Thanks for trying, Lakesh."

Lakesh tilted his head in an unspoken questioning.

"Trying to make it seem less than it could be," Kane muttered. He escorted Lakesh and Domi along the corridor toward the ops center. "But my job is to look for the worst-case scenario. Let's simply assume that one of those snake-faced bastards survived *Tiamat,* and he's making some moves."

"It's your job to be prepared for the worst. It's my job to look at all possibilities equally," Lakesh replied, trying to keep up with Kane's long strides, spurred on by his tension. "Both are important, and let us do what we do best. This is part of the synergy that has kept us going all this time."

Kane nodded grimly, slowing to accommodate his two companions, realizing the effort Lakesh expended to maintain his pace. "The only synergy I want is the blending of a bullet and an Annunaki face. I'd thought that we were done with the fucking overlords."

"The only one who died for certain was Lilitu," Lakesh said. "With our rogue's gallery, unless you see the corpse, they truly cannot be discounted. And even then, some whose corpses we've beheld as forever stilled…Colonel Thrush, Enlil, Sindri…"

"Sindri was just beamed into a storage pattern, no corpse to 'behold,' as you put it," Kane corrected, his voice taking on a derisive tone that usually accompanied any mention of the miniature transadapt genius. While Kane reserved a murderous rage for the overlords, the wolf-lean warrior harbored a deep-down annoyance for Sindri.

The three people entered the redoubt's ops center, where Bry, Brigid Baptiste, Grant and Brewster Philboyd were waiting. Bry and Brigid were at one of the computer workstations. Philboyd and Grant were sitting at a desk, throwing cards down in a quick game of War. With Kane's entry, Grant seemed relieved, obviously tired of the card game.

"Glad you finally showed up," Grant grumbled. While Kane was an imposing figure, Grant was truly menacing. Taller than Kane, with a thick, powerful build, Grant was also a former Magistrate. Not only was the ex-mag one of the finest combatants Lakesh had ever observed, but also his massive strength was coupled with an uncanny skill at piloting nearly any craft, air, land and sea.

"Not again," Kane replied, looking over to Philboyd.

"Grant, the game's called War. Do you fight fair?" Philboyd asked.

"It's a card game. You're not supposed to cheat," Grant replied. "What's the fun in that?"

"Now, this is hypothetical because I am not a cheater—" Philboyd began.

"Yes, you are," Grant interjected.

"Let us know when you two are finished," Brigid spoke up, a chilly disdain for Grant and Philboyd's minor quarrel weighing on her words.

"Busted," Kane said with a grin. He leaned in

conspiratorially to his friend. "Besides, who else are you going to play cards with?"

"I dunno. I was thinking my partner," Grant retorted.

"Maybe if I catch amnesia and forget how much of a hustler you are," Kane said. He looked at the monitor where Bry and Brigid were busy. "That's the contrail from the dropship."

Brigid adjusted her spectacles on her nose. Years of constant reading as an archivist had left her vulnerable to eyestrain when going over fine imagery and small print. "We can't tell who was piloting the dropship. It could be anyone who gained access to one of them. We spotted the transsonic atmospheric distortions in the island chain that used to be Greece."

Lakesh frowned. "It has to be something important for the surviving overlords to risk exposure. As far as we knew, when *Tiamat* was destroyed, they all died."

"Hard to believe that something as old and big as *Tiamat* could die," Grant grumbled. "The big bitch might be down, but I don't think it's forever."

"By the time she recovers from her injuries, we'll hopefully be long dead," Lakesh noted, referring to the living megalithic ship on which the Annunaki had ridden to Earth. "Preferably of old age."

Brigid let loose a cleansing breath, pushing away the horrifying thought of *Tiamat*, the miles-long living chariot of the gods, reawakened to spread more destruction. The starship had more than enough power to scour all life from the surface of the planet. Its crippled and comatose state had accounted for lessened stress in her life, though the thought of an active Annunaki overlord was hardly reassuring. "Right now we are looking at some footage recorded from a recent conflict in that region."

Bry's fingers danced over the keyboard, and a bird's-eye view flashed on the monitor. "The footage is about twenty minutes old, and we only caught the tail end of things."

The monitor's image sharpened until Kane and Lakesh could see the presence of massive sets of coppery metallic heads and shoulders, like living statues, leaving behind a morass of green-and-black corpses.

"I've double-checked the math, and the dead creatures are about a shade over five feet tall, and they are identical, at this magnification at least," Bry explained. "They resemble the humanoid reptilian mutants that used to roam across the remnants of the United States."

"Scalies," Lakesh mused. "But they were exterminated by a concentrated pogrom."

"Here on the North American continent, but you have to remember that these mutants could be artificially created," Brigid said.

"If they're about five feet tall, then how big are those constructs walking away?" Lakesh asked.

"Approximately twelve to fifteen feet, and almost half as wide," Bry stated. "What did you call them, Brigid?"

"Mecha," the archivist said. "A generic term for robotic combat vehicles."

"Giant robots," Lakesh murmured. "Larger than the ones we encountered in China. And heavily armed by the looks of them."

"Close-ups of the shoulders correlate with late-twentieth-century machine-gun designs. Belt-fed rifle caliber," Bry noted. "Grant recognized them, and utilizing the known dimensions of the weaponry, calculating the rest of the robot's size was easy."

Grant smirked as he shuffled his deck of cards absently. "Brigid wants to go meet with the group that owns the robots. They seem fairly decent, according to this footage."

"Decent?" Lakesh asked. "That's a refreshing change. How did you determine that?"

"We caught a flash of an explosion while scanning the area. On image enhancement we saw that a trio of robots was assisting a line of local villagers against the mutants," Brigid said.

Bry cued up the footage and Lakesh watched the battle from above. He was surprised to see one of the mecha detonate an explosion at its own feet to stanch the tide of attackers. He was even more dazzled when the chest plate of the robot swung open. He couldn't see inside the torso of the robot, but apparently there was someone inside.

"It looks like one robot is talking to the others about the friendly-fire incident at the start of the recording," Kane noted.

"So they're piloted craft," Lakesh mused. "And they have rules of engagement to protect outlying communities."

"You noticed the lack of industrial capability in the town, as well," Brigid said.

"If they only have bolt-action rifles and pitchforks to deal with a mutant horde, I doubt that those people have a garage to tighten the nuts on a battle robot," Kane interjected.

"Precisely. Indeed, there aren't even any vehicles on the premises," Lakesh added.

"I am fairly curious," Brigid answered. "But Bry and I have been running comparisons between the one prone mecha being dragged back to base. Any pilot taller than five feet would be cramped inside even the most generous of compartments for the robots. Domi is well over the limit for riding in the chest, let alone operating the device."

Domi tilted her head. "Maybe Sindri's people?"

"The transadapts," Kane agreed. "The tallest of them were just over four feet. And if you have a lab that can breed scalies, you can whip up a batch of transadapts, as well."

"Trouble is, those strange little monkey men would be in conflict from the critters from the selfsame lab. And the transadapts we've encountered are hardly friendly and generous toward humans," Grant said.

"You're also talking about an abandoned people who had been slaves," Brigid countered. "Not being oppressed and forced into submission to humans would have a good effect on them."

"Rottenness isn't a matter of genes," Domi murmured. "Remember Quavell?"

The meeting room grew quiet as each of the Cerberus staff present remembered the Quad-Vee hybrid who had taken refuge along with them for several months while she was pregnant. The Cerberus explorers had initially believed that the infant had been sired by Kane when he had been captured and pressed into stud service to revitalize the frail, genetically stagnant hybrids. When it turned out that another had fathered the child, Kane and his allies continued to protect Quavell and her baby. Quavell died, however, due to complications of childbirth brought on by the genetic transformation from the slender, delicate hybrids to the larger, more powerful Nephilim, the servants of the Annunaki overlords who had also been awakened by *Tiamat's* signal. Especially present in the minds of those around Domi was the albino girl's shift from hatred and loathing of the panterrestrial humanoids to love and compassion for the hybrid woman.

It was a reminder that though they all had become open-minded, the nature of humanity was to harbor prejudices, something made very apparent by their encounters with the Quad-Vees and the transadapts.

"What's powering the robots?" Domi asked. "Doesn't look like it smokes like a Sandcat."

Brigid looked back to the screen, and Bry, on cue, called up the image of the downed robot. "Kane, you remember the Atlantean outpost that Quayle had discovered?"

Kane nodded. "Yeah. You missed out on that. I'm sure you would have loved the place. All kinds of wall carvings, and a metal called orichalcum that blew up when sunlight touched it. Took out the whole joint."

Brigid leaned past Bry and tapped a few keys, drawing up a subscreen. "Greek philosophers like Plato discussed Atlantis at length. One of the things mentioned was the legendary gold-copper alloy that was the hallmark of Atlantean society. Seeing it as a staple of decorations and animatronic statues in city plazas seems at odds with the unstable explosive compound you described."

"Fand told me what the stuff was called," Kane responded. "Besides, the outpost was a couple thousand years old and under the ocean. Who can say that the seawater exposure didn't rust it or cause some kind of other imbalance, like dynamite left sitting too long? Maybe kept away from rust-inducing salty humidity, it's great."

Brigid shrugged. "You stated that it was stored in a vault, under excellent storage conditions. However, it could be akin to a high-energy metal like uranium. I wish you'd brought back a sample."

Kane sneered. "Quayle kept me kind of busy for that. Plus, that whole sunlight-making-it-go-off-like-a-grenade thing dissuaded me."

Brigid locked eyes with Kane for a moment. Though the two shared an enormous affection for each other, it was commonplace for them to push each other's buttons even in the most casual of conversations. "In its stable format, orichalcum could easily prove to be a reliable power source. Given Grecian familiarity with Atlantean mythology, it's quite possible that these robots may be artifacts from an outpost placed in Greece. Or it could be a component of a highly durable alloy."

"Given the artifacts we've found around the world, it's very possible that Atlantis itself was the beneficiary of Annunaki and Tuatha de Danaan technology," Lakesh added. "The orichalcum that Kane discovered could be a manufactured element, along the lines of plutonium. But the most important thing is that they have apparently mastered a lost form of technology. We had a glimpse of it in Wei Qiang's at the Tomb of the Three Sovereigns."

"Those suckers were strong, but still only man-size. Basically, semi-intelligent muscle. Double their size and give them a thinking person at the controls, you've got some considerable power on your side." Grant nodded, for emphasis, at the image on the monitor of lifeless, scaled mutants and their shattered muskets being shoveled into a mass grave. "I wondered how those robots did what they did, I mean programming wise. They reacted to our actions with some reasonable responses."

"Ancient forms of computers have been discovered. The most prominent of these is the Antikyteria Mechanism," Philboyd answered. "The Antikyteria was an analog gear-style computer that was capable of charting star patterns. It's a fairly simple looking design and more minute versions of that gear, working in concert, could form a non-circuit-board style computer."

"Didn't Archytas also mention that he possessed an automated, steam-powered, wooden robot pigeon?" Lakesh asked.

"Around 200 B.C.," Brigid confirmed. One of the former archivist's strongest interests was research into out-of-place artifacts, examples of modern technology originating in historical eras. Philboyd seemed slightly put out that she fielded the question regarding robotics, but was used to her need to provide an explanation. "It was capable of flight, if I recall correctly."

"So they could have airborne mecha," Kane said grimly.

"Potentially," Brigid said. "But I'd presume that it would simply be more efficient to hang one off the bottom of a Deathbird. I'd consider a Manta, but the damaged armor appears ill suited for orbital use."

Grant took a deep breath. "Fifteen feet tall. Plenty big, but not as big as some of the monstrosities in myths."

"Like Talos or the Colossus of Rhodes," Brigid mentioned.

"How big would those be?" Domi asked.

"Descriptions are inconsistent," Brigid explained. "And they could have been highly embellished as mythology advanced. Talos could reasonably have been about forty to sixty feet tall, and the colossus about twice that."

Domi looked back to the robot lying on its back. "Well, it's nice to know that we have friendly folks in control of that technology. I can see why we'd want to hook up with them right away."

Philboyd nodded. "The Greek robot pilots can fight, and they have an advanced form of technology. It'd be like the Tigers of Heaven had our Mantas from the start."

"And if the snake-faces are back and in action," Grant began, "we can use that kind of fighting power."

"Which explains the presence of a dropship in the region," Kane grumbled. "The Greeks represent a possible enemy, and the overlords don't want to have to deal with them."

"You're right. We'd better assemble an away team to meet them," Lakesh urged. "Especially if they can be potential allies."

"With a heads-up, we could make invaluable friends," Brigid noted. "What could go wrong?"

Philboyd paled, remembering the conflict with Maccan, a Tuatha prince, that had been sparked when the Outlanders visited the Manitius Moon-base for the first time. Grant and Kane looked at each other silently.

"Suit up," the two partners said in harmony.

"I'm coming, too," Domi added.

"We might need backup from CAT Beta," Kane said.

"Then I'll be on scene. If necessary, the rest of my team will pop in," Domi said. "One of the ex-mags can substitute for me."

Brigid Baptiste sighed. In asking the rhetorical question, she'd thrown out temptation for fate. She groaned softly. "Time to break out the battle bra again."

Chapter 3

Diana was just another wheelchair jockey in the meeting hall, sitting with the rest of the pantheon of hero-suit drivers. Zoo, Airy, Pollie and the rest were arranged around a bisected corpse illuminated by a searing white cone of light. The separated torso had been seared. Cauterized wounds from Airy's thermal ax had sealed in the dead thing's juices behind walls of charred flesh. The face had been cleaned up, and it was at once handsome and intimidating. Though finely sculpted, the face's beauty was sheathed in fine-scaled, lizardlike armor. Diana tried to shake off her imaginings of this creature's angelic magnetism, even in its sleep of oblivion.

She had to remind herself that this being had been fighting alongside the Tartarus mutants, joining them in a raid on a New Olympian settlement. The mutants were mass murderers, bred for attacking and exterminating humans. The wake of death and terror that Thanatos's minions had left was something that Diana would never forget. She reminded herself of the scaled thugs' horrific actions every time she touched her fused, fire-scarred cheek or forehead. The handsome snakelike humanoids that were related to the lifeless thing under the blazing light were allied with the monsters that inspired Diana to sacrifice her remaining leg so that she could fit into the cockpit of a hero suit.

The orichalcum-framed battle suits had been designed around slighter, smaller creatures. As such, even a small woman like Diana had been before the Tartarus raids had scarred and mutilated her, was too large for the cockpit. The metal caps on her thigh stumps and the cybernetic port adjacent to her lower spine were less a reminder of her wounds than they were badges of her empowerment. Her half-destroyed face was a brand of the evil that rose from the Tartarus vats.

No matter how beautiful the stranger was, the ugliness of his allegiance was unmistakable.

ZOOs, the chief of the pantheon, looked at her. His furry features made his nickname of Zoo all too appropriate. "Recognize what the creature is wearing, or are you still caught up looking into his eyes?"

Diana bit back a response as she examined the burnished metal sheathing the corpse's limbs and torso. "Secondary orichalcum. The color is a bit off, but he's clothed in it."

"It's more than just that," Zoo, the Zeus of the New Olympians, noted. "It's woven, nearly cloth-like, and far more flexible than anything we've ever seen except in one instance."

Diana's mind flashed to Hera's skintight armor.

"Airy's ax carved through it, but we're talking about a blade swung by a one-and-a-half-ton war machine. You can see the discoloration there and there where our small arms struck it. Bullets penetrated its limbs on only straight hits. Anything less turned into a glancing blow."

Hera looked at the bisected stranger, her silvery fingertips touching as her mind seemed to be caught in a storm. She rapped her metal-clad knuckle on the inert body's thigh. "Someone not only knows how to mass-produce secondary orichalcum, but has enough to give it out like clothing."

"How'd he get in that?" Ari "Airy" Marschene, the pilot of Are5, asked. "It's not like that getup's got a zipper."

"In a way, there is," Hera noted. She rolled the top of the torso over, revealing a knot-shaped mechanism high between the strange visitor's shoulder blades. None of the eleven pilots of the pantheon needed to be reminded of the similarity between the device and the one that enabled their goddess-queen to enjoy the protection of impenetrable silver-and-gold skin. The same knotted base for ropes of molded smart armor was a cybernetic port that Hera had been able to reverse engineer in order to allow the pilots to control their robotic war suits. Hera fiddled with the device until ribbons of metal retracted, folding back into a capsule around the cybernetic hub. The metal had only peeled away from the torso and arms, the lower part of the corpse still clad in its glimmering armor.

Zoo wheeled over as Hera pried the mechanism from the back of the corpse. "An almost exact match."

Zoo's burly arm reached out and picked up the severed forelimb, still wearing its glove of secondary orichalcum armor. Around the wrist of the grisly trophy, three tendrils of mechanical cable ended in snakelike heads. "Though apparently it still maintains its shape without the proper command impulse."

"Careful with that," Ari said. "When I went after him, he fired a burst of energy from the device still on his wrist. It had enough power to smash one of my axes. It was like nothing I'd ever seen. It's a lot more focused than Pollie's Greek fire sprayers."

Hera plucked the blaster-equipped wrist from Zoo's grasp. She seemed to be weighing it against the cyber-module in her other hand.

"So what is all of this?" Diana asked. "What has you so nervous?"

Hera looked balefully toward Diana. "I want this technology. I want all of this. If we had a hold of this kind of weaponry, we could drive Thanatos and his mutants into the ocean. If these become common among the spawn of Tartarus, we'll be swept from the Earth."

"Give me a half-dozen Spartans, and I'll run a reconnaissance," Diana answered. "A quick raid, and we'll see if this was the only one, or if there are more."

Hera shook her head. "No."

"But—" Diana began in protest.

"Do not make me repeat myself, girl," Hera snapped.

The wheelchair-bound pilots all fell silent. They had never seen their goddess-queen this agitated in the years that they had known her. Most of all, they had never imagined that Hera would have growled a threat at any of them, let alone Diana, the girl who was Hera's surrogate daughter. The menace hanging in the air, however, was unmistakable.

"Zoo, come on," Hera barked, urgency speeding the words from her lips. "I'm taking this back to my lab."

The queen and her amputee consort left the conference room without another word.

Diana watched silently, feeling a knot of nausea forming just under her sternum. The goddess who had raised her up from a useless cripple had delivered her a rebuke before her peers. After all she had done for the pantheon, earning herself a role as named pilot of a hero suit with blood and sacrifice, Diana stung as she was discarded, tossed aside like a petulant child. Ari wheeled over to her.

"Di, baby…" Ari began, affection purring under his words as his deep brown eyes studied her fused mask of a half face.

"Just leave me alone," Diana answered curtly. "I'm too old to need sitting."

Ari swallowed, regretting his choice of words. The high-tech war-avatar pilot made no secret of his love for the straw-haired girl who commanded the robotic huntress. He also was very clear and careful to always treat her with respect, even though Diana had cut herself off from interpersonal ties, feeling herself unworthy of romance. He reached out to take her delicate fingers in his grasp. "Di, something is worrying Hera. Otherwise, she wouldn't be so on edge. I mean, there's a fucking alien lying on the table, and he had a laser gun and bulletproof armor. Look at it."

"I have been," Diana answered. "It's almost human, though. An alien should be…alien, shouldn't it?"

Ari glanced at the angelic reptilian once more.

"Think about it," Diana continued. "Two eyes. Two ears, vestigial as they are. Nose. Mouth. Arms. Legs. This could be something out of those cheesy old vids about the starship, where they distinguished aliens with bumps on their forehead or just some rubbery makeup."

"This is a lot more convincing than latex," Ari said. "It looks like the big brother of the Hydrae horde. The one that got all the good genes, while the others are just crappy copies."

"That's why Hera's so scared?" Pollie interjected. He'd remained taciturn as his two friends,

Ari and Diana, spoke. "Think this critter is the one who supplied the template for Thanatos's clones?"

"It's possible," Diana murmured. Her friends could tell that she was in retreat, curling back into her shell. All she could think about was Hera's bitter rebuke.

Diana wheeled her chair back to her quarters, alone. Hauling herself into her bunk, she finally allowed herself to give way to the sting of tears.

THE INTERPHASER'S HUM FADED in Kane's ears, and mistlike energy plasma dissipated around him. His keen pointman's instincts kicked in, sweeping the area where they'd emerged. The interphaser's design was a godsend after years of employing conventional mat-trans units. The psychic and physical trauma that accompanied traditional gateway jumps was greatly minimized if they used the interphaser instead. The interphaser exploited naturally occurring vortices that were spread around the globe and even on other planets. The energy points had been mapped by the Parallax Points Program, which they had discovered on Thunder Isle and the input into the interphaser.

The sky blazed a burned orange marking the sunset, and the mountaintop ruin was silent, save for the baleful calls of terns that hovered on thermals watching the strange appearance of Kane and his companions. Kane could smell the brine of the ocean—the Aegean, he'd learned from Brigid.

He set down his war bag and jogged to the edge of the weathered and cracked stone floor. Behind him, Brigid, Grant and Domi set about stowing their own equipment bags. Grant made certain to secure his huge rifle case. The container was taller than Domi was, but there was a crack in the stone floor large enough to secure it. Brigid and Domi elected to leave behind their Copperhead submachine guns and the bandoliers of grenades in their war bags. Kane and Grant opted to keep their Copperheads with them. The four Cerberus exiles were on a first-contact mission, and the two men would be out of place without something heavier than Sin Eaters in their forearm holsters. However, if all four showed up packing enough guns to fight a war, it would send the wrong message.

Kane and the others had been around enough to balance shows of strength with diplomacy. Grenades and Grant's monster Barrett rifle were stashed away for contingency in the event of betrayal and disarmament. The extra weaponry disappeared under a camouflaging tarpaulin that Grant covered with dirt.

Kane pulled a pair of compact field glasses from a pouch on his equipment belt slung over his shadow suit. The high-tech polymers of the uniform conformed to his powerful muscles, providing nearly complete environmental protection from all but the most inhospitable climates. While not able to withstand rifle rounds like his old Magistrate polycarbonate armor, the shadow suit still offered minor protection against small arms and knives. In return, the new suits granted greater ease of movement and offered protection against radiation and temperature fluctuations. Kane also noticed that the shadow suits were far less intimidating than the ominous black carapaces of their mag battle armor.

"No movement," Kane announced. He turned to see Brigid Baptiste tracing her fingers over the surface of a weather-beaten column. "Any ideas what this was?"

"Considering that many of the vortices were recognized by ancient peoples as places of power, aided by the influence of the First Folk, this could have been an oracle. This isn't Delphi, but it has a similar layout," Brigid answered. "Sadly, nothing of archaeological significance remains."

"So you won't be distracted by shards of pottery," Kane returned with a wink and a smile.

Brigid shook her head. "No. The only thing that could be found here would be in the form of resonant psychic energy."

Kane raised an eyebrow. "Oh, right. Because the oracles were manned by ancient psi-muties. The nodes' energy would increase their perceptions."

"That's a very good theory," Brigid congratulated. "You've been doing some reading?"

Kane shrugged. "Continuing education. With all the crap we've encountered, and all the telepathic trespassing that's gone on in my head, it helps to be prepared. Granted, I'm going off of digital copies of the *Fortean Times* in the redoubt's library."

Brigid smiled. "I remember when you asked for that archive disk. I thought it was just to get more information on Atlantis."

"That's where it started," Kane admitted. "A lot of the theories in those old rags sounded crazy. But after slugging it out with Quayle in the outpost, I had a feeling we'd eventually run across Atlantis itself. Along the way, other articles caught my eye, mainly from personal experience."

"We know for a fact that the Annunaki took the roles of the Sumerian and Greek gods, among other identities," Brigid noted. "With that knowledge, some of von Danniken's alien-god theories come off much more plausibly…if you're willing to ignore the obvious sloppy interpretation of an Aztec sacrifice's guts being mistaken for the tube hookups on an ancient space suit."

Kane shrugged. "Lazy speculators, or just plain gullible nuts."

He sighed, getting back to the business at hand. "We seem to be on a peninsula. There's a land bridge leading down from that cliff. So far, I don't see any movement that would indicate the locals are aware of our presence."

"Thank heaven for small favors," Brigid replied.

Kane continued to scan the countryside when suddenly a column of blue-white electrical fire speared down into the land, creating huge clouds of debris and smoke from the earth. He recoiled from the power and the violence. At first, he thought it was a lightning bolt, but the searing slash of energy was too focused, too intense and lasted far too long to be a simple work of nature. Flames licked up from charred ground, and sprawled in the scarred landscape, burned corpses steamed. The dying sunset had been blotted out, overwhelmed by the brilliance of the sky fire. Cries of fear and suffering echoed in his ears, and he could smell the sickly scent of roasting human flesh.

Despair surged through him when he realized that he had been grasped firmly by Grant. Kane blinked away the flashes, and the sights, sounds and smells faded.

"Kane?" Grant asked, as if he were repeating himself. The big ex-Magistrate's Sin Eater retracted back into its powered forearm holster, though Grant appeared confused at what had caused Kane to stagger and reel.

"No, of course you wouldn't have seen that," Kane muttered. "It wasn't real."

"See what?" Domi replied. She still hadn't put her handgun away. "You froze for a moment, then started backing away from the edge."

Kane looked around the ruins. "The oracle helped me experience a psi-mutie vision."

"What did you see?" Brigid asked.

"Lightning," Kane said. "But it wasn't natural lightning. It was a weapon, and it tore the ground apart. And it was focused. It left swaths of charred corpses in its wake."

"Zeus, the king of the Olympian gods, had a quiver of thunderbolts forged for him by Hephaestus. Zeus's thunderbolts were so powerful, they could destroy even the greatest monsters in the land," Brigid said. "That myth could have its basis in an Annunaki weapon."

Domi's nose wrinkled. "This shit's getting weird."

"You asked to come along," Grant chided. He glanced back at their hidden stash of weapons. "Monsters, other gods, cities, too, right?"

Brigid nodded. "Zeus obliterated anyone with his thunderbolts."

"So nothing in our bags is ever going to match that kind of firepower," Grant announced. "Let's just head down the bridge and meet the locals before Zeus drops the sky on us."

Kane nodded in agreement, finally past the harrowing realism of his momentary psychic flash. "Good plan."

The arcs of future lightning were still harshly inscribed on his mind's eye, an ominous premonition of hell peeling back the sky and incinerating the earth below. He couldn't dismiss his dread, and so he threw himself into his work. Maybe knowing the potential tragedy looming in the future gave Kane the power to prevent it.

It was as good a coping mechanism as any.

THE FURTHER THEY GOT from the oracle, across the ramp of stone and packed earth sloping down from the ancient temple's remains, Kane's senses grew clearer, returning to normal. As his senses sharpened, he realized that they were not alone. He shot a glance toward Domi, knowing that her own feral instincts were also preternaturally sharp. She was on edge.

Grant picked up on his two allies' silent, brief exchange. "Where?"

"Feels like we're surrounded, on at least two flanks," Kane explained.

Grant nodded. The hilly, rolling terrain was covered with sparse scrub, making it difficult for anyone to hide any closer than the hillcrests that bracketed them. Only the tops of the ridges provided sufficient concealment, as well as a good commanding view of the rut they passed through. Even with the deepening shadow of evening, their stalkers would be behind the ridges. The massive ex-Magistrate flipped down the faceplate on his black polycarbonate helmet, and vision-enhancing optics were engaged. While the shadow suits and mandibular implants had superseded most of Grant's old armor's protection and communication functions, the image-intensifying and night-vision capabilities of the black helmets were too valuable to surrender. The Mag helmet was also one of the few pieces of equipment that Grant was able to perform repairs on without compromising the fit of the Magistrate armor piece.

A heat source flared on a ridge, a head poking over the hilltop. Grant locked on to it, but the figure disappeared quickly. Still, he had enough for cursory identification. "Humanoid. Scrawny, hairless and naked according to the signature. Mammalian core heat."

"Naked?" Kane asked. "Then it's not the robots laying out this welcome mat."

"More like the mutants we saw on satellite view," Brigid said. "Strange that they have reptilian skin, but mammalian endothermic metabolisms."

"Strongbow's old crew were scaly faced, as well," Grant said. "Though they had remnants of facial hair."

"Makes you wonder about the so-called scalies often referenced in the *Wyeth Codex*," Brigid said.

"Less ancient history, more current events," Kane grumbled. His own faceplate was down, his pointman's instinct working together with the advanced electronics of the Magistrate helmet.

"There is some historical relevance. Zeus's greatest enemy was the monster Tiamat, mother of a million tormenting beasts," Brigid noted.

"*Tiamat* is dead," Kane said coldly.

"Our *Tiamat*," Brigid responded. "But look at places like the Archuleta Mesa, or the attempted use of Area 51 to produce Quad Vee hybrids. Two locations that had the technological potential to create biological constructs. It stands to reason that if Greece is a location for Annunaki-designed robots, there might also be the technology for creating monsters. Literally the womb of Tiamat. The First Folk are a prime example of Annunaki genetic tampering."

Kane's brow furrowed under the polycarbonate visor. "So whoever played Zeus the first time, long ago, made his own rogue's gallery?"

Brigid shrugged. "The towns in these islands are heavily fortified. That bespeaks an ever present, hostile enemy in herdlike numbers. Especially considering the corpses shoved into the mass grave and the amount of damage those poorly armed humanoids were able to inflict on a single robot, we must be dealing with some sort of cloning facility."

Kane hadn't slowed his pace, and he could hear Brigid panting as she tried to keep up while applying her intellect to the problem at hand. "So they'd be akin to the mutant herds that roamed the American wasteland after the war. Bred specifically to be alien, of animalistic intelligence and a hostility toward nonaltered humans, they would be a perfect means of keeping the surviving population in check until the Program of Unification."

"Can you think of a better way to isolate communities?" Grant asked.

The two ex-Mags scanned the hilltops with their light-amplification lenses. The ground was cast in an eerie green haze by the helmet units. Though

Domi and Brigid didn't have the high-tech head-gear, Domi's sensitive albino eyes were accustomed to the darkness, and Brigid was wearing a light-weight Moonbase visor. Brigid's eyewear was slightly bulkier than a pair of sunglasses, but the lenses were polarized to allow protection against intense light sources as well as having a built-in LED UV illuminator and lenses that filtered the tiny lamp into the visible spectrum, as well as amplifying ambient light. Still, the tall archivist envied the telescopic targeting option on Kane's and Grant's Mag helmets.

"So far, it looks like we have only one shadow," Grant said.

"It feels like more," Kane countered. He looked to Domi. She nodded, then strode off quietly.

"Be careful, girl," Grant whispered over his Commtact. The admonition brought a smile to the albino's face, a moment of cherubic warmth before her porcelain features hardened into a grim battle mask.

"You know they're going to wonder where she went," Brigid warned.

"Good," Kane replied. "That will force them to divide their focus. I'm going up ahead to further disperse them. Stay close to Grant."

Brigid looked as if she was going to protest, but held her tongue. There were times when the four Outlanders operated as a democracy, applying individual skills and expertise to solving their mutual dilemmas. On the other hand, when being hunted by an unknown number of enemies in the countryside of a far-flung, shattered nation, Brigid would defer to Kane's warrior knowledge and hard-contact experience. His combat abilities and finely honed instincts provided him with almost instantaneous strategies that would allow the explorers to remain safe and secure from hostile foes without dithering or debate.

Brigid was also irritated by the implication that she was a less capable combatant than the highly trained former Magistrates and the feral albino girl. Compared to most of the rest of the world, she was a formidable survivor of globe-spanning conflicts. But she realized that though she could handle herself in a dangerous situation, when surrounded by a small horde of snarling mutants, reason dictated that the lifetimes of combat endured by Kane, Grant and Domi gave them an edge. Kane's warning to stay near the towering Grant was not an insult, just common sense. A lightning-quick assessment also provided her with the insight that she and Grant would form the hinge of the two-flanked counterattack by Kane and Domi. Grant needed Brigid's backup as much as she needed him.

Grant simply nodded at his partner, and Kane advanced fifty yards ahead of the pair.

Kane wasn't certain if the mysterious stalkers had access to the same optic technology that he and his allies possessed, but he doubted it. The massive warbots would be more likely to possess advanced cameras, but their stealth would be negligible compared to the scrawny mutants that Grant had spotted. From the satellite pictures, they seemed to be more proficient at using their muskets and bayonets as spears rather than rifles, which meant the complexities of electronically enhanced vision would be beyond their limited mental scope. However, if the mutants had sharp, animalistic senses, Domi's transformation to shadowy midnight wraith would be insufficient camouflage. Even with her shadow suit already blended to the darkened terrain by fiber-optic technology and the addition of a blackened head rag covering her bone-white hair and a scarf wrapped around her nose and jaw, the acute night vision of predatory animals would allow her to be spotted easily. Kane recalled, however, that most reptilian hunters didn't rely on vision when they stalked at night.

The girl would stand a chance, and even if the hunters did come at her, she'd hold them off long enough for Kane and Grant to even up the odds.

This far from the oracle's influence, and minutes separating him from his jolting psychic flash, Kane trusted his instincts again, and he felt as if violence were about to break loose like a driving rain. He activated his Commtact. "Domi, eyes on targets?"

"Ten muties close to you," Domi replied in her clipped, tense vocal cadence. When her adrenaline kicked in, she reverted to her old, primitive way of talking, dropping articles. "Dozen back by others. Haven't seen me."

Kane seized his Copperhead from its spot on his web belt. "Definitely muties."

"Too hunched, scrawny," Domi answered. "Bald and ugly, and think they can sneak up on me."

Kane smirked in appreciation of the feral girl's guts. Though Domi could, and did, survive with nothing more than a knife and clad in a few rags in the wilderness, her years at Cerberus gave her an appreciation for more complex tools in concert with her sharp senses. "It feels like they're ready to make a move."

There was a grunt over the Commtact, and Kane froze. Before he could call out, something registered on his visor, an infrared trace in his peripheral vision. "Grant, on our left."

"Just spotted that one," Grant answered. "Looks like we're being herded. So the numbers that Domi announced are probably double. This could get rough."

"What else is new?" Domi grumbled.

"What happened?" Kane asked.

"Banged knee getting behind rock," Domi responded. "Caught glimpse of muties across way."

"We're going to be boxed in, and that's going to suck. Time for us to make some noise," Kane responded. He transferred the Copperhead to his left hand and flexed his forearm tendons. The sensitive actuators in the holster for his Sin Eater launched the folding machine pistol into his grasp with a loud, intimidating snap. Back when he was a Magistrate, enforcing the law for Cobaltville, the lightning appearance of the deployed side arm broke many a criminal's will to fight. Now, the sudden appearance was the trigger for gibbering yammers of dismay from hilltop mutants.

"That got attention," Domi announced before, off to Kane's right, the throaty bellow of the albino's Detonics .45 split the night.

Kane raced, broken-field pattern, toward the surge of infrared contacts on his left on the ridge across from her position. His charge was met by a half-dozen misshapen heads popping up in response to rapid movement. They peered over the spine of the hill, and a volley of musket balls rippled down from the group.

One of them smacked, wet and hot, against Kane's chest, stopping his forward charge as if he'd slammed into a brick wall.

* * * * *

Don't miss the gripping conclusion of
PANTHEON OF VENGEANCE
coming in August!

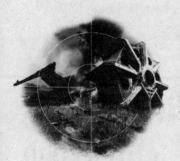

ROOM 59

A nuclear bomb has gone missing. At the same time Room 59 intercepts a communiqué from U.S. Border Patrol agent Nathaniel Spencer. But as Room 59 operatives delve deeper into Mexico's criminal underworld, it soon becomes clear that someone is planning a massive attack against America…one that would render the entire nation completely defenceless!

Look for

aim AND fire

by

cliff RYDER

GOLD EAGLE®

GRM593